THE
MOUTHLESS
DEAD

Also by Anthony Quinn

The Rescue Man
Half of the Human Race
The Streets
Curtain Call
Freya
Eureka
Our Friends in Berlin
London, Burning
Molly & the Captain

NON-FICTION
Klopp: My Liverpool Romance

THE
MOUTHLESS
DEAD

Anthony Quinn

a

abacus
books

ABACUS

First published in Great Britain in 2025 by Abacus

1 3 5 7 9 10 8 6 4 2

A CIP catalogue record for this book
is available from the British Library.

Hardback ISBN 978-0-3491-4692-8
Trade paperback ISBN 978-0-3491-4693-5

Typeset in Caslon by M Rules
Printed and bound in Great Britain by
Clays Ltd, Elcograf S.p.A.

Papers used by Abacus are from well-managed forests
and other responsible sources.

MIX
Paper | Supporting
responsible forestry
FSC
www.fsc.org FSC® C104740

Abacus
An imprint of
Little, Brown Book Group
Carmelite House
50 Victoria Embankment
London EC4Y 0DZ

The authorised representative
in the EEA is
Hachette Ireland
8 Castlecourt Centre
Dublin 15, D15 XTP3, Ireland
(email: info@hbgi.ie)

An Hachette UK Company
www.hachette.co.uk

www.littlebrown.co.uk

For Tom Grant

When you see millions of the mouthless dead
Across your dreams in pale battalions go,
Say not soft things as other men have said,
That you'll remember. For you need not so.
Give them not praise. For, deaf, how should they know
It is not curses heaped on each gashed head?
Nor tears. Their blind eyes see not your tears flow.
Nor honour. It is easy to be dead.
Say only this, 'They are dead'. Then add thereto,
'Yet many a better one has died before'.
Then, scanning all the o'ercrowded mass, should you
Perceive one face that you loved heretofore
It is a spook. None wears the face you knew.
Great death has made all his for evermore.

CHARLES HAMILTON SORLEY

1

He had wandered along port side and stopped to lean against the rail, absorbed by the heaving, tussocky swell of the water, its blue distances braided with white like veins in marble. He found he had a taste for staring at the waves as they bumped drunkenly along; for observing how, whipped up by the wind, they started piling and tottering and crashing against one another. The previous night they had stirred so massively that it seemed impossible the boat should ride them – a ceaseless *whump, whump* against the bows, and the comical tilt of the deck. It was almost seesawing. He cowered in his cabin, fearing the ocean was about to overwhelm them.

It never did. In the morning the ship ploughed on, the sea restored to its ponderous sway. The disturbances of the night were behind them, dissolved like a bad dream. He was drinking in the bright morning, when of a sudden, about fifty yards ahead, a flash of something silvery darted across his eyeline. Another, and then another came, until a shoal of them were leaping in sequence as neatly as a Busby Berkeley chorus line. Fish that could fly! He laughed to see them, and looked round for another passenger to share the moment – but it was early, and he was alone. Later, at lunch, he learnt that flying fish weren't actually capable of powered flight, they simply launched themselves from the water and used their pectoral fins to glide for a few hundred feet. 'To escape predators', came the explanation.

He thought about the verb *to fly*. Obviously its principal meaning was to move through the air, as those remarkable fish did. But the word had multiple nuances, including *to flee*, to escape. He remembered a teacher at his grammar school explaining the word in *Macbeth*. When Banquo and Fleance are ambushed by the killers, Banquo urges his son not to run but to 'Fly, good Fleance, fly, fly, fly!' More curious still, it contained an opposite meaning – not to flee but to attack, as in to *fly at* someone, or to *let fly*. In falconry the word didn't even require a preposition: hawks fly rooks. He liked this word that faced forward and back, that both pursued and ran away, that looked for a fight and took to its heels.

'Why don't you fly? Everyone flies now,' said a friend when he first announced his plan to visit New York. Not everyone. He had reached his middle fifties without ever having boarded an aeroplane, or ever wanting to. He had been born in 1892, of a generation that was not inclined to be airborne – much like Neville Chamberlain, ill and grey-faced, obliged as Prime Minister to take his very first flight at the age of seventy, to go to Munich and talk to Hitler. What was more unnerving to him at the time, the prospect of being shunted in a metal tube through the clouds, or negotiating over the future of Europe with a madman? He was dead, poor Chamberlain, just over a year later, from cancer. That plane was a bird of ill-omen. Now the world shall remember him only for his moment on the airfield, waving the piece of paper – his white flag.

Whenever anyone asked him about flying he would reply with the joke of the two caterpillars gazing at a butterfly overhead, one saying to the other, 'You'll never get me up in one of those.' In any case, he regarded the calm of an Atlantic cruise not merely as a pleasure but a requirement. If he were to compose this memoir he would need the meditative view of the horizon, the wide stroll of the deck, the civilised rhythms of life on board. Most of all he would need the monkish confines of his cabin, where he might lie on his cot, smoking, reading, or scratching away in his little notebook, a few words at a time. It was his fancy he should take to the cloistered life, for he could stand a great deal of solitude. Perhaps only the man who has known a lifetime of institutional routine can truly appreciate this boon: time to oneself. Not that he meant to shun company. If he tired of his cell he could take the clanging staircase to the deck, roam the lounges, park himself at the bar and chat with whosoever of the other 1,522 passengers happened to pass by – which was, he noted, almost exactly the number of souls lost on the sinking of the *Titanic*. He would keep that to himself.

He called it a memoir, but he knew it was not exactly that. He didn't want to give an account of his life, eventful as it had been. He had lived through two world wars, one of them as a soldier, and the reign of five different monarchs. He had served as a police officer for nigh on thirty years, in which time he had pursued as many cases – and probably solved as many – as any other copper had done. On retiring as a detective inspector earlier that year he was pleased, though hardly flattered, to hear his career described as 'distinguished'. It was the word that got bandied around upon the retirement of any long-time public servant who had managed not to disgrace himself or damage the office. For the most part he conducted himself with honour; he didn't consider himself a hero, or a coward. He had carried out his duties with diligence, upheld the principles of law and order, earned the respect of his colleagues. So he told himself.

He might have looked back on his years in the force as quite unexceptional had it not been for the accident of a single case that was, in its time, wildly notorious, and had become in the years since the material of legend. The crime was a domestic murder, but the circumstances surrounding it, the investigation and trial following it, and the outcome attending it, had elevated the case to the cloud-capped peaks of unfathomability. That titan of newspaper criticism, the lately deceased James Agate, was not alone in calling it 'the perfect murder', insofar as every piece of evidence had been examined, every solution mulled over ... and still the identity of the murderer remained unsolved. It had become a classic of criminology, and it was his purpose to shed some light, howsoever faint, into its labyrinthine darkness.

He found himself enjoying the ocean-going life. The ship was, he realised, a floating miniature of the native class system. Those subtle differences that passed beneath the surface of 'polite society' on terra firma were magnified here in unignorable proximity; indeed, they were openly demarcated: first class, and second class. It seemed they had done away with steerage, though he couldn't be certain. The first-class lounge was redolent of a suburban golf club wherein ample-bottomed Rotary stalwarts and their wives played bridge, drank gin, read *The Times*, and warily engaged their neighbours in games of softly-softly one-upmanship ('Were you not at Cowes this year?'). The second-class lounge, where he ventured in a spirit of anthropological curiosity, turned out to be much the same, except for a more plentiful supply of peanuts, poker instead of bridge, and no jewellery worth stealing. Mindful of the novels and films set on board liners he had expected to bump into card sharps, hot-eyed vamps, cashiered officers, a flighty heiress or two. So far the company had been wanly prosaic. Passengers drifted about like sheep, mute, incurious, waiting for their next big feed.

He doubted the quality, of the food at least, but his fellow cruisers appeared to down it very willingly. A man next to him at breakfast dined on grapefruit, cornflakes, bacon and eggs, toast and marmalade, black pudding – and then asked the waiter to bring some kippers, which he thought rather heartless of him. Luncheon, following close on its heels, involved boiled salmon, chicken livers or veal escalope, served with salad leaves that looked not so much wilted as depressed. On the next table were the mother and daughter he had first spied on the gang-plank at Southampton. The former was a thin-lipped fusspot, well-dressed, fiftyish, with a stridulous note in her voice that sounded like an unoiled hinge. The latter was a somewhat plain girl, awkwardly tall, and (he deduced) unmarried, which would explain her mother's pernickety ways, chivvying her along and scolding her if she slouched. Plain, and a touch poignant in the hopeful little smile she would flash at a stranger, as she did to him when they happened to catch one another's eye in the lunch queue.

On seeing them at the rail in the afternoon he sidled over for a chat.

'So you've found your sea legs, then?' he said to the girl,

recalling her stricken pallor when the boat began its lurching waltz yesterday. But now the hesitant expression on her face conveyed alarm.

'I beg your pardon?' she said in a strangled voice, as though he had just made a grossly unwelcome advance. It must have been the mention of 'legs'. He asked, more straightforwardly, if she had recovered from her seasickness. At that her features relaxed and she smiled in affirmation. The mother – Mrs Tarrant – had turned a coldly inquiring eye on him, her mouth tensed at the intrusion, so he introduced himself with all politeness.

'Key?' she said in echo of his name. 'We once had a vicar named Key. Remember, Lydia?'

The girl nodded, and, as if his clerical namesake had some-how sanctified his existence, they were all amiability after that. The pair were taking a holiday together while the husband, a director at Shell, was on a posting abroad. Miss Tarrant – Lydia – was perhaps twenty-nine or thirty, and patient with Mother. She also made allowances for her petty-mindedness. When two middle-aged ladies bustled past them in a cloud of cigarette smoke and laughter Mrs Tarrant's muttered remark ('dreadfully common') brought a blush to the daughter's face, followed quickly by an apologetic wince in his direction. Both were impressed on learning of his former occupation. The police officer was a figure to be either feared or reverenced; he could always tell which side people fell on.

'And by your accent I'd say you're from somewhere up north,' said Miss Tarrant. 'Scotland, is it?'

He laughed. 'Not that far north. Liverpool. Born and raised.'

And so he yarned a little about his professional life as they loitered at the rail and the ship heaved along, throwing up flashpowder trails of white in its wake. He polished up some favourite cases, small change, worn smooth as old sixpences but no less fascinating to his new companions, who knew little of robbery and assault and the career criminal. He found it gratifying to have listeners of such innocence, for almost every tale of wrongdoing tended to reflect a certain cavalier dash upon the teller – the one who had braved the violent streets. He declined, however, to mention the case uppermost in his thoughts. He felt he needed a clear run at it, in the quiet of his cabin, and that to offer a peep around the curtain at this stage might put him off his stroke.

By the time they had finished talking the sky had assumed a grey, bilious complexion and the deck was empty of other passengers. They gazed down from the stern on the receding miles of ocean, and Miss Tarrant said, in a musing voice, 'Just look at all that water we've left behind – how it seems to be racing after us!'

'Let's hope it doesn't catch us up,' he replied.

2

Liverpool, January 1931. A bleak and cheerless month, in a city feeling the first bite of the Depression. It was still the largest port in the country, but the ships came down the Mersey less frequently now. The transatlantic passenger trade had gone south, and the docks were at the start of a long decline. Work had become scarce. In the morning your breath clouded on the raw blue-misted air, you stamped your feet like the rest of them waiting at the stop for trams and buses. The roads forlorn at twilight; the tall-shadowed, fog-shrouded evenings when you felt the damp in your bones and heard the distant lowing of horns from the river. The rumble of the Overhead Railway, like a ghost train. To cross the town at night was to wade through a murk of coal smoke and smuts, through dank, clinging smells from tanneries, breweries, factories, while the salt air from the estuary filled your nose and throat. You would pass blurred figures huddled on steps, wonder at the soot-stained courts and the lives cramped within their narrow walls, glimpse dread in the cobbled lanes and passageways. He had known streets in this city that policemen feared to venture down.

Further north lay Anfield, whose red-bricked terraces huddled tight against the winter cold. Dreary but respectable, graceless but sturdy, this was a neighbourhood of the aspirant lower-middle classes, clerks, publicans, shopkeepers, the worker bees of the Liverpudlian economy. Houses where they kept the front doorstep scrubbed and the net curtains clean. Anfield, where the Wallaces lived, at 29 Wolverton Street. William Herbert Wallace had met his wife Julia while he was working for the Liberal Party in Harrogate. The couple moved to Liverpool in 1914, and Wallace took up a post as an agent collecting insurance premiums for the Prudential Assurance Company. They were now both in their early fifties, had no children, and led a quiet life together. If friends or relations came to call they would be entertained in the parlour, sometimes with music: Julia played the piano, Wallace accompanied her on the violin.

He also belonged to the Liverpool Central Chess Club, which convened twice a week at the City Café on North John Street. Here the story properly begins. At 7.15 p.m. on the evening of Monday 19 January, a phone call came through to the club and was answered by a waitress.

A man's voice asked, 'Is Mr Wallace there?'

The waitress replied that she wasn't sure, pushed open the door of the telephone booth and looked over the room. No sign of Wallace, but she spotted the club captain Samuel Beattie and asked him to deal with it. Beattie told the caller that Wallace was expected that evening for a club fixture – his name was posted on the noticeboard. The man explained that he had some business to put Wallace's way and asked to leave a message: the insurance agent should call at his home, seven-thirty tomorrow evening. He supplied his name, R. M. Qualtrough, and his address, 25 Menlove Gardens East.

About half an hour later Beattie spotted Wallace across the room, engrossed in a game. He went over to deliver the phone message. Wallace looked blank: Qualtrough? He'd never heard of him. But he made a note of the appointment and address, in block letters. Business wasn't so steady that he could turn down work, even from a stranger. He discussed the matter on his way home that night with a fellow clubman and neighbour, James Caird. The following day, Tuesday 20 January, brought rain. Wallace took a tram to nearby Clubmoor where he did his collections. He was a familiar figure in these streets, a tall, gaunt man, bespectacled and moustached, with a long stride. His stiff collar and tie lent him an elderly Victorian aspect, and his sallow complexion hinted at something valetudinarian: he had been troubled by a kidney condition for years.

At two o'clock he had completed his morning rounds and returned home. Julia was suffering from a cold. Over lunch they talked about his appointment that evening with Mr Qualtrough. Menlove Gardens was located four miles south, in a leafy residential district known as Calderstones; they occasionally visited the park there. Julia agreed that he should go; there might be work for him. The rain had gone off, so Wallace left behind his mackintosh in the hall before setting out again for Clubmoor, where he continued his calls until late afternoon.

At six-thirty that evening Wallace said goodbye to Julia and set out from Wolverton Street on his errand. He walked south and caught a tram on Belmont Road, then a second tram at the junction of Lodge Lane and Smithdown Road, asking the conductor if he knew the address he was bound for. The man didn't, but told Wallace he should change at Penny Lane. Ten minutes later he alighted from the tram and boarded another for Calderstones, and again inquired about directions from the conductor; as they were passing a road off Menlove Avenue he advised his passenger to alight – that was Menlove Gardens. Wallace nosed around this triangular network of roads for some minutes. He had found Menlove Gardens North, and South, and West, but to his bafflement there appeared to be no Menlove Gardens East. He asked several passers-by if they knew the address – none of them did. He retraced his steps and knocked at 25 Menlove Gardens West, thinking the address might have been misheard, but the woman who answered the door knew nothing of a Mr Qualtrough.

He stopped to ask a policeman on his beat, and then at a post office and a newsagent's, where he was offered a local directory to consult. His inquiries all drew a blank; there *was* no Menlove Gardens East, and apparently no Qualtrough either. Tired and bewildered, Wallace crossed the road and caught a tram back to Anfield. At eight-forty-five John and Florence Johnston were leaving their house on Wolverton Street by the back door when they encountered Wallace, their next-door neighbour, in the shared back entry. He appeared to be in some confusion. He explained that he'd been out for a couple of hours and had returned to find both front door and back fastened against him. Johnston suggested that he try the back door again; if it still wouldn't open he would try it himself. Wallace re-entered the yard at the back of his house, and this time the door opened without trouble. The Johnstons waited while he disappeared inside, and for a full minute nothing was heard. Then footsteps returned: Wallace, pale, agitated, his voice in a tremble – 'Come and see. She's been killed.'

He led his neighbours into the house, through the hall, where the parlour door stood open. There, crumpled across the rug in front of the gas fire, lay Julia Wallace, the left side of her head a pulpy mess of bone, brain tissue and blood. A stunned silence held for a moment; then Wallace, immobile over his wife's body, stooped down and felt her left hand. Mrs Johnston, in shock, also leaned down to touch the dead woman's hand. Johnston told them he was going to fetch the police, and hurried off. In the kitchen Wallace found that a cabinet had been wrenched open and a cashbox containing Prudential money rifled. Upstairs, in the middle bedroom, he found an ornamental jar containing a roll of pound notes untouched. In a seeming daze he returned to the parlour, Mrs Johnston in attendance. Once more they stared at the scene in mute horror, until Wallace, edging around his wife's corpse, bent forward to examine something. Tucked under the right shoulder was a mackintosh. 'Is that yours?' asked Mrs Johnston. He took a closer look, and confirmed it, yes, it was his. This too was soaked in blood.

The first policeman on the scene was a constable, Williams, who examined the murdered woman. He felt her right wrist, found a faint warmth but no pulse. He listened as Wallace recounted the story of his evening in Menlove Gardens. Then both men searched the house. There was nothing untoward upstairs except for some disarray in the front bedroom where the bedclothes had been half torn away, exposing the mattress, and some of Julia's hats and clothes had been thrown onto it. Back downstairs Wallace pointed out the broken cabinet and the cashbox, from which he thought perhaps four pounds had been stolen. None of Julia's money had been taken from her handbag.

Next to arrive was the police pathologist, Dr MacFall, an avuncular character with long experience in murder cases. He set to work immediately in the blood-spattered parlour. Examining the corpse he deduced that the killer's first blow had caused the gaping wound at the left side of the head; multiple other blows had crushed the skull and caused blood to spurt over the floor and the walls. It was almost certain she had been sitting down when her assailant struck her. More difficult to determine was when she had died. The two methods of estimating the time elapsed after death were body temperature, and the progress of rigor mortis. The latter was known to be unreliable, yet for some reason MacFall chose this method to make his vital calculation, and omitted to cross-check it by measuring the body temperature. It was nearing ten o'clock when he first examined the body, still warm, and he subsequently asserted in his report that death had most probably occurred about two hours before his arrival: that is, around eight o'clock that night.

It was a few minutes after ten when CID showed up at the house. Hubert Moore, the superintendent, examined the crime scene and quickly consulted with PC Williams and another sergeant who had been waiting in the kitchen with Wallace and the Johnstons. They soon established that there was no sign of forced entry, no sign of a struggle with the victim – and no sign of a murder weapon. Some money stolen, a disordered bedroom, but nothing else. There was no telephone at the Wallace house, so Moore drove to the station in Anfield Road to telephone the police headquarters at Cheapside, Dale Street. They in turn alerted each police division, launching a city-wide search of lodging houses, night houses, beer vaults, pubs, railway stations. At this stage the only fix they had on the culprit was the likelihood of his clothes being bloodstained.

By eleven o'clock the house at Wolverton Street was swarming with detectives, police photographers, medical orderlies. The hunt for the killer was underway.

3

Key remembered the conversation as if it were yesterday. It was the morning after the murder, Wednesday, and he was at home in Falkner Street when the phone started to ring.

'All right, son?' said Ged McMahon, DI, one of his oldest friends on the force. He was calling from the Anfield bride-well, where the investigation was partly based. 'Surprised not to see you here last night. You've heard about –'

'Wolverton Street. They got anything?'

'We've started house-to-house this morning. Nobody knew her that well – the missus, I mean. He was in the interview room till about four, we're still getting the story straight – seems he was out on business, Menlove Avenue, for a couple of hours. When he got back the missus was dead on the floor, her head stoved in. Repeated blows. Blood, brains, the lot. But it's a queer one, this.'

'Where's Wallace now?'

'He stayed the night with his sister-in-law on Ullet Road. Has to report back at Cheapside in an hour.' McMahon paused. 'You sound terrible by the way.'

'Stinking cold. When you say "queer" ...'

'Well, s'far as we can tell, there's no motive. Few quid stolen, nowt else. The woman's locked the back door, so she must have opened it again to someone she knew. Husband's the chief suspect, as ever, but he's got this alibi that's – tram conductors, people on the street he talked to, even one of ours on the beat. He was miles away, so he couldn't have been bashing her brains out.'

Key gave a sigh of resignation. 'Well, if he's at Cheapside I'd better get along there.'

'Sounds like you should be in bed.'

'I have been. But it turns out I've also got a useful perspective on this case.'

'Oh aye?'

He allowed himself a pause. 'I know Wallace.'

There was a brief stunned silence. 'You're kidding me. How?'

'Chess. We're in the same chess club.'

The revelation provoked a similar surprise later that morning. The phones at the station apparently hadn't stopped ringing since news of the murder got out. Two detectives were working on Wallace in the interview room: Key spied him through the peephole for a few moments but didn't intrude. At this stage he wasn't sure it would be helpful. Superintendent Moore, on hearing of their acquaintance, asked Key to accompany him in the car to Wolverton Street. One of the sergeants was at the wheel.

His voice was metallic with the cold, and he apologised for his sneezing. Moore shook his head, as if it were of no account.

'You know him well?' he asked, squinting sidelong at Key.

'Not really. We've only talked at the club, and neither of us are regulars. I suppose we first met about three years ago.'

Moore, a softly spoken Irishman, pondered this for a moment. 'And what sort of character?'

'Mild-mannered. Shy. Studious – he's interested in chemistry, keeps a laboratory in a spare bedroom. Big reader, philosophy and that.'

'What about her?'

'Don't know her. I mean – I didn't know her.'

'But he talked about her?'

He shrugged. 'Occasionally. He told me she worried about him – his health isn't good. He had a kidney removed years ago, and he takes medicine for the other one. Could be why he's quite melancholy.'

'Melancholy?' Moore echoed, with a sniff. He turned to gaze out of the car window as the Anfield terraces rolled by. After a measured silence he said, 'I don't get the impression, from what you're telling me, of –'

'No, he's the least likely wife-killer you could meet. I mean, we know it's always the quiet ones, but Wallace ... I don't think he's capable of it.'

Moore fell silent again, brooding. Key had a sense that his premature judgement of the case was of no special interest to him.

'Ever play him at chess?'

'A few times. He was useless.'

A deep guttural noise emanated from inside Moore: a sort of laugh. 'No wonder he's melancholy.'

A large crowd was waiting as they arrived at Wolverton Street – neighbours, kids, press, the usual gawpers and ghouls. Police were on the door, front and back. He followed Moore into the house, every room being meticulously picked apart and scoured for clues; they could hardly move in there for the forensics. And big-wigs, in their big overcoats. In the parlour Moore had joined MacFall, the Chief Constable Mr Everett, and the City Analyst, Professor Roberts. Herbert Gold, another detective, was there. They were discussing the 'splash area'. The carpet, the walls, the pictures and photographs on the walls, Wallace's violin case, the paper cover of the score on the music stand – all spattered with blood. So why, asked Moore, was there not a single speck of it on the suit of clothes Wallace had worn on the night? It was at that moment Key realised that Moore was already convinced Wallace was the murderer. It seemed they all were.

Roberts meanwhile was complaining that sloppy work on the previous evening had contaminated the crime scene. Several policemen filing in and out of the small bathroom had failed to find anything incriminating – Roberts reckoned they had been trampling evidence 'under their hobnailed boots'. But later MacFall discovered something that had been overlooked; using a pocket torch he located a small clot of blood in the lavatory pan. It was minuscule, but it was something. The scene still didn't add up. As MacFall argued, the killer would have been spattered all over his face, clothes and boots, and yet neither the bathroom nor the kitchen betrayed any evidence of a clean-up. 'So how – *how* – could he have left the house with blood on him like a butcher's apron?' What further perplexed them was the mackintosh that had been left tucked under the corpse's shoulder. Closer inspection revealed that the mac had been badly scorched, possibly by the gas fire. Asked about this on the murder night Wallace said he'd worn the coat in the morning but had left it hanging in the hall that afternoon; he had no idea why it had been burnt. Nor did anyone else.

While they were in the house DS Bailey arrived. He had been investigating the name of the mystery caller, and had found fourteen different Qualtroughs living in the Merseyside area. He had interviewed them all and found nothing to connect them with Wallace or the phone message. On hearing this Moore said, 'We should interview the girl who took the call at the City Café. And the captain of the chess club. Maybe they remember something about his voice.' Key stepped forward and volunteered to go; he knew Beattie already, and felt curious to hear what he had to say about Qualtrough. Moore nodded, and he was on his way.

The case had set the city alight. It was all they were talking about, in the pubs and caffs, on the streets. Every fresh report in the *Echo* was seized upon like holy writ. Key's own parents were obsessed with it. Four years previously they had moved to a new house in Cromptons Lane, a five-minute walk from Menlove Gardens. They were tickled to have their neighbourhood suddenly thrust into public notoriety, his mother repeating, scandalised, 'Menlove Gardens *East* . . .', as if the bogus address itself were somehow proof of wrongdoing.

Upstairs on the tram into town he earwigged two old boys as they considered the matter. 'There'll be money involved,' one muttered wisely to the other. 'Well, he works for the Pru, dusn'e? Biff and a bang and he's got her life insurance.' He could have leaned over to correct them on that point. Wallace's record of employment at the Prudential was beyond reproach, and his personal savings had made him secure. He would not stand to gain by bumping off his wife.

But he merely listened to them chunter on.

At North John Street he descended the steps at the City Café and found the waitress, Gladys Harley, who had taken the call that Monday evening. She didn't recognise him. He asked her about her routine. That evening she'd answered the telephone 'maybe ten times' between four and eleven, when she knocked off. Yes, she remembered the caller being put through by the operator. Could she recall what sort of voice he had? Miss Harley shrugged. 'Just an ordinary voice.' From round here? he asked. She nodded, but her vagueness suggested she'd forgotten the voice almost as soon as she'd handed on the call. He then went off in search of Beattie, tracking him down to his office at the Cotton Exchange a few minutes away.

He was prepared for the questions. The voice of the man identified as Qualtrough was 'educated': he said he wanted to talk to Wallace in particular, about something in the nature of his business – a favour for his girl. Beattie had known Wallace for a few years, and the man who rang the club that evening was not him. On that point he was adamant. Would he recognise the voice again? 'Yes, probably.' Then he asked Key a question – did the police have a suspect? Key shook his head, though he must have realised that the circumstantial evidence so far pointed in one direction. They talked of the chess club for a while, but as Key was leaving he said, 'Mr Wallace – he's a gentleman, you know. He couldn't have done a thing like that.' Key thanked him for his time, and left.

Rumour bristled on the air. On the Thursday two vital pieces of evidence emerged. The first concerned a milk delivery boy, Allan Close, who had called at 29 Wolverton Street on Tuesday evening; Mrs Wallace had answered the door to him. He told the police that this had been at quarter to seven. It would almost certainly have been the last time anyone saw Julia Wallace alive. The second discovery was equally significant. The police had managed to trace the origin of the telephone call from Qualtrough. It had come from a call box in Anfield, at about seven o'clock on the night of 19 January. The operators at the exchange were interviewed – they too had heard Qualtrough's voice. There had been some footling about the caller confusing the A and B buttons on the phone. But it was the location of the call box that most intrigued Superintendent Moore. As well as being four hundred yards from Wallace's house it was only a few steps from the tram stop, where Qualtrough would have caught a car into central Liverpool.

Another curious conversation then came to light. After a long day of questioning, Wallace had left the police station and was passing a tram stop on Lord Street when he happened to encounter Beattie and James Caird coming from the chess club. It was late in the evening, and the men exchanged greetings. Talk soon turned to the case. Wallace asked Beattie if he could remember at what time he had taken the call on Monday evening – it was 'important' to him, he said – and the latter replied that it must have been about seven o'clock. Wallace, plainly anxious, asked him if he could be a little more 'exact'. But Beattie could not; moreover he advised Wallace not to discuss the case any further lest his words be misconstrued. The whole of this conversation was reported to Moore, who asked Wallace about it next day. What did he mean when he told Beattie the time of the phone message was important? Wallace replied that he'd had 'an idea', though he wouldn't explain what it was. He admitted that talking with Beattie about the call had been a mistake.

The following night after work Key met up with Ged McMahon at the White Star, near Mathew Street. They always drank there, he wasn't sure why. Of all the hundreds of pubs in town the White Star was probably one of the smallest, certainly one of the pokiest, and usually full to the door. It must have been habit, he supposed. He'd lost count of the times they had sat at that corner table, with the bevelled mirror throwing back the bar's reflection and the ceiling mustard-coloured with tobacco smoke. The landlord there was pally with them because they turned a blind eye to the lock-ins.

They would have been drinking bitter, or mild.

'The Super's got this bee in his bonnet trying to work it out,' said McMahon. 'If the kid delivering the milk saw Julia Wallace at 6.45, and Wallace caught the second tram on Lodge Lane at 7.06, that gives him twenty-one minutes to –' he counted them off with his fingers – 'murder his wife, clean up, dispose of the weapon – whatever it was – fake a burglary, bolt the doors, walk to the stop at St Margaret's Church, wait for the tram, travel a mile and a half to the next connection.'

Key shook his head. 'It can't be done.'

'That's what I thought, until Moore got a bunch of us to do his "tram test". He sent us out in pairs to time the journey on foot from Wolverton Street to the second tram stop. We were at it all afternoon doing relays. I was paired with Jimmy Dent.'

'Dent – do I know him?'

'Young feller, nice enough. Two blind spots, though ...'

'Two?' he queried.

McMahon nodded. 'His eyes.' He spluttered into his beer, laughing.

'Anyway,' he continued, 'shortest time we managed it in was twenty minutes. Some did it in seventeen. One pair did it in *fifteen*, but it turned out they had to sprint to catch the tram – not something yer fifty-two-year old could do.'

'And Wallace is frail to start with.'

'So the thing was a bust. All it proved was that Wallace couldn't have left the house later than 6.49 on the night of the murder. Given the milk boy's claim of seeing the victim at 6.45 that gives Wallace four minutes to have done her in and cleaned up. Which would take some doing.'

Key agreed. 'Took you longer than that to get to the bar and back for these pints.'

Though he fancied him for the murder, Superintendent Moore was forced to concede that everything Wallace had said about his movements on the night of 19 January and the following night had been checked and verified. The three principal determinants of a crime – motive, means, opportunity – were far from secure. Opportunity was in doubt after the tram test. As for means, the latest on the murder weapon came from the Wallaces' charwoman, who said a small poker was missing from the fireplace in the kitchen. And an iron bar was supposedly missing from the parlour.

'Who keeps an iron bar in the parlour?' McMahon wondered aloud.

Regarding the third determinant, however, Moore believed they were getting somewhere. Wallace was known to have been treated for a kidney complaint at a Liverpool hospital. The surgeon dealing with his case had testified that Wallace's physical condition was such that it might affect his mental capacity and provoke him to violence. So Moore had identified the motive: his suspect was a madman.

Key was sceptical on that score. His acquaintance with Wallace, while far from intimate, was enough to convince him that he was sound in mind, if not in body. He had never shown any sign hitherto of mental infirmity. Even if he had temporarily taken leave of his senses, who was to say he would have resorted to violence – against anyone, let alone his wife of sixteen years?

'He looks more like a poisoner, doesn't he?' McMahon said abruptly. 'I mean, Wallace's type doesn't go for the blunt instrument. Too messy. He would have been mixing up solutions in his laboratory, like Crippen.'

Key shook his head. 'You've got him all wrong. If he really couldn't bear being married to her I think he would just have disappeared, fled the country. Caught the slow boat to Valparaiso, maybe. But he wouldn't have murdered her.'

McMahon was staring at him. 'You seem very sure of yourself. Maybe you'd like to put a little wager on it? Five quid says he's the killer.'

He was holding out his hand expectantly. 'Done,' Key said, taking it.

'You just have been, son,' he replied.

Over that weekend more evidence emerged about Wallace's movements on the murder night. A young typist, Lily Hall, told detectives that she had seen Wallace talking to a man not far from Wolverton Street. She had been on her way to the pictures, and recalled the time of the sighting as 8.35 p.m., about ten minutes before the Johnstons encountered Wallace trying to get into his house. Moore presented this information to Wallace, who denied having spoken to anyone on his way home from Menlove Gardens. The police put out appeals to the public in the hope of identifying the mystery man: no one came forward. The episode was inconclusive, but it twitched the veils of mystery already surrounding the suspect.

At Cheapside the following Monday Key happened to run into Wallace. It was the first time he'd spoken to him since the murder. Drained and depleted, he seemed to have aged quite alarmingly. A suppressed appeal flared in his eyes. His obvious worry was that the senior detectives on the case were convinced of his guilt – he added that Moore especially had it in for him. Key told him not to panic; however determined Moore was on a conviction he simply didn't have the evidence.

'What about Parry?' Wallace asked. 'Have they interviewed him?'

'Yeah, but I haven't seen the transcript yet.'

'You read my statement, though, haven't you – the second one?'

'Of course. They all know what Parry's been up to.'

These assurances didn't seem to have any effect. Wallace stared off in that blindfold way of his, as if he hadn't taken in anything that had been said. He had developed a nervous habit of gnawing the inside of his cheek. Key wanted to tell him to desist (it made him look guilty) but Wallace was in such a fragile state he kept quiet; it would be heartless to put him under more pressure. Just then Gold and a couple of other detectives appeared, and Key chose that moment to leave, telling Wallace he would be in touch.

Richard Gordon Parry was a former associate of Wallace's

at the Prudential. A single man of about twenty-two, he had a history of juvenile convictions including vandalism and theft. He had been with the company for three years, during which time rumours swirled around him. In his statement Wallace recalled that when he'd been ill with bronchitis in December 1928, Parry had taken over his collection round for two or three days a week. He would call on the Wallaces at their home and became well acquainted with their 'domestic arrangements'. After a while Wallace noticed small discrepancies in the accounts. He spoke about this to Parry, who eventually admitted he had not paid in full what he had collected; he apologised, and promised to set the matter straight. This was not the first time he had been caught out. Months earlier the amounts he paid in at the company's head office were found to be short. This came to the notice of the Prudential superintendent, Joseph Crewe, who rather than dismiss the young man decided to speak to his parents. Parry's father, who worked at the City Treasury, came to the rescue, offering to pay thirty pounds to settle accounts. So a scandal was averted.

Wallace named another man, Joseph Marsden, who had also filled in for him during his illness that winter. Like Parry, who had recommended him, Marsden was a louche, unreliable character who had also been caught cooking the books at the Prudential. Now, in 1931, he was working as a bookmaker's clerk in Birkenhead. That Wallace had employed one chancer as his sub-agent was perhaps a misfortune. To have employed two ... In any event both men became familiar visitors at Wolverton Street and knew that the cash-in day for Prudential agents was Wednesday; they also knew that Wallace kept the money in a cashbox on top of the bookcase in his kitchen.

Tuesday, the day of the murder, would be the most opportune time to lay hands on it.

If Wallace intended to create an air of disrepute around these two men he had succeeded. Both had a grudge against the Prudential, their former employer, and might have targeted the Wallace household as easy prey. With the man of the house temporarily diverted to Menlove Gardens Julia Wallace could have answered the door to either one. Perhaps the plan to steal the cash had gone wrong, someone had panicked and Julia had been the victim of a bungled larceny.

Key asked one of the desk sergeants for a transcript of the Parry interview, and saw that it had been conducted by Alec Moran, another CID detective he was friendly with. He called him up. He said that Parry had been co-operative and showed no sign of nerves during the hour-long interview. Did his alibi check out? It did. On the Tuesday evening Parry visited the house of a friend named Olivia Brine, thirty-nine, married, about 5.30 p.m. Mrs Brine's fifteen-year-old nephew called about 6 p.m. They talked about arranging someone's birthday party. Both Brine and the nephew stated that Parry left the house about 8 p.m. He then went in his car to call on Lily Lloyd, his girlfriend, who lived at Missouri Road in Clubmoor. He stayed there until about 11 p.m.

Key wondered if there was any chance one or both of the women were covering for him. Wasn't there a period of time unaccounted for, between his leaving the Brine house and his calling on Lloyd? 'Yeah, I wondered about that, too,' said Alec, 'but when I mentioned it to the Super he said no further inquiries were necessary.' 'Isn't that a bit odd?' There was a pause at the other end of the line, and Alec's voice dropped to a confiding volume: 'You'd have to ask him. But I've heard that Parry's dad and the Super know one another – maybe he was doing his mate a little favour.'

There was something else about Parry they couldn't square. Given his propensity for petty thieving one would have assumed he was short of money. Yet Wallace had also mentioned in his statement that Parry kept a motor car. How could he possibly afford it? Alec didn't have an answer either.

That was Monday afternoon. Later, Ged McMahon rang Key at home. Wallace had been arrested that evening at his sister-in-law's house on Ullet Road. Moore was one of the arresting officers. Charged with the wilful murder of his wife Julia, the accused was now under lock and key at Cheapside.

4

Key couldn't remember if it was Wednesday or Thursday. A disorienting aspect of life on board was that the days blurred into one another. The previous evening he had attended the formal dinner, and dressed for it, in fact. The pressed white uniforms of the crew, decked out with frogging and insignia, recalled the sailor suits of his Edwardian boyhood. His own dinner suit had an air of mustiness, the sort to which old clothes are prey. He went rather heavy on the cologne in an effort to mask it.

His head was still in turbulence from a dream. He was riding on the top deck of a tram, the old Liverpool type in red and cream livery, not the 'Green Goddess' that replaced it. It was quite the clanking old beast, that tram, heaving out of the Mersey mist like a giant sarcophagus, engine wheezing, interior illumined by the pickled yellow light you only ever found there. When it rained the inside of the windows became steamed up from the soaking mackintoshes and coats of people packed close together. The conductor's bell made its lonely clang – the same Wallace would have heard that night on his journey to Menlove Gardens. They had a distinctive smell, those tramcars, fusty, frowsy, as if the tobacco smoke and body sweat of a million passengers had soaked into the moquette lining of its seats.

In this dream he seemed to occupy a semi-official capacity, stalking up and down the aisle checking on the passengers, a random assortment of people he knew – former colleagues on the force, distant relatives, friends, felons. Perhaps he was there to ensure their safety, for they could feel the car roll and pitch. (During the blackout years the tram's lights would suddenly die and plunge them into darkness – you felt the fear, either of the bombs or else the opportunist pickpocket.) Visible at the head of this tram was a woman, dressed in black, her back turned to him. He kept trying to make his way towards her but the other passengers insistently blocked the aisle, unwilling to let him approach. Why? Meanwhile the motion in the car was more frantic, rocking from side to side. People cried out in fear. Who the black-clad woman was he never discovered, because a moment later he awoke – the rocking no longer that of the tram but the waves beneath him. He felt relieved, as if he had escaped something – impossible to know what.

Not only had Key been invited to join the Captain's table, he had the honour of being seated next to the man himself. It proved a chastening experience. Captain Jarrett was a lean, bearded man of about his own age, eyes narrow as blades ready to slit open his unsuspecting guests. He was from Carlisle, on whose pronunciation he was pleased to correct Key ('*Car*lisle'). He had two conversational quirks. The first was a disconcerting private smile, not because you'd amused him but because he seemed to have amused himself. The second was his tendency to pause: whenever you made a remark or asked a question he would wait before answering, in which time your words would echo back to you as those of a blabbermouth. He was laconic and mysterious, like a character out of Conrad. He smoked a pipe, of course.

Over langoustines and sea trout they talked about Key's time on the force, and what he had planned for his retirement. When he admitted to beginning a sort of memoir the Captain paused, and said, 'I suppose a great many men believe they have a story to tell.' Key felt rather stung by that. His implication seemed to be ... *and most of them are deluded.* But then Jarrett recovered his manners and suggested Key make use of the ship's library. The man on his other side was a high-up at Cunard, from Surrey, pie-faced and amiable, with whom he shared some idle chat. But he couldn't help feeling magnetised by the Captain's enigmatic aura. While not quite friendly he had more about him than the Cunard chap, and Key hoped he might establish a link, however tenuous. Eventually one came up: they had both served at Third Ypres, though in different sectors. They traded a few stories in the close-mouthed way of old soldiers. He had lost a younger brother out there, along with many friends. But worse was to come. Demobbed in early 1919 he returned home just in time to find both of his parents and grandmother in the last throes of life: they had succumbed to the flu epidemic, and perished shortly after. 'I'm sorry,' Key muttered, in useless sympathy; but Jarrett gave a shrug and talked about the loss as if it had happened to someone else. Either he was slightly inhuman or magnificently phlegmatic.

Dinner over, the port and cigars came out. Key didn't trust himself to pass the decanter, let alone take a glass from it. Jarrett, who had drunk steadily all evening, seemed unaffected by his intake. The mood felt dangerously expansive, and when talk turned to the intricacies of detective work Key's natural reticence gave way. 'There's one case in Liverpool that became very notorious,' he said. 'I dare say you read about it at the time – the Wallace murder, in 1931.'

The Captain squinted uncertainly, so he explained. 'An insurance agent named William Herbert Wallace was accused of murdering his wife, though his alibi on the evening of the crime was watertight. It became known by some as "the perfect murder" because it seemed only Wallace could have done it, and yet he was manifestly innocent ...' He had kept his eyes on Jarrett as he spoke, expecting some twitch of recognition to register on the Captain's face. None came.

'In Liverpool, you say?' he asked.

'Yes, but it became of national interest. It was all over the papers, for *years* –'

To his astonishment Jarrett was shaking his head. Famous or not, it was news to him. Key offered a few more details of the case, but it was clear the Captain had lived in perfect ignorance of the whole boiling lot. 'But in my defence,' he said, 'at that time I was in the Merchant Navy, sailing around the remotest regions of Canada. We didn't see many English newspapers over there.'

Key felt the home truth cold in his gullet. Hitherto he had imagined that tribesmen in the remotest regions of Mongolia had heard of the Wallace case and its impossible conundrum. He had been mistaken. The Captain was a man of the world, and if this legend of criminology had yet to impinge on him, who was to say how many others it had failed to reach? The evening rather lost its bounce for him after that and he sidled off to brood upon his vanishing consequence in the world. On the way past the lounge he happened to spot Mrs Tarrant and her daughter playing whist, and went over to say hullo.

They gave him a friendly welcome, and Miss Tarrant – or Lydia, as he now called her – asked him to stay for a nightcap. From her flushed features it seemed she'd also had one or two. They talked about their respective evenings, and Mrs Tarrant was impressed to hear he'd been a guest of the Captain. Key gave a brief and favourable account of him, omitting to mention his remarkable admission of the night. 'He does sound an interesting man,' she said, so Key promised to introduce her when an occasion offered. Lydia, in mischievous mood, asked him if he'd read a story in *The Times* recently about a well-off family in Manchester who'd been taken in by men posing as CID officers with a warrant to search their house. Having bound and gagged the wife, her daughter and a maid, the gang broke into two safes and made off with over £1,500. The husband, who'd been at the races that afternoon, was alerted by a police broadcast on the loud-speaker system.

'But Mr Key,' Lydia continued, 'is there a way of telling a real police officer from an impersonator? Don't we trust the man who claims to be the law?'

'They probably had fake badges,' he replied. 'And a lot of nerve.'

The girl looked at him, with a half-smile. 'Why, we believe *you're* a police officer, but only because you've told us.'

'Lydia,' said her mother, sharply. 'I think that's quite offensive to Mr Key. Of course he's an officer.'

'No, no, you're quite right,' he replied, fishing an old CID card from his wallet to show them. 'Appearances can be deceptive. And strictly speaking I'm not an officer. As of this summer I'm retired ...'

Lydia gave a giggle, and said, 'There's something too funny about this story. The name of that family they robbed is Guise. Now can you guess what the husband is called? Ivor. *Ivor Guise!*'

Mrs Tarrant only tutted, but Key chuckled along. *I've a guise* ... They were still smiling about it, he and Lydia, as they said good-night and repaired to their berths. It pleased him to think how much they enjoyed one another's company.

5

At ten o'clock on the morning of Tuesday 3 February 1931, Wallace stood against the rail of the dock in the Stipendiary's court at Dale Street. Wearing a black overcoat over his dark suit, he looked calm, though tired. The room of course was packed to the door. Seated along from Key were Moore, Everett the Chief Constable, and the Assistant Prosecuting Solicitor, Mr Bishop. The court rose as the magistrate entered and took his seat. Once the room had settled Bishop stood up and began to set out the case against the prisoner. Key remembered his statement being riddled with small errors and inaccuracies, and wondered whether he had been properly briefed.

By now most knew the story well enough – the phone call to the chess club, the message from Qualtrough, Wallace's trip to Menlove Gardens the following night. The main points of the prosecution were, first, that the message was sent to the accused by Wallace himself, posing as Qualtrough; that the mackintosh found beneath the victim's shoulder was used by Wallace in the act of killing to protect himself from blood spatter; that the robbery of four pounds from the cashbox had been obviously staged by the accused; that the killer's use of the bathroom upstairs indicated it was Wallace himself – an intruder with blood on his hands would have used the sink in the scullery, a few steps from the murder scene and convenient for escape via the back door; finally, that the absence of a murder weapon also made the housebreaker theory unlikely, for if a stranger had murdered the woman he would not take his weapon away.

Bishop then applied for the prisoner to be remanded for eight days. The Stipendiary asked the accused if he had anything to say. Wallace held the rail and addressed the court quite clearly: 'Nothing, sir, except that I am absolutely innocent of the charge.' Key looked to his right and saw the Super exchange a look with the Chief Constable. A moment later Wallace was remanded in police custody and taken down to the cells. Before he was transferred to Walton jail he was permitted to telephone a solicitor. The man he chose was Hector Munro, a young lawyer who also happened to be a member of the Liverpool Central Chess Club. Wallace didn't know him at all, though he may have recognised Munro's name, given his office was in the same building as the Prudential on Dale Street.

The next morning the police case against Wallace was laid out for the public's delectation in the Liverpool *Daily Post*. Reported verbatim in black and white with a photograph of the accused it made bleak reading. Munro had immediately set to work and unearthed a new witness for the defence. A newspaper delivery boy named James Allison Wildman was prepared to swear he had seen Allan Close delivering milk to the Wallaces' door as late as 6.38 p.m. on the night of the murder. He knew it was this time from having glanced up two minutes earlier at the clock of Holy Trinity Church on the corner of Breck Road. It was dark, but Wildman made out Close in the light from the open door of number 29, waiting for his milk can to be returned. If Julia Wallace was alive and well at this moment it confirmed the near-impossible timeframe allowed to Wallace to commit the murder and carry out the clean-up: eleven minutes.

After a further remand of eight days, committal proceedings in the case opened on Thursday 19 February. Wallace was represented in court by Sydney Scholefield Allen, who would tangle a number of times with Bishop, the police prosecutor. The latter was seen to perform as if addressing a jury rather than an inquest, and his insinuations provoked the defence to object. What the court required was 'cold, hard facts', he argued, not a constant barrage of Mr Bishop's opinions. Scholefield Allen argued, fairly, that whatever was said in the court would be reported in the press that evening. These reports would be read 'by people wise and people ignorant', and one should bear in mind that a jury of twelve would be selected from those same people to try a man for his life. Bishop was prejudicing the case against Wallace simply by inflaming the imagination of the public. 'The public are not judging this case,' replied the magistrate.

On it went, day after day, the jostling crowds outside, the public gallery full to capacity with spectators, the witnesses on the stand coming and going, the sudden hush at a particularly lurid testimony. When MacFall described the wounds on the victim's head 'as if a terrific force had driven in the scalp, bursting it in parallel lines', Key glanced up at the dock. Wallace, his head bowed, sat in absolute stillness. One had to wonder how much more of this he could take. On the fifth and sixth days of the inquest huge numbers besieged the court and many were turned away. On the seventh and last day the press got the moment it had been waiting for. At the invitation of Scholefield Allen, DI Gold read an extract from Wallace's diary, tenderly describing a walk with his wife through Stanley Park in winter frost. The public gallery was stunned by the sight of Wallace, overcome and weeping, a handkerchief pressed to his face. The magistrate called an adjournment for lunch, and Wallace sat there until he recovered his composure.

In his cabin Key leafed through a file of loose newspaper cuttings, from the *Echo* and the *Post*, from *The Times*. Yellow at the edges now, and yet those early months of 1931 came back to him as fresh as paint. On that last afternoon at Dale Street the clerk read out the formal charge. Wallace rose, and for a moment it seemed he might not hold his nerve to speak. But he kept going. 'I plead not guilty to the charge made against me, and I am advised to reserve my defence . . . The suggestion that I murdered my wife is monstrous. That I should attack and kill her is to all who knew us unthinkable and unbelievable, all the more so when it must be realised that I could not gain one possible advantage by committing such a deed. Nor do the police suggest I gained any advantage.

'On the contrary,' he continued, the emotion quavering in his voice, 'I have lost a devoted and loving comrade. My home life is completely broken up and everything that I hold dear has been ruthlessly uprooted and torn from me. I am now left to face the torture of this nerve-wracking ordeal. I protest once more that I am entirely innocent of this terrible crime.'

A total silence fell on the court. Then the presiding magistrate cleared his throat and announced that Wallace would be committed for trial at the next Liverpool Assizes. The prisoner, having exchanged words with his defence, was taken down. The crowds poured out of the court, dispersing on the street in a mutterish echo of gossip and laughter, as crowds do. Only an hour to go before the evening paper hit the stands, when the arguments would start all over again.

How Wallace survived the tension of those weeks was difficult to imagine. Confined to the hospital at Walton jail under the observation of medical officers, he passed the time reading or playing draughts with fellow prisoners, most of them illiterate or mentally defective. He was permitted an hour's walk in the morning, and a half-hour in the afternoon. His most frequent visitors were his lawyers, Scholefield Allen and Hector Munro.

One afternoon Key went to visit him; being the only friend he had on the force it seemed the least he could do. They talked in the prison grounds, away from prying ears. He was not in good spirits – that much was to be expected – and needed encouragement for his prospects at the trial. His barrister was to be Roland Oliver KC, the Recorder of Folkestone, and a man held in high regard. For some years he had been Junior Crown Counsel at the Old Bailey, and had appeared in several well-known criminal trials of the day.

Wallace had also had good news from Munro. At the Prudential HQ in London the union had met and agreed to pay his entire defence costs. Munro reported that he had been closely questioned about his client by members of the executive, and by the end of the session there wasn't a single person in the room who doubted Wallace's innocence. The council set up a defence fund for him and drafted their own manifesto. It was circulated to Prudential members all over the country and quickly raised £500, while the company itself contributed £150 and agreed to keep his position open for him.

'That's very decent of them, isn't it?' Key said.

Wallace agreed, though his expression was distracted, and forlorn. He had received some terrible letters, he said, from strangers cursing him as a wife-killer and 'wishing damnation on my soul'. Key told him he should ignore them; stories of public interest always attracted a lunatic element. Tormenting the innocent was simply an outlet for their madness.

'They didn't sound lunatic,' he said, quietly. 'They sounded disgusted.'

Some other subject was required to divert him. Key, spotting a chess set in his cell, suggested a game, but Wallace only shook his head. The gloom seemed to shimmer about him, like the aura of a cursed saint. Key had got up to leave when he felt a hand on his arm. 'And Parry? Last time you said he was under investigation.' 'He still is,' he replied. 'We're working on his alibi. There seems to be a discrepancy, but it's going to take a little more time.' Wallace looked at him, and said, 'Time is what I don't have.'

In March the news landed with a splash that Edward Hemmerde KC had been offered the prosecution brief in the Wallace case. It was a controversial appointment by any standards. Hemmerde's name had caused a stir both in and out of court for years. His early career seemed to mark him for greatness. An outstanding silk, he was elected as Liberal MP for East Denbigh at the age of thirty-five, and later nominated as Recorder of Liverpool. He also enjoyed some success as a playwright. But the high-flyer hovered too close to the sun, and after switching allegiance to the Labour Party in 1920 he was passed over for legal office. Gambling debts and ill-advised ventures in the stock market came home to roost, and the popular press had a field day with his reputation. Sorrows did not come single spies: his wife divorced him, and not long after came news from East Africa that his twenty-three-year-old son had died in an accident. Despite his office as Recorder, the City of Liverpool snubbed him whenever legal representation was required. A long feud simmered between him and the Corporation, with pointed offences on both sides.

In this atmosphere of mutual antagonism the announcement of the brief caused a sensation. It appeared that Hemmerde himself regarded the City's offer as an olive branch, and he had snatched it with alacrity. But the stakes were already vertiginous. If he were to lose the case and Wallace walked free, his career would be up in flames, this time with no prospect of a comeback. If, however, he were to secure a conviction his good name would be restored, and his rackety past forgiven if not forgotten.

'How are you feeling about yer fiver now?' Ged McMahon asked him when they encountered each other on the steps at Cheapside.

'Quietly confident,' Key replied.

'Your man doesn't look up to a long trial. He looks like *death*. And he won't get any mercy from Hemmerde.'

'Doesn't matter, they still don't have the evidence. There's not enough there to convince a jury. I'll offer you double or quits.'

McMahon laughed in surprise. 'Do you know something I don't?'

He shook his head. 'Just considering the facts, mate – like you should.'

'All right,' said McMahon, rubbing his hands. 'Ten quid. I'm looking forward to this!'

6

Wednesday 22 April, 1931. St George's Hall is not only the greatest of many great buildings in Liverpool, it is also the best situated, directly opposite the entrance of Lime Street Station. Visitors piling out of the trains there are confronted by an edifice that rivals anything in Rome, or Athens, or London come to that. You think this merely an exaggeration of local pride? You should look for yourself. That long colonnaded portico and its plaza in front can hold its own for majesty anywhere in the world. The Wallace trial had found a setting worthy of its significance.

On this rain-whipped April morning crowds had mobbed the front steps, hoping for a seat in number one court. Here was a legal set-piece nobody wanted to miss. By ten o'clock the courtroom was a restless hive of murmurs – which ceased abruptly on the clerk of assize calling for silence. The entry of the judge, Mr Justice Wright, brought the assembled to their feet. As he took his place Wallace, brought up moments before, looked out from the dock. On his left, in two serried pews, sat the jury. Above him was the press gallery; it had never been so tightly packed. Nor was there room to budge in the public gallery.

In the well of the court the lawyers prepared to go in to bat. Key noticed Wallace nod to his junior counsel, Scholefield Allen, seated alongside Hector Munro. The clerk rose again, and said: 'William Herbert Wallace, you are indicted and the charge against you is murder, in that on the twentieth day of January, 1931, at Liverpool you murdered Julia Wallace. How say you, William Herbert Wallace, are you guilty or not guilty?'

The prisoner replied, 'Not guilty.' The jury was sworn, and the stage now set for the prosecution to begin.

In his opening address Hemmerde admitted that the Crown could suggest no motive for Wallace to murder his wife. But that should not affect their judgement of the matter. If the facts pointed unequivocally to the conclusion that the accused *had* done the crime, motive was neither here nor there. 'This is not a case where you will be in any way concerned with other possible verdicts such as manslaughter,' he continued. 'If this man did what he is charged with doing, it is murder, foul and unpardonable. Few more brutal murders can ever have been committed; this woman literally hacked to death for apparently no reason at all. Without an enemy in the world she goes to her account, and if you think that the case is fairly proved against this man, that he brutally and wantonly sent this unfortunate woman to her account, it will be your duty to call him to his account.'

The prosecution deputy, Leslie Walsh, dealt with the cross-examination of the operators at the Anfield Telephone Exchange. Louisa Alfreds and Lilian Kelly had both talked to Qualtrough, who had asked for Bank 3581, and both recalled his voice as 'ordinary'. Kelly confirmed that the caller had made a mistake in pressing button A and told her that he 'hadn't had his correspondent yet'. Their supervisor Annie Robertson then came to the witness box, and testified that she had made a note of the call at 7.20 p.m., as was usual when such an enquiry was placed; her pencil note read NR – 'no reply'. The waitress Gladys Harley – the one I'd interviewed – was called, and answered pretty much the same questions I'd put to her. The café served about a hundred customers a day, and she verified the positioning of the noticeboard with its names of chess club members and their match appointments. Then Samuel Beattie gave his testimony about R. M. Qualtrough's call on the evening of the 19th, and his passing the message on to Wallace. The defence, Roland Oliver, wanted to know exactly what he recalled of his conversation with Qualtrough.

'The part I am interested in particularly,' said Oliver, 'is the part in which the voice told you about the business, whatever it was. Can you remember what the voice said about that?' Beattie: 'Yes. I told him that Mr Wallace was coming to the club that night and he would be there shortly, would he ring up again. He said, "No, I am too busy; I have got my girl's twenty-first birthday on and I want to see Mr Wallace on a matter of business; it is something in the nature of his business."'

There followed questions as to the tone of the speaker's voice – 'strong and confident', according to Beattie – and whether it was anything like Wallace's voice. 'Certainly not,' he replied. 'Does it occur to you now it was anything like his voice?' asked Oliver. Beattie: 'It would be a great stretch of the imagination for me to say that it was anything like that.'

The witnesses came and went: the milk boy who had de-livered to Wolverton Street the night of the murder, the tram conductors, the various parties Wallace had consulted during his futile search for Menlove Gardens East, and the police who had conducted Moore's tram tests, including Ged McMahon. Also Joseph Crewe, superintendent of the Prudential, who had known the accused for twelve years. He recalled Wallace visiting his home in Green Lane several times: he was learning to play the violin, and Crewe had offered to give him lessons.

Asked to give a character testimony Crewe was forthright. He regarded his colleague as 'an absolute gentleman in every respect'. Q. 'Have you ever seen any sign of violence or ill-temper about him?' A. 'None whatever.' Q. 'Scrupulously honest?' A. 'Absolutely'. Q. 'What about his accounts, were they always in order?' A. 'Always to a penny.'

After the court adjourned for the day a bunch of senior detectives stopped for a drink at the Legs of Man, a lively pub at the corner of Lime Street and London Road. About ten minutes later Key joined them at the bar, where Ged McMahon had found himself the target of some chaffing. Most of the questions put to him on the stand had concerned the timing of the trams, and required from him either a 'yes' or a 'no'. Alec Moran was at his dryest. 'Always respect a feller who can hold his nerve under questioning,' he said, and mimicked the orotund tone of Roland Oliver KC. 'On your second experiment, which took eighteen minutes, did you board the tram at the Church corner at 6.52? DI McMahon took a deep breath: Yes. Tellin' yer, this lad won't crumble under pressure.' They all laughed along, Ged included. He seemed glad to have done with it. It was one thing to give eye-witness evidence in a murder trial; quite another to stand there answering questions about Liverpool tram routes.

The second day opened with the Wallaces' neighbours, Mr

and Mrs Johnston, testifying about the night of 20 January. Florence Johnston remembered meeting Wallace in the back entry of Wolverton Street at 8.45 p.m. He had just returned home and asked her whether she had heard anything 'unusual' that evening; she replied, 'No, what has happened?' Wallace then explained that he had just tried both his front door and back and found them locked against him. Mr Johnston advised him to try again, and if it didn't open he would try to force it. When Wallace went back to do so he said to the couple over his shoulder, 'She will not be out; she has such a bad cold.' When he tried the back door this time it opened, though it was some minutes before he re-emerged. The Johnstons separately recalled a light going on in the back bedroom, then a match was lit and flickered in the little 'workshop' or laboratory. Q. 'When he came out to you what did he say?' A. '"Come and see; she is killed".'

Then they went through the kitchen to the parlour, where Julia Wallace's body was lying across the rug. A long exchange followed between witness and prosecutor about the exact disposition of the body and the furniture in the room. Mrs Johnston had some difficulty in squaring this with her memory of it on the night. The photograph of the crime scene made it look very different from the actual thing.

Her testimony was not without its moments of grim comedy. When asked if Wallace had spoken while the police were searching the house she replied, 'Yes; he did say "Julia would have gone mad if she had seen all this",' meaning the strangers knocking about the house. Before the police arrived he was quite collected, she said, but when they were alone in the kitchen he had twice broken down in tears.

The Wallaces' charwoman, Mrs Draper, caused a stir when she said that things were missing from the house on the morning of the 21st. One of them was a small poker that was kept in the kitchen; more alarmingly, an iron bar kept by the fireplace in the parlour was also gone. It was apparently used for cleaning spent matches and cigarette ends from under the gas fire.

Undoubtedly the highlight of the day was the arrival of MacFall, the pathologist. The court had been patient during the longueurs of circumstantial evidence. Now came the gory detail. MacFall quickly got down to describing the corpse of Julia Wallace; by his calculation rigor mortis had set in around four hours before he'd begun his examination, at 10 p.m. Hemmerde probed him for a margin of error on this timing. Possibly an hour out, replied MacFall, on which reckoning Wallace could have been in the house killing his wife at seven o'clock. Photographs of the blood spatter from the victim's head were passed around. Judging from the trajectory of the drops MacFall believed she had been sitting in front of the fireplace, with her head a little forward and turned to the left, as if talking to someone. The bloodstains were so small the judge had to use a magnifying glass. MacFall said there had been ten blows to the head, and then corrected the number to eleven. After the first blow death would probably have followed immediately. (Q. 'The head is lying upon the floor when the ten blows are struck?' A. 'Yes, lying much in the position as seen in the photograph.')

In the afternoon came more troubling, though less gruesome, testimony from MacFall. Questioned about the demeanour of Wallace on the night of the murder, the pathologist replied, 'I was very much struck with it. It was abnormal.' Q. 'In what way?' A. 'He was too quiet, too collected, for a person whose wife had been killed in the way that he described. He was not nearly so affected as I was myself.' Q. 'Do you happen to remember anything in particular that led you to that conclusion?' A. 'I think he was smoking cigarettes most of the time. Whilst I was in the room examining the body he came in smoking a cigarette, and he leant over in front of the sideboard and flicked the ash into a bowl. It struck me at the time as being unnatural.'

A murmur went round the courtroom. Hemmerde now saw the moment to prompt MacFall into upping the ante, and he obliged: 'I formed an idea of the mental condition of the person who committed this crime. I have seen crimes, many of them of this kind, and I know what the mental condition is. I know it was not an ordinary case of assault or serious injury. It was a case of frenzy.'

'We may have already formed that opinion,' the judge remarked drily.

Oliver, seeking to limit the damage, now engaged MacFall in a testy back-and-forth on the subject of mental instability.

Q. 'If this is the work of a maniac and he is a sane man, he didn't do it. Is that right?' A. 'He may be sane now.'

Q. 'If he has been sane all his life and is sane now it would be some momentary frenzy?' A. 'The mind is very peculiar.'

Q. 'It is a rash suggestion, isn't it?' A. 'Not in the slightest. I've seen this sort of thing before, exactly the same thing.'

Q. 'The fact that a man has been sane for fifty-two years and has been sane while in custody for the last three months would rather tend to be prove he's always been sane, wouldn't it?' A. 'No, not necessarily.'

49

Q. 'Not necessarily?' A. 'No, we know very little about the private lives of people or their thoughts.'

Q. 'I want to deal with evidence and not speculation.' A. 'You asked me, I think.'

Q. 'Let us go back. You have told the jury that you were very much struck with his callous demeanour?' A. 'I was.'

Q. 'Why did you not say so at the Police Court?' A. 'Because I was not asked.'

Q. 'You do not mind volunteering things. You have been volunteering things for the last five minutes.' A. 'There is a great deal I would like to volunteer that my Lord has pulled me up on.'

Q. 'I will get this fact from you: Not one word about his demeanour was said by you at the Police Court?' A. 'No.'

Q. 'Although you gave evidence for a long time and in detail?' A. 'Yes.'

This wouldn't be the last time the defence exposed MacFall's inconsistency. Oliver now moved on to the question of the bloodied mackintosh and how it came to be burnt. 'Suppose it was round her shoulders and she collapsed,' he said, 'do you not see the possibility of the mackintosh falling into the fire and getting burnt too?' MacFall agreed there was a possibility. There had arisen a theory that the killer had worn the mackintosh over his naked body, thus ensuring against bloodstains on his clothes. But whatever his state of dress, Oliver proposed, the killer would have been splashed with blood. 'On his left-hand side I think he would,' MacFall replied.

Q. 'What about his right?' A. 'No, I don't think so ... You don't find the blood so much on the hand that holds the weapon.'

Q. 'The last blows being probably struck with the head on the ground there would be blood upon his feet and the lower part of his legs for certain, wouldn't there?' A. 'I should expect that.'

Q. 'And his face?' A. 'Yes.'

Q. 'And his hair?' A. 'Yes, but more likely upon the face.'

MacFall, having admitted that he had not made any notes on the progress of rigor mortis in the deceased, now got into difficulties. He agreed that a powerful and muscular body would be affected by rigor much more slowly. So a frail woman such as Mrs Wallace would probably be affected more quickly? 'No, she would be rather delayed if anything,' he replied. The judge noticed the contradiction, and Oliver made a point of going through the argument again.

'Was this a feeble and frail woman?'

'Yes.'

'Then she would be likely, would she not, to be more quickly affected by rigor?'

'A little.'

'Then why did you say "rather longer" just now?'

'Not rather longer than a muscular person.'

'You are not arguing the case, are you?' Oliver said.

'No. I wish to state what I found.'

'You know what's at stake here?'

'I do.'

'Bearing in mind that this feeble and frail woman would be more likely to be affected by rigor, are you going to swear she was killed more than three hours before you saw her?'

'No, I'm not going to swear,' MacFall replied. 'I am going to give an opinion, and I swear that the opinion I give shall be an honest one.'

At this the judge interposed, 'Then what is your opinion?'

'My opinion was formed at the time that the woman had been dead about four hours.'

'Now that I have reminded you that, she being feeble and frail, rigor would come on quicker, does that move your opinion?'

'No.'

'It doesn't?'

'No.'

'You don't think she was killed four hours before you saw her?'

'I do.'

'You *do*?'

'That is your honest opinion?'

'Yes.'

'You saw her at half-past ten?'

'Yes.'

'So if she was alive at half-past six, your opinion is wrong, is it not?'

'Yes.'

'Doesn't that convince you what a very fallible test rigor mortis is?'

This was the point at which MacFall could have got off the hook by agreeing that the pathology was unreliable. Everyone knew that rigor mortis was an inexact science, and MacFall better than most, yet he refused to budge. 'I am still of the opinion,' he insisted.

'Do you think the milk boy imagined seeing her alive?' Oliver asked, nearly incredulous.

'I don't want to think of the milk boy and what he saw at all,' was MacFall's petulant reply.

His had not been an authoritative display of professionalism, thought Key. As police officers they all took notes, all the time; to hear that MacFall, a professor of forensic medicine, had failed to take a single one on the night of the murder was a surprise. It tended to undermine his entire testimony, because whenever he was cross-examined about timings nothing he said rang true.

The second doctor to take the stand that afternoon was, if anything, even less convincing. Like MacFall, Hugh Pierce had not taken any notes, and was even vaguer about the timing. Having examined the corpse at 11.50 p.m. he estimated that death had been 'some few hours' previous. The judge interrupted: '"Some few hours" means nothing ... I don't know what that means.' Pierce then revised this to 'about six o'clock', with a margin of error of two hours either side. This estimate was shown to be so broad as to be useless. After more inconsequential exchanges Oliver cut his questioning short. 'I will leave it there, my Lord.'

One could but marvel at MacFall's arrogance, and ignorance. That a professional should be so underprepared was bad enough; that he had also tossed around psychological speculation like confetti was irresponsible. His picture of Wallace's apparent coolness on the murder night had damaged the defence. And his insinuation of how little one knew about people's 'private lives' would have planted a seed of doubt in the jury's thinking. Was this placid-looking insurance man actually other than he seemed?

That question must have been foremost in the court's mind when Wallace entered the witness box on the third day. His pallor was wraithlike. Ged McMahon had got him right:

he looked like death itself. His voice on first replying to the defence counsel was husky, and then became clearer. Oliver, having dealt with the chess club evening, addressed the crucial hours of six to nine o'clock on the 20th. He put a direct question to the accused: 'Did you lay a finger upon her? Did you lay a hand upon your wife at all that night?'

Wallace considered this a moment. 'I think in going out of the back door I did what I often enough did. I just patted her on the shoulder and said "I won't be longer than I can help".' He had obviously misconstrued the question. 'I did not mean that,' said Oliver. 'Did you do anything to injure her?' 'Oh no, certainly not.'

There followed another long retread of his search for Menlove Gardens East, including his encounter with a 'genial' policeman on Green Lane, his eventual return home and the discovery of his wife's body. Oliver then gave him an opportunity to answer MacFall's recollection of his 'cool and collected' demeanour once the police had arrived and the house was being searched. Wallace replied that it was an effort on his part to *appear* 'as calm and cool as possible', since 'I had to do something to avoid breaking down'. This admission would at least remind the jury that he was in a vulnerable state of mind.

The counsel moved on to the possibility of someone calling at their house that evening, and which people Julia Wallace would have been likely to know and admit.

Q. 'Looking at it now, if someone did come and give the name of Qualtrough to your wife on that night, do you think she would have let him in?' A. 'Seeing I had gone to meet a Mr Qualtrough I think she would because she knew all about the business.'

Q. 'It is only a matter of speculation?' A. 'Yes.'

Q. 'If she had let him in where would she have taken him?' A. 'Into the front room. There is no question about that.'

Hemmerde's cross-examination of Wallace was by turns pernickety and aggressive. He rained questions on him in such profusion it seemed the aim was to tire him out, like a boxer jabbing his opponent, waiting for him to drop his guard. He asked about the piano in the parlour, about his friendship with Joseph Crewe, about the money he had collected that week, about the phone box Qualtrough was alleged to have called from.

Q. 'Has anyone ever left a message for you before at the City Café?' A. 'No.'

Q. 'Or has anyone ever left such a message for you anywhere?' A. 'No.'

Q. 'You must have realised he had not the slightest idea as to whether you got his message or not because no one knew you were going to be there?' A. 'Yes.'

This was a point on which the defence could have objected, for anyone who had glanced at the club noticeboard in the weeks before the murder would have seen that Wallace was scheduled to play on Monday 19 January. Beattie had told the man on the phone that he expected Wallace shortly. So an unknown caller could have watched Wallace leave home for the City Café at the appointed hour.

Hemmerde returned to the fact that Joseph Crewe, his Prudential colleague, and a resident of nearby Green Lane, would have known about the existence or otherwise of Menlove Gardens East. If he was puzzled by the address why didn't he simply ring up Crewe and ask him? Wallace: 'I could have done that but I didn't think of it.' Having been in the witness box for two hours Wallace looked strained and close to exhaustion. Hemmerde now went on the attack.

Q. 'Does not the whole thing strike you as very remarkable, that a man who does not know you should ring you up for business in another district and expect you to go there, and yet without knowing whether you had gone there or not come and wait outside your house for the chance of murdering your wife?'

A. 'Yes.'

Q. 'It is a curious thing, is it not?'

A. 'Yes.'

Q. 'It would have been easier for him, would it not, to have given a right address a little further off?'

A. 'I suppose it would.'

Q. 'If you had been given a right address, of course, you need not make a number of inquiries. One would have been sufficient. You follow what I mean?'

A. 'Yes.'

Q. 'The wrong address is essential to the creation of evidence for the alibi. Do you follow that?'

A. 'No, I do not follow you.'

Q. 'If you had been told Menlove Gardens West, the first enquiry would have landed you there?'

A. 'Yes.'

Q. 'If you are told of an address which does not exist, you can ask seven or eight people, every one of whom would be a witness as to where you were.'

A. 'Yes.'

Q. 'So, to a man who was planning to do this, a wrong address would be essential to his alibi?'

A. 'Yes.'

Hemmerde, in another agonising round of questions, returned to the moment Wallace arrived back at Wolverton Street. His initial supposition on finding the doors fastened against him was that his wife might have gone to post a letter. But on the Johnstons turning up in the back entry he said, 'Have you heard anything unusual?' In a statement to DI Gold at Cheapside Wallace had said, 'I thought someone was in the house when I went to the front door because I could not open it, and I could not open the back door.' Hemmerde asked him if he remembered saying that.

'No, I do not,' replied Wallace.

'Do you still think that when you were there you thought there was someone in the house?'

'No, I do not.'

'You have given that theory up?'

'Yes.'

'Did you ever believe it?'

'I might have done at the moment.'

Hemmerde finished by casting doubt on the claim that there was genuine trouble with the locks on the front and back door.

Q. '... you now say that when you came back from Menlove Avenue that night, you are convinced that the front door was bolted, but the back door was only stiff?' A. 'Yes, that is so.'

Q. 'I put it to you that the front door was in the condition it had been for a very long time, and the back door was the same?' A. 'As far as the locks are concerned, yes, that is so; the back door had been like that for years, sticky.'

Q. 'Had you ever known before the key not to turn in the lock?' A. 'No, and we had not been unable to get in with our keys.'

Q. 'How long were you trying altogether to get in that night?' A. 'Not many minutes – possibly half a minute on the first occasion, and I would go round to the back, possibly four or five minutes altogether, not more.'

Q. 'You could not open the front door?' A. 'No, I could not get it open.'

Q. 'But you saw the Superintendent open it at the very first time?' A. 'Yes, that is true.'

Q. 'Close the door and go out in the street and open it without any difficulty?' A. 'But I could not open it because the bolt was on it.'

Q. 'But the key?' A. 'I said the key slipped back.'

Q. 'You never told him that?' A. 'I don't know if I told him that, but I tell you that.'

After another flurry of minor testimonies the judge decided to close proceedings for the day. The summing-up would be made the next morning.

That Saturday, 25 April, Key had breakfast with Ged McMahon, Jimmy Dent and Alec Moran in the dining room of the Imperial on St George's Place. They were in high spirits. Alec and a few others were off to Anfield that afternoon to watch Liverpool play Man Utd in the Lancashire Senior Cup. Key would drop by on his parents for tea, as he always did on Saturday.

They were debating the latest and most outlandish rumour to emerge in the case. In his statement the milk boy, Close, said that having knocked at number 29 with a delivery between 6.30 and 6.45 he had returned moments later on seeing that the milk can had been taken in. The front door was now open, and he waited for a minute until Mrs Wallace came out to give him the empty can. She asked him about his cough, and told him to hurry home out of the cold. He said the hallway was dark when they talked.

'Which makes a problem,' said Ged. 'How could she have come to the door if she was already lying dead in the parlour?' None of them had an answer to that, so he continued. 'Well, the kid definitely talked to *someone* there. The theory is – it was Wallace, dressed up as his missus.'

Key burst out laughing at this. 'That would be funny if it wasn't so grotesque.'

Alec said, 'Well, it would explain why her clothes and hats were scattered on the bed upstairs. And we know it was dark in the hall.'

'Dark? Even if that milk boy hadn't noticed that Julia Wallace suddenly had a deep voice and a moustache, he couldn't have mistaken her height. Wallace was about a foot taller than her. Even a drag artist couldn't carry that off.'

'In any case,' said Ged, 'the prosecution decided not to raise it. They didn't want to get the kid confused.'

'He wouldn't have been the only one.'

Breakfast done, they crossed the road to the Hall, where the queue had been forming since the early hours. It snaked around William Brown Street and into St John's Gardens. It started to rain as they took the steps up to the entrance. The others knew all about the bet McMahon and Key had on the verdict. Ten quid was a fair sum in those days, and yet neither of them were serious gamblers. Key would have a five-bob treble whenever he was at Haydock Park, and McMahon did the pools every week. So why did they set the stake so high? Perhaps it was the equal force of certainty that provoked

59

them. McMahon really did believe, along with most of their colleagues, that Wallace was guilty and that the court would convict him. Conversely, Key had good reason to believe that no jury could say beyond doubt that this man had murdered his wife.

It was finally the turn of Mr Justice Wright, in his blood-coloured robe, to sum up the case. Until now Wallace had regarded the proceedings in an attitude of imperturbable calm, almost indifference. He kept his arms folded. Now, as the end-game approached, he looked more animated, leaning forward in his seat, chin resting on his balled-up fist. His focus upon the Bench was absolute.

Wright began by warning the jury not to judge the case on what they had read and heard in the weeks before the trial; only the evidence presented in the courtroom mattered. 'This case, I should imagine, must be almost unexampled in the annals of crime. Here you have a murder committed on an evening in January, in a house in a populous neighbourhood, and you have that murder so devised and so arranged that nothing remains which would point to anyone as the murderer, no signs of anyone having come into the house forcibly, no fingerprints, no marks of blood anywhere – I mean apart from the marks due to the actual commission of the crime round the woman's head as she lay there.'

As for the evidence, they had to accept that it was circumstantial. And yet the value of such evidence might vary infinitely. The real test of it was this: 'Does it exclude every reasonable possibility? ... If you cannot put the evidence against the accused man beyond a probability which is not inconsistent with there being other reasonable possibilities, then it is impossible for a jury to say: "We are satisfied beyond reasonable doubt that the charge is made out against the accused man."

'Then again, the question is not: Who did this crime? The question is: Did the prisoner do it? – or to put it more accurately: Is it proved beyond all reasonable doubt that the prisoner did it? It is a fallacy to say: "If the prisoner did not do it, who did?" It is a fallacy to look at it and say: "It is very difficult to think the prisoner did not do it"; and it may be equally difficult to think that the prisoner did do it. The prosecution have to discharge the onus cast upon them of establishing the guilt of the prisoner, and must go far beyond suspicion or surmise, or even probability, unless the probability is such as to amount to a practical certainty.'

Once again came the narrative of Julia Wallace's last moments on earth, perhaps hearing a knock, answering the door and leading her killer – all unknowing – into the parlour, where she sat and lit the fire. Was the first blow to her head delivered from the front? Or had the assailant taken her completely by surprise? Of the burnt and bloodied mackintosh it was also difficult to judge. Perhaps Mrs Wallace had momentarily put her husband's mackintosh over her shoulders when going out into the yard; if she was still wearing it at the moment of attack it would explain how the coat was burnt as she fell in front of the fire. It was perhaps significant that Wallace had never disowned the mackintosh, either to the Johnstons in the immediate aftermath of discovery or to the police later that evening. If he were the killer would he have left an item of his own clothing so conspicuously close to his wife's dead body?

As to the single clot of blood on the lavatory pan in the bathroom, the judge dismissed it. The scientists examining it deduced that coagulation could not have occurred in less than an hour after the murder. No one could tell how it got there, and within the more vexing mystery of how the killer had disposed of his bloodied clothes it seemed an irrelevance.

The most crucial element of the case, the judge continued, lay in the timing. Would the prisoner have been able, in the narrow frame of time allowed, 'not more than ten minutes', to carry out his purpose? 'It is perfectly true that if he planned and executed this scheme he would have had everything ready and everything would have gone, in the way of execution, with the utmost precision and rapidity. But there was a lot to do, you must consider. And twenty minutes afterwards he was found, at six minutes past seven, apparently completely dressed and apparently without any signs of discomposure, on a tramcar twenty minutes' journey from his home. Therefore he must have worked with lightning rapidity and effectiveness. It does not follow that he did not do it, but you have to be satisfied that he did do it.'

In concluding, the judge once again acknowledged the wholly perplexing nature of the case, and the obvious difficulty a jury must have in reaching a decision. There seemed so little in the end to incriminate anybody. 'If there was an unknown murderer, he has covered up his traces. Can you say it is absolutely impossible that there was no such person? But putting that aside as not being the real question, can you say, bearing in mind the strength of the case put forward by the police and by the prosecution, that you are satisfied beyond reasonable doubt that it was the hand of the prisoner, and no other hand, that murdered this woman? If you are not satisfied, if it is not established as a matter of evidence, as a matter of fact, of legal evidence and legal proof, then it is your duty to find the prisoner not guilty.'

He then invited the jury to retire and consider their verdict. The whole court seemed to let out a breath. The twelve jurors filed out. Wallace vanished down the stairway leading to the cells below. After the tension of the counsels' addresses and the summing-up a mood of exhaustion had settled. Key looked along the row where several of his colleagues sat, all staring straight ahead, glassy-eyed. He rose to stretch his legs. In the corridor outside he saw Moore and Gold, their heads together. It was half-past one by now. Alec Moran sidled up behind him.

'Well?'

'If they take any notice of that judge, they'll acquit.'

'He took long enough, didn't he?' Alec said, glancing at his watch. 'At this rate I'm not gonna make the game.'

'I'm sure that's playing on the jurors' minds,' Key replied.

They went outside for a smoke and a coffee. The Mersey sky had that off-white shade of milk on the turn. But the rain had gone off. They walked up London Road a while, and turned into Pembroke Place. A large furniture shop at number 5 was shuttered and closed. On the fascia above was a mirrored sign.

A. KEY Furniture. Est. 1872. Alec looked at it, and then at Key.

'Is that you?'

He nodded. 'Arthur Key. My grandfather. I used to work here as a kid during the holidays, deliveries and that. My uncles run it.'

'You gonna take it over?'

He gave a half-laugh. 'What, and miss all of this?'

They turned back, and as they came in sight of the hall

Jimmy Dent was on the steps, frantically waving. 'They're back!'

So here it was. They took their seats just as the judge reappeared. Up in the dock Wallace was standing, flanked by two warders. Behind him he had laid his overcoat on the chair. McMahon pointed this out, and murmured, 'Optimistic, isn't he?'

The jury presented their poker faces; only the foreman remained standing. The clerk of assize addressed him. 'Members of the jury, are you agreed upon your verdict?' They were. 'Do you find William Herbert Wallace guilty or not guilty?'

'Guilty.'

There came a collective gasp – of amazement. *Guilty?* Key was almost too stunned to follow the words, though he remembered later when the judge next spoke he was wearing the black cloth on his head. 'William Herbert Wallace, the jury after a very careful hearing have found you guilty of the murder of your wife ... only one sentence ... The sentence of the court upon you is that you be taken ... thence to a place of execution ... hanged by the neck until ... God have mercy on your soul.'

He looked up at Wallace, who maintained a remarkable appearance of calm, as he had throughout the trial. Key had a sudden fear that he might look across the court and find his eye, but he stared dead ahead. And then they took him down.

'I'll accept cash or a cheque,' whispered McMahon, though he looked rueful about it. A reward for my hubris, Key thought. He had not properly conceived of anything other than Wallace's acquittal. Alec made for the tram to Anfield, the rest went to the Legs of Man.

'Give us a brandy,' McMahon said to the barman, 'we're in shock.'

When he took out his cheque book and a pen, Ged said, 'There's no rush, son.' Key felt his hand shaking as he wrote. Guilty. *Guilty.* The word tolled like a bell around his brain. *Do not ask for whom . . .*

'There'll be an appeal,' said Jimmy Dent, who'd detached himself from another bunch of drinkers to join them. 'I mean, what kind of jury convicts someone on evidence like *that*?'

'A deaf one?' someone said. Even Ged looked troubled. While he believed Wallace *had* done it he also knew the meaning of 'reasonable doubt'. The jury could only have mis-understood the advice of the judge.

Key had another couple of large ones and yet remained weirdly sober. The alcohol had somehow lost its stupefying power. Eventually he left Ged and the others to it. On the steps at Lime Street a newsboy had hold of the latest edition. 'MERR-DA TRIAL,' he cried. 'Wallace to 'ang!'

He walked back to Falkner Street, passing on the way another *Echo* vendor, howling the very same thing.

7

Key was teaching Lydia how to play chess. An apt pupil, though she hadn't come close to beating him. 'Impetuous,' he remarked of her latest false move: her self-reproach came in tinkling laughter, and she continued, unembarrassed.

He had made fast friends with the Tarrants. Even the mother had grown on him. Prim and snobbish she may have been, but beneath that brittle social carapace one glimpsed a stifled sense of fun. Possibly marriage had ground it out of her, though for all he knew the husband was the life and soul. He sometimes found her looking at him in a way he could only describe as wistful. Did she dream an alternative life as a copper's helpmeet? There were worse fates, he supposed. But it was doubtful she'd have found their society very congenial.

Lydia he had liked from the start. She too had surprised him, or rather he realised his first impressions had been misplaced. A plain girl, as he thought, yet being in her company at close quarters was having an odd effect; the distinctive mobility of her features, her manner of addressing people, the fetching way she moved her slim pale hands transformed her, not into 'a beauty', but a person one was charmed to look at. It was confounding. The eye could play such tricks ...

In between their games he encouraged her to talk about her life. East Sheen, he gathered, was a suburb close to Richmond Park, respectable and dreary (she said) in the way so many London suburbs are. She had lived there with her parents and younger brother up to 1940. At school she had discovered a facility for languages – French, German – which she felt minded to turn to account in the war effort. A friend told her of a job at the War Office that involved putting checks on 'subversive elements'; they were recruiting women to read the letters and papers of foreign travellers, prisoners of war, bogus refugees and the like who might be passing information to the enemy. Most of it was drudgery, but once or twice she scored a bull's-eye, such as the occasion she was handed a French cookbook confiscated from a man who claimed to have employment on a merchant vessel. Lydia studied the book and noticed that some of the recipes had faint pencil markings in the margin. On a hunch she took it to an operative in counterespionage, who quickly worked out that it was a cipher about British shipping lanes.

'So you were actually codebreaking as well as censoring,' he said.

Her laugh in reply modestly disowned the idea.

Long hours in an unheated London office during the blackout made the journey back to East Sheen an extra inconvenience, so she moved into a house in Bayswater with friends. There had been perilous times, including a Blitz night when they were bombed out, but camaraderie and a spirit of adventure got her through. 'We worked all day and then went dancing in the evening – the Berkeley, or the 400 Club in Leicester Square. A lot of nice-looking men in uniform and girls in pearls squashed up together. To be honest I had the time of my life.'

Key wondered if she'd had a sweetheart, but hesitated to put her on the spot. Perhaps it was that he couldn't bear to hear that she'd been jilted or – worse – bereaved. Whatever had happened, the freedom she had enjoyed in those years lasted until the day her department was disbanded and she was out of a job, surplus to requirements. The return to life back at home seemed to have been an anticlimax. But she was without self-pity, a sort of bravery in itself.

'Could your father not find you a job?'

'I don't know what I'd be good for. There's not much call for single women without academic qualification.'

The chess board lay forgotten on the table between them. Lydia suggested they go for tea at the Palm Court; she liked to hear the string quartet that played there in the afternoon.

'Should we not ask your mother to join us?' he said as they set off.

'She's in her cabin with a cold compress to her forehead. One of her headaches.'

'Oh dear . . .'

'Don't worry. She'll be fighting fit again by dinnertime.'

They decided to take a long way round via the deck. It was mid-afternoon, the light pearly and the sea in one of its benign swollen phases. Seagulls wheeled about in the sky. They had reached the taffrail, and as they looked down on the ship's wake unspooling in parallel furrows, he remembered Lydia's comment about the waves seeming to chase them.

Then another quite different line came back to him. '*Caelum non animum mutant qui trans mare currunt.*'

Lydia looked round. 'What?'

'Horace. A poet of my schooldays. "They change their skies, not their souls, those who rush across the sea." In other words, you may travel as far as you please, but you're still stuck with yourself.'

'That's rather cheerless,' she said, after a moment. 'So you have Latin?'

'I've forgotten most of it. All those hours of parsing, reciting. Bits of Horace or Virgil ambush my tired old brain now and then.'

'Where were you at school?'

'Oh, a Jesuit college in Liverpool. Salisbury Street. I dare say it was a useful place to be if you were bright. If you weren't – well, it was best to keep your head down. The "Js" prized elitism and competitiveness, often among themselves as much as the pupils. And they ruled by fear.'

'Did they beat you?' she asked.

He laughed. 'Most of us. You've heard of a ferula?'

He explained to her, with a certain degree of relish, the school's notorious system of punishment. The ferula was made of whalebone with a hard rubber surface, about the size of a shoe-horn. If a teacher judged that a boy had done wrong he wrote out a bill – a red slip with name, offence, number of ferulas, signature – and handed it to the offender. He would then have to present this bill to whichever teacher was on discipline duty within twenty-four hours. The waiting for some would be an agony greater than the punishment itself. The number of strokes to the palm varied according to the nature of the infraction; three, six, nine, twelve, or – among the more sadistic – twice twelve. He remembered the strange throb of heat and numbness that lingered in the hand for hours afterwards.

'They weren't noted for their mercy. And it wasn't always for misbehaviour. Some teachers would deal them out for poor work. Which caused a *lot* of resentment, quite often on another fellow's behalf.'

Lydia's voice had dropped to an undertone. 'The brutes . . .'

He shrugged. 'It wasn't all bad. And they did provide a first-rate classical education.'

She shook her head, distress in her eyes. 'What a horrible way to treat a child. How they could –' Her voice gave out. He had told the story in a spirit of cavalier reminiscence, but had reckoned without his listener's tender sensibility. Something about it had really upset her, and he was sorry.

'Crossing the Atlantic from east to west you tend to meet far more weather than if you go west to east. You get these ridges of high pressure coming at you full in the face, like a roller-coaster. But going the other way, from New York to Europe, if you time it right you can catch the same tailwind for the duration of the voyage.'

There were about fourteen at table that evening with the Captain, who was giving the company fair warning of some lively weather systems ahead. There had been rumours of a hurricane brewing, but Jarrett assured them that the threat had been downgraded to a tropical storm. Mrs Leverton, a red-faced matron of Newbury, Berkshire, asked, 'How close are we to this, er, storm?'

The Captain was nonchalant. 'We should have flat calm for at least a day. I don't think we're going to have any great trouble when it arrives.'

Key detected the professional's bedside manner there, putting his passengers at ease. Mrs Orme, who was Mrs Leverton's widowed sister – or was it the other way around? – asked him if he would be leading the dancing at the Farewell Ball.

'I'm no dancer, alas. But I expect you all to be there on Saturday night – we take the event very seriously on this boat.'

Mrs Orme pointed out that Saturday was in fact the penultimate night of the crossing. What about Sunday evening?

'We like to allow passengers a day of recovery following the Ball. And Sunday gives the crew a chance to clean up the vessel before we dock.'

Key laughed inwardly at that 'day of recovery' – Jarrett's language was at its most euphemistic this evening. What he meant was that they'd be hungover. As the table conversation broke into pairs Mrs Tarrant, seated on his right, turned an expectant look on him. 'Are you prepared, Mr Key, to trip the light fantastic?'

Her tone carried the faintest glimmer of flirtation.

'I shall do my best, Mrs Tarrant, though I was never in great demand at the Liverpool Police ball.'

'Were you expected to bring a partner?'

'If one could be found,' he replied, with a jaunty hoist of his brow. This seemed to encourage her.

'So you're a confirmed bachelor, then?'

'I'm not sure about "confirmed". That suggests an element of volition on my part, whereas I've come to regard bachelorhood as a matter of fate.'

He could sense her next question from the momentary pinking in her cheeks. 'Was there ever the possibility of a Mrs Key?'

He gave a deflecting sigh of regret in answer. Better to leave the matter ambiguous and give Mrs Tarrant something to wonder about. He reached for the bottle of wine to top up her glass, and asked about her headache.

Key could have told her the story, of course, though he wasn't sure he understood it any better now than he had thirty-five years ago. In those early years of the century his family lived at a house on Lord Nelson Street, at that time one of only two private residences on the terrace. It was large enough to accommodate his parents, uncles Chas and Frank, two maids, a cook, his sisters Cinny and Maud, and himself. Next door lived his aunt Ada and her husband, George, along with their three kids. Both houses were the property of Arthur – the furniture man – and his wife Elizabeth, who ran the largest fruit and veg stall in St John's Market. For a family that had escaped from Ireland – the children of immigrants, like everyone else in the city – they had made good, and in an economy as precarious as Liverpool's they were positively well-off. When his great-grandfather Thomas stepped off that Dublin boat in the late 1840s his surname was McKee: soon after he shortened it to Key, on the grounds that an English-sounding name was more likely to prosper. A Key decision, you might say.

Lord Nelson Street runs parallel to Lime Street Station, so the boy grew up to the sound of trains, hundreds of them every week, arriving, depositing, collecting, departing. They couldn't keep the windows in the house clean for more than a day with all the smoke and smuts. Back then the place was mad-busy, you'd hear all sorts of different languages, on the street, in the pubs. Sailortown, Babel-town. Liverpool was where you came to get the boat to America. The waterfront was the last of England most emigrants ever saw. A city of farewells, and departures. It was not a place people came back to any more.

As a kid he helped at the shop on weekends, riding on the back of horse-drawn carts piled high with furniture, when horses vastly outnumbered motor vehicles. They went all over town with deliveries, and sometimes he'd pick up an extra bob or two in tips. They attended Mass every Sunday at St Vincent de Paul on Hardy Street, near to where Thomas McKee first rented in a lodging-house. Five rooms, home to at least three families at a time. (The house came down in the thirties, to no one's lament.) That church was the reminder of where they'd come from. The tribes all descended for the Sunday ritual, God's plenty on parade, families like theirs in muted best – the men in frock-coats and hats, the women in bombazine with lace veils over their face – while nearer the back of the church crowded the more numerous poor, barely able to clothe and feed themselves but still offering coppers when the collection plate came round. Those piteous undernourished faces sometimes came back to him. What on earth were *they* giving thanks for?

Even the Jesuits were hard-pressed to explain that one.

The year was 1911, in that very hot summer. He remembered it because it was the long-awaited moment they peeled away the massive scaffolding at the Pier Head to reveal the Liver Building, with its double clock-face and those two birds perched impossibly high. The sight of it stopped people in their tracks. Birds thou never wert ... and yet he couldn't stop staring at them. He was then at the University, a history student – the first of the family to attend such an institution. So much for his mother's hopes of his entering the priesthood. It was never a serious prospect for him. He had the Jesuits to thank for that.

The city, as he recalled, had come to standstill with a general transport strike – dockers, sailors, railwaymen, the lot. Later that summer a union meeting outside St George's Hall turned into a riot when police charged the crowds. It became so violent they sent the army in. And did he care a rap about any of this? His nineteen-year-old head was turned quite another way. It had begun when a bunch of them went along to a dance at the Wellington Rooms on Brownlow Hill. Whatever else might grind to a halt, nothing in Liverpool derailed the quest for entertainment, for music and ale and dancing. Their partners would have been drawn from the tiny pool of women at the University, or else sisters and cousins recruited for the occasion. In that grimly homocentric world they were strangers to female company.

The circular ballroom, with its frieze of dancing maidens running along the walls, had an Austen-like formality at odds with the crowd and its loud, sometimes loutish mood. Cologne and cigar smoke hung heavy in the air. He would never have met her but for the Paul Jones halfway through, that long winding dance wherein you start with one partner before joining a circle and, as the music changes, partnering with the person closest to you. Thus did he find himself holding a dark-haired girl whose fluid, light-stepping movement across the sprung floor felt a world away from his own mechanical waltzing. (Maud, his older sister, had been a despairing dance instructor at home.) She wasn't that tall, but she carried

74

herself with a graceful air of assurance: the floor seemed hers to command. Somehow he took heart from this, and with concentration managed to steer them around the room quite competently.

At the end she looked up and said, with an ironic twinkle, 'Thank you for not treading on my toes.'

It was only at this moment that he got a close look at her, and was half stunned to realise how pretty she was, the dark brows framing her tawny eyes, a straight nose and an interesting olive-coloured skin. He first thought her colouring Mediterranean, though her accent was as strong as his. He heard himself thanking her in return and asking if she might care for another dance later. Possibly his request sounded stiff, because she half laughed before taking out her dance card with its little pencil attached by a ribbon. She asked his name and marked him for a valse and a polka.

'Two?!' he exclaimed, flattered.

'This card doesn't fill itself, you know.' She smiled, a smile that began in her eyes and ran down to her mouth in two lines of delight. He liked this reply, which seemed to mix something forthright and self-deprecating at once. He asked her name, and she told him. Esmé Levinson. *Esmé*. It sounded an enchantment in itself.

'I'll look out for you.'

She nodded her agreement, and faded back into the throng. From that moment his gaze didn't stray from her, talking with her friends, or dancing with one new man after another. This became disconcerting, and he found himself hoping, unreasonably, that these partners of hers were toe-crushers, or brutes with bad breath. When he saw her smile at them he felt agonised. The gang he had arrived with were having a high old time, none of them too fussy about who his dance partner might be, but he couldn't be so carefree any more. It was Esmé and no one else he wanted in his arms.

That night he waltzed himself to tatters, and asked permission to accompany her home. Quite a walk, as it transpired. The trams were on strike, and she lived way south in Sefton Park, but what did that matter to him? He would have walked her to Llandudno and back if she'd asked. She was two months away from her eighteenth, had just started as secretary to an insurance broker in town. The boss was someone her father knew. She had two sisters, like him; she played violin and piano. And her favourite dance was the polka. They talked all the way to her front gate. The tree-shadowed streets off the park, lamplit and bosky, suddenly felt tremulous with romance. How else could they be, now that he knew *she* lived there? Something made him hang back in the shadows as the front door opened and a light glimmered on the porch. She didn't wave, but she turned her face back in his direction, which seemed a private way of saying good-night.

Over the following weeks he took every chance to be in her company. If she had a lunch hour free they would have sandwiches on a bench by the Pier Head, or else he would take her to the Kardomah for tea and cake. In the evening they might have a drink after work, and then the delight of walking her home. They didn't need a tram anyway, the nights were sultry and the parks – first Prince's, then Sefton – were beautiful in their heavy midsummer foliage. As they sauntered very slowly under the trees and he listened to Esmé's light, level voice it seemed the darkening blue distances of the park enveloped them in a dream, a gliding dream of companionship. They talked only to one another; he never met her friends, nor she his; they had no need of anyone else. He loved to stare into her eyes, to make out the flecks of tawny gold inside the green. If he'd known how to he would have written sonnets to her. She laughed when he told her that.

'Who are you – John Keats?' she said. He must have looked hurt, because she then said, in a softer voice, 'You could write me a letter, if you liked.'

'But if I can see you every day there's no need to write you a letter.'

She made a face that suggested he'd missed the point. But there was nothing wrong between them, not for an instant, until the news about them got out. One evening after dinner his father took him aside. Was it true about this girl he'd been seeing – Esmé something? He confirmed it, and anticipated the objection. I know she's seventeen, he said, but she's eighteen in September – that's adulthood, really. His father shook his head sadly. Her age wasn't the problem. He looked at him for a moment, uncomprehending. 'You know what she is, don't you?' The penny dropped. Of course he was aware that Esmé was Jewish, but it impinged on him no more than the particular scent she wore, or the tiny mole on her cheek.

'I'm sure she's a nice girl –'

'She's more than nice,' he told him.

'Your mother's upset about it. She doesn't want you to –' His tone was mortified, and he wondered how much of this came from her rather than him. His father dealt with Jews all the time, as clients, as customers, in the day-to-day running of the shop. The piano tuner who came to their house was Jewish. The doctor who'd attended his sister in the sanatorium when she had TB was Jewish. But there was no gainsaying Papist bigotry. From schooldays he'd heard them called 'Jew-boy' and 'sheeny'; he laughed at jokes about their meanness and sharp practice. That was the way they were. It didn't mean he disliked them.

'I want to marry her.'

Why did he say that? No word of marriage had ever passed between him and Esmé. But confronted by outright disapproval he was stung, and felt he should raise the stakes. His father retracted his chin in surprise.

'Come on, son, don't talk daft. You know once her parents find out they'll feel exactly the same about you. They won't want their daughter knocking round with an RC.'

In his naivety he'd not considered this possibility. He and Esmé had talked of their parents, and he had made light-hearted allusion to his mother's piety. But the subject of 'faith' hadn't bothered them. They had tacitly accepted their upbringing as a difference, not as a potential for conflict. It shook him. He was disbelieving at first, and then angry, so angry he decided to have it out with his mother. If his father was regretful, she was implacable. She took it amiss that he should even object to giving up 'a Jewess'. She remarked, stiffly, on the dangers of people not 'keeping to their own'. To this he reacted with some heat, though he didn't care to recall the words he used. He was certain it was nothing like she had ever heard from him before.

His urgent mission now was to talk to Esmé. This was in the days before most families had a private telephone, so he took it upon himself to call at her house the next morning. A mistake? He began to think so when a lady – her mother, or else an aunt – answered the door and found an agitated young stranger asking if Esmé was at home. From her guarded, sharp-eyed expression he instantly understood how little welcome he was, and the door seemed about to close when Esmé appeared in the hallway. The door was left ajar while a whispering confabulation went on behind it. A sense of decorum made him step back off the porch.

Some moments later she emerged, pale and flustered. Confusion chased over her features: he had violated an unspoken pact between them, namely that their relationship was something private, and now he was obliged to explain. He didn't know how much he should tell her. A deep mortification oppressed him; to disclose his parents' feelings on the matter induced a shame too scalding to touch. As they crossed into the park he offered her a halting account of what had been said. She listened, without interrupting, until he'd finished.

He turned to her, hoping for some word of consolation. What she said surprised him: 'And what about you? Does my being – make a difference?'

'Of course not! How can you ask me that? It's *you* I care about, not your being – what you are.'

'But Jewish is what I am,' she replied, gravely. 'Maybe you don't care now, but one day you might. If – just say if – we ever had children, wouldn't you want to raise them Catholic?'

The coolness of her reasoning wrongfooted him. 'Isn't this – it doesn't seem – I haven't thought about it.'

'Maybe you should. One day it might really matter.'

He stopped dead still; he faced her, put his hands on her shoulders. 'Esmé. Don't talk like this. You said you loved me. Do you?'

His voice had cracked, and Esmé, calm until now, turned her face away. He waited for her to speak. When she looked back her eyes had gone filmy.

'Yes. I do,' she said, but in a voice so choked with emotion he felt panic, not reassurance. He had to be practical, but what plan did he have? They couldn't run off – neither of them had money – and in any case he hadn't the boldness of youth to break from everything he knew. Before they parted they made avowals. Piety and religion could go hang. They loved one another, that was all that mattered.

But it wasn't. That same week his father was invited to the Levinson home to consult with Esmé's parents. His forecast regarding their attitude was correct. Mr and Mrs Levinson were apparently so alarmed at the prospect of their daughter marrying out that they thanked his father and gave him an assurance that Esmé would now be under strict instruction to stay away from him – as if he were a medical danger, like the mumps. He was at a loss. What was wrong with finding love where it fell?

Misgivings first took hold when he called at the insurance office where she worked in Castle Street and a message was sent down: Miss Levinson was not available. He patrolled outside her building at the closing hour, one day after the next, and saw no sign of her. He eventually had it from a colleague of hers that Esmé had left town for a few days – a precaution of her parents, he assumed. The days dragged into weeks. He expected to have word from her. He remembered the day she told him he could write her a letter, if he liked. So at last he did. As far as he was concerned his feelings were unchanged: he loved her, and if she felt the same way that was all he needed to know. *Please write*, he implored. He sent it care of her employers, reasoning that any letter addressed to her home would be intercepted.

He waited, fretful and restless. He waited as the days elided into weeks, the weeks into months. Did she receive his letter in the end? If she did, then her silence told him to desist. If she didn't ... That was the torturing thought, the straw he clung to, believing he might hear from her still. Where was she? He didn't know her friends so he had no way of finding out. Months later he would wander across Sefton Park, imagining he might run into her. But he was searching for a ghost. Esmé was gone, spirited away by an unknown hand. Here was his lesson in tribal antipathies. A young woman might disappear to save a family from disgrace.

Did it inflame a resentment against his parents? He didn't recall it so. However bitterly he regarded his loss, he was a dutiful son – the only son they had – and continued to be. But he came to realise that their interference had changed him; he knew after that he could never really trust them. Some of the blame in it he accepted as his own. If he had been bolder, had acted more decisively once movement against them was afoot, things might have been different. He had allowed fate to take charge, and did nothing as love turned to cinders, ashes, dust. The shock came late: he *did* hear from her. Perhaps a year had gone by when he found an envelope dropped through the door, addressed to him. There was no letter inside; just a dance card, from the Wellington Rooms, with his name pencilled against the last valse and polka. It had been hand-delivered. There it was, still in his wallet, creased with age.

8

It must have been a lunch hour, since he was the only one in the investigations room when the Super summoned him to his office. Moore had been in a quietly triumphant mood since the verdict against Wallace. An appeal had already been lodged, but among the high-ups at CID a general belief prevailed that they had got their man. Privately, Key was amazed at this complacency. No matter that the conviction flew in the face of all that doubt; professional experience held that Wallace *must* have done it, because no one else could have.

Moore got straight down to business. 'I've just had a call from a garage in Moscow Drive. Manager there says one of his staff served a feller named Parry, the night of January twentieth.'

'Parry – Wallace's friend at the Pru?'

Moore nodded. 'The lad who reported it works there nights, so we can't talk to him until this evening. Can you be ready to go at ten?'

Atkinson's Garage in Stoneycroft was a family-run business. As well as car repairs and maintenance they operated a fleet of taxis, a round-the-clock venture that made the place quite a social hive for private clients and assorted night owls. Moore and Key arrived there in the car just as the night staff were clocking in. The manager served them coffee in his office upstairs, then brought over an employee named John Parkes. He was a local lad, in his twenties. He had known Gordon Parry since they were at school in Lister Drive, knew him pretty well, though didn't consider him a friend.

'Why not?' asked Key. 'You fell out?'

'No, no. I just didn't trust him, you know. Gordon Parry's been in trouble round here, on the rob an' that.' He looked out the window. 'The boss always tells us to keep an eye out when he's around.'

So Parry's reputation as a petty thief preceded him, and yet by all accounts he lived quite well and owned a motor car. So why was he always in need of money? Parkes shrugged. 'I dunno. I think he might have got the car from his old man.'

The 'old man' was a big-wig at the City Treasury, and known to be friendly with the Super. But Moore, poker-faced, only said, 'Tell us about the night of January twentieth. You were on a late shift?'

'Yeah. I got here about eleven o'clock ... there was a bit of a crowd. Someone said there'd been a murder in Anfield that night, and we talked about it for a while.'

Parkes reckoned it was around 12.30 in the morning when Parry arrived in his motor at the garage. There seemed nothing unusual in his mood, he said, though he had 'obviously' been drinking. He asked Parkes to wash the car for him, which he did with a high-pressure hose, inside and out. They talked as he worked on the car, mostly about Parry's trouble with his ex-girlfriend, Lily Lloyd. He'd recently given her the elbow but she wasn't going quietly. 'It didn't bother him, though.' Then Parkes noticed a leather glove stuffed into a box, so he pulled it out to save it from getting wet. He noticed the glove had dark stains on it, and said that it looked like blood. At which Parry suddenly snatched the thing from his hand, saying, 'If the police got hold of that, it would hang me!'

Key looked up from his notebook. 'Those were his exact words?' He repeated the sentence back to him.

He nodded. 'I asked him what he meant – whose blood was it? But Parry just shook his head and laughed. He said, I'm just kidding yer. He was often like that, you know, sort of theatrical – one minute dead serious, the next laughing fit to bust.'

Moore, listening to this in pointed silence, now spoke. 'So it was a joke, then – about the glove incriminating him?'

Parkes gave a considering shrug. 'I'm not sure. He might have meant it, but with Parry you can't always tell.'

'When he arrived, did he have any blood on his clothes?'

'No, I don't think so.'

'What about the car – any blood there?'

'There might have been –'

Moore clicked his tongue impatiently. 'Did you see any blood in the car – on the floor, on the seats?'

'Well, the light wasn't good, so I couldn't be sure. All I know was that Parry wanted that car washing down good and quick.'

Once the car was cleaned to his satisfaction Parry paid him five bob, and after more chat drove off. The garage hand was worried, however, and next morning told his boss the story we'd just heard. 'And what did your boss say?'

'We both knew Parry was a bad'un. Boss said I shouldn't get involved.'

'So all this time you've been sitting on possible evidence in a murder case. What changed your mind?'

Parkes shrank a little at the Super's reproving tone. 'Well … When they found Wallace guilty I wondered if they'd made a mistake. Not that I was certain Parry done it. But I reckoned I should inform the police.'

'Better late than never, I suppose,' Moore deadpanned.

His sarcasm went undetected by Parkes, who said, 'You don't wanna see an innocent man hung.'

'Hanged,' Moore corrected. He stood up. 'Right. If anything else occurs to you, Mr Parkes, give us a call. But don't leave it another four months.'

The interview was done. On their return downstairs the manager showed them the inside of the garage where Parry had parked his car that night. Overhead, hanging from a roof beam was a metal armature, and coiled about it a long power-hose. They were walking out towards the car when Parkes caught up with them.

'Something else I've just remembered,' he said, with an earnest expression. 'You know you asked about Parry's clothes – if there was blood on them? I heard from someone who lives round here that Parry had borrowed fishing gear from them a few weeks before the murder.'

'Fishing gear?' Key repeated, taking out his notebook again.

'Yeah, an oilskin cape and a pair of waders that come up to 'ere. Which would shield you, like, from any – you know – splash.'

Moore and Key glanced at one another. 'And you saw Parry in possession of these things?'

'No, not meself,' he replied. 'But I do know that the feller who lent the gear to him never got them back.'

Moore sniffed. 'Waders and oilskin cape. Have you made a note of that, detective?'

Key nodded, and they thanked him again for his time.

On the drive back into town the Super was incredulous. 'Fishing gear! Does he imagine Julia Wallace's murderer turned up at her door dressed like the bloody Ancient Mariner?'

'What about the bloodstained glove and Parry's talk about hanging? I don't think he invented that.'

'He's an attention-seeker. He'd probably heard about the murder and thought he'd spin a yarn to the gullible lad who washed his car. It's a prank, nothing more.'

'A morbid kind of prank,' Key mused. 'Shall we call Parry in again?'

'I don't see the point. The alibi from the Brine woman is solid. I don't doubt young Parry's a thief and a crook. I've heard as much from his father – he's been bailing him out for years. But murder? He hasn't got it in him.'

Key was still wondering. He could see that the story of the fishing gear was probably meaningless, and that Parry was a joker. But that he *might* have been a visitor at Wolverton Street that evening was not absolutely impossible, and Moore's dismissive attitude to his being a suspect was in itself baffling.

Had Parry's old man actually put the arm on him?

The following week, on Friday 15 May, Key was in a train carriage with a number of plain-clothes detectives escorting Wallace from Lime Street to London. The hearing at the Appeal Court was scheduled for the following Monday. Munro and Oliver intended to argue that the verdict of guilty was unreasonable – tantamount to saying that the Liverpool jury had made a grievous error. This had never happened since the Court of Criminal Appeal was set up in 1907, so a ruling in Wallace's favour would be unprecedented.

Having a private conversation with the prisoner was ticklish, but Key managed to speak to him just before they whisked him off to Pentonville. Wallace wanted to know what his chances were; Key replied that he should be confident of a reprieve, though privately he was far from certain. The tide of opinion was pushing so hard against him, and the absence of another suspect so damaging, that even his most optimistic supporters were beginning to doubt.

He asked about Parry again, and Key told him of the conversation with the garage hand. 'Moore dismissed it completely. He said that feller's been reading too many "true crime" stories.'

Wallace muttered grimly, 'They're all against me.'

Key assured him they were not. 'You'll leave this court a free man.'

Ten minutes later they took him off in a Black Maria.

He next appeared on the Monday morning at the Royal Courts of Justice. In the dock he stood tall, straight-backed, cadaverous; his high collar and spectacles lent him the aspect of an Edwardian schoolmaster. The judges filed in: the Lord Chief Justice, Lord Hewart, took his seat between Mr Justice Branson and Mr Justice Hawke. Roland Oliver stood and addressed the court, expressing the main argument of the appeal: a man who might well be innocent had been convicted of murder and sentenced to death. Before him on his desk lay a transcript of the judge's summing-up at the Assizes in April.

'A man cannot be convicted of any crime, least of all murder, merely on probabilities, unless they are so strong as to amount to a reasonable certainty ... If the circumstances of this case, as

I shall hope to persuade the court, were such that they did not exclude other reasonable possibilities, then a jury could not and ought not to have been allowed to find the appellant guilty.'

Not allowed – in other words the case should have been withdrawn from the jury to obviate any miscarriage.

Oliver then dealt with the night of the murder. The salient point here was that Wallace could not have been the quick-change artist the prosecution effectively portrayed him to be. It would have been impossible for him in the aftermath of his violent act either to destroy or to clean his clothes between 6.30 and 6.45. The idea that he was naked while committing the murder was patently absurd.

Oliver now turned to the near-certainty of the jurors at the trial being predisposed before they knew they would be trying the accused. Such had been the gossip around the case that some of the jury were inevitably subject to bias, and did not base their verdict solely on the evidence they heard in court.

As for the relationship between Wallace and his wife the weight of evidence suggested that they were a devotedly fond couple. Nothing about their life together indicated any hint of strife or hostility, nor was there any suggestion of another woman in the case. Money could also be ruled out as a motive. Wallace had savings in the bank of £152, while Julia had £90 of her own; no suspicion attached to their personal finances. But someone else might have been induced to murder Mrs Wallace knowing that her husband kept money in the house – even though in the event only £4 was stolen.

Having dispatched the vexing question of Wallace's 'demeanour' at Wolverton Street when the police arrived – this was MacFall's misleading claim that the suspect had been cool and collected – Oliver went on to present two 'absolutely crucial' questions of the case. 'The first of them was this: Who sent the telephone message, or rather, did the prosecution prove that the appellant sent the telephone message of the nineteenth? If he did, he was guilty; if he did not, he was innocent. The second was this: At what time was Mrs Wallace last seen alive?' Oliver argued that there were several credible witnesses who could have testified that she was seen alive later than 6.30, but the police didn't call them. Instead, they staked their case on the evidence of a milk boy who had allegedly noticed the time that evening by the clock of Holy Trinity Church. He himself later told other people that he had seen Mrs Wallace at about 6.45. 'As I have said, every minute of that time is vital to the appellant; if you get to anywhere near a quarter to seven it would be fantastical to suggest that he could have been the murderer, but that is how the matter was dealt with by the prosecution.'

Oliver pressed home this argument. Could Wallace, infirm as he was, have rushed straight from the brutal murder of his wife without cleaning himself or his clothing and jumped straight on a tram? As to the time of the killing, a newspaper that had been pushed through the letterbox at about 6.30 was later found open on the table. Was it likely that after committing the murder Wallace would have picked up the paper and laid it there?

'What one looks for in this case and completely fails to find is any piece of evidence which is not consistent with innocence.'

The defence finished with another plea to the three judges. 'What I might venture to suggest is that, if at the end of the case for the Crown your lordships cannot say there is any fact that has been proved, which fairly and necessarily involves the guilt of the appellant, you have not proved the guilt of the appellant. You cannot build up a case, Mr Justice Wright says it himself in the summing-up, by a number of pieces of suspicion, or a number of pieces even of probability; you have got to bring guilt home with certainty, and if your Lordships think, after this hearing, guilt in this case has not been brought so, then you have not only power under the Act, but you would interfere with the verdict of the jury.'

Oliver's speech had lasted nearly four hours. As a corrective to the Liverpool jury's verdict it was as cogent and thorough as one could have wished. He had made the case not only that Wallace hadn't murdered his wife but that he oughtn't to have been on trial at all.

The following day it was the turn of Hemmerde to speak for the prosecution. He rejected the defence's claims that the jury had been prejudiced – and that the police had been at fault with the witnesses, coaching some and suppressing others: 'I take full responsibility for everything that was done in this case, and the police had nothing whatever to do with the conduct of it.'

Having got that off his chest, Hemmerde rehearsed the case he had mounted against the defendant in Liverpool. If Wallace were innocent the jury had to accept the story that the murderer telephoned, on the night before the murder, a man whom he had never met and who he had no reason to know would ever receive his message, that he acted on the assumption that Wallace had received the message, and that he entered the house intending to rob, whereas there was no evidence of any search for money, and jewellery in the bedroom had not been taken. The condition of Julia Wallace's body was not consistent with the theory of murder by a man who had entered the house to steal. A thief would not have committed a murder of such viciousness.

The jury were entitled to reject the theory put forward by the defence. The only alternative was the version of the facts advanced by the prosecution, and the evidence in support of that was strong. The mass of detail pointed to the likelihood that Wallace was the caller, and that once his actions thereafter were traced the jury was led irresistibly to conclude that 'it all fitted together like a jigsaw puzzle'.

At the conclusion – another four hours – Key looked over at Wallace, seated in a side gallery between two warders. He remembered Ged McMahon's description of him in the run-up to the trial at Liverpool: 'He looks like death.' It was true; even with the breath of life in him he couldn't have looked more deathly, eyes sunken deep in their sockets, skin waxen and pale.

But would his journey to the grave now be halted – or hurried? They waited in the corridor, close-mouthed, while the judges were out conferring. The court was filling up again, and the mood was feverish. He overheard a reporter striking a deal with a boy to occupy one of the outside phone boxes for him – there was always a stampede for them once the verdict was out. Just after 4.15 a call came for silence, the assembled pushed to their feet and the judges trooped back in.

If ever there was a moment Key's faith faltered it was then. Some lowering phantom had flitted out of the darkness to prey on him. His breathing had become shallow, and he felt a toppling dizziness. As a boy he'd had a habit of fainting – once in a dramatic collapse at a school assembly – but he had not been troubled as an adult. He was about to scramble his way out of the row he occupied when, in a collective motion, the court sat down. Forcing himself to stay, he could feel the light-headedness of nausea swirling in wait. There seemed not to be enough air in the room. He must have gone white, for a detective – plain clothes, not one of the Liverpool mob – asked him *sotto voce* if he was all right. He nodded, thanked him, and sat tight.

Then the Lord Chief Justice was speaking: '... Three facts are obvious. The first is that at the conclusion of the case for the Crown, no submission was made on behalf of the appellant that there was no case to go to the jury. The second fact which seems to be obvious is that the evidence was summed up by the learned judge with complete fairness and accuracy, and it would not have been at all surprising if the result of the trial had been an acquittal. The third obvious fact is that the case is eminently one of difficulty and doubt.'

He continued: 'We are not here concerned with suspicion, however grave, or theories, however ingenious. Section Four of the Criminal Appeal Act of 1907 provides that the Court of Criminal Appeal shall allow the appeal if they think that the verdict of the jury should be set aside on the ground that it cannot be supported having regard to the evidence.' He then cleared the police of any 'imputation' as to their fairness. 'The conclusion at which we have arrived is that the case against the appellant, which we have carefully and anxiously considered' – he held his breath, it seemed for minutes on end – 'was not proved with that certainty which would justify a verdict of guilty ... The result is that this appeal will be allowed, and this conviction quashed.'

Not guilty.

Wallace was walking out of the court a free man. Down the other end of the row Key caught sight of the Super, his expression hard as granite. He felt relief – such relief that it might have been his own escape from the hangman's noose. Desperate for air, he joined the massing crowd as it edged towards the exits. Newsmen were calling Wallace's name, asking for a comment. Two detectives shouldered him down the corridor, where they stopped to let him put on his coat and bowler hat. Just before they reached the big double doors Wallace turned back and looked at the surge of faces around him. He picked out Key, and briefly lifted his hand.

Outside, the crowds had closed in, and cheers were raised for the reprieved man. Flash bulbs cracked in celebration. Some smart friend of his had been making provision, for the next thing they knew Wallace had disappeared into a cab, and the cab disappeared down Fleet Street. Key crossed the road and bought a postcard at a newsagent's. He took it into a pub, sat down and wrote to Ged McMahon. *Wallace a free man. I'll have my tenner back, and another ten for the win.*

9

He first noticed the young man at breakfast, yarning away to the Captain at his table. The latter, characteristically, said little in reply, though the ironic look he kept trained on his loquacious companion said enough. That afternoon he spotted him again as he was playing the tables in the casino, first at blackjack, then at roulette. The youth was wearing a bow tie, V-neck sweater and grey flannels, like an aspiring Wooster. He stood by to watch as Key loaded what remained of his chips on red. The ball performed its skittering dance around the wheel – *tock tock tock tock tocktocktocktocktock* – and landed on red.

'Bravo!' came the cry behind him.

Key said over his shoulder, 'You must be a lucky charm – that's my first win all afternoon.'

'Put it all on black,' he said. Without thinking much about it Key did so. Another rattle of the wheel, and black came up. The young man told him to leave it on black, and Key laughed drily. 'I'll quit while I'm ahead, thanks. Perhaps I can buy you a drink with my winnings?'

They parked themselves on stools at the bar next door. He introduced himself as Teddy Absolom. He was late twenties, jolly, apple-cheeked face, dark hair slicked back tennis club-style. Well-spoken, the voice light. He wore co-respondent shoes in cream and brown leather, and chose a Stinger from the cocktail menu. He was much more like the sort of cruise passenger Key had envisaged meeting. They clinked glasses.

'And what's your line of work? No, don't say, let me guess.' Teddy squinted at him consideringly. 'Something in the services, perhaps. A pilot?'

Key smiled. 'Never been in a plane in my life.'

'Hmm. In the military, then. I can see you on the parade ground . . .'

'Getting warmer. I was in the Army, many years ago.'

'Or something to do with the law?'

'You're good. Detective Inspector with the Liverpool CID. Retired.'

They talked a little about the war. Teddy had been rejected for service – flat feet – which suited him fine. Film had been his obsession since boyhood. He started as a dogsbody at the BBC, making tea, lugging cameras, a runner and clapper-boy on public information films. Then his number came up. A friend of his knew a director who required an assistant on a film he was making about the auxiliary fire service in London's East End. The director turned out to be Humphrey Jennings, and the film was *Fires Were Started*.

'I saw that. Twice, as a matter of fact. It was remarkable.'

'D'you think so?!' he cried. 'We were terribly proud of it.'

'A difficult job, I imagine.'

Teddy confirmed it. 'We'd been through the worst of the Blitz by then. But trying to reconstruct it felt nearly as dangerous. So exhausting and filthy, and we all got burned. We

95

were working fourteen hours a day in these conditions. The collapsing walls, warehouses up in flames ... you wouldn't believe the risks we took.'

'How did you get on with Jennings?' he asked.

'Oh, we all adored him. None of your tyrant in jodhpurs. It was first names, beers together after work. He really got the team spirit going. He didn't spare himself, at all, so we didn't either. Some chaps you work with are quite sloppy, or make it up as they go along. Not Humphrey – he had it all worked out on paper before we started shooting.'

'I liked the scene of them singing around the piano. And of course the warehouse fire was tremendous.'

Teddy bugged his eyes at the memory. 'D'you know, I almost killed one of the actors in that scene. William Sansom – he played the new recruit – had to go up on the blazing roof. Humphrey, or someone, told me to empty a bucket of water over him before he started the climb. Well, by accident I picked up a bucket of paraffin and emptied *that* over him. In the chaos nobody noticed, but poor old Sansom was drenched in flammable fuel with showers of sparks and flash fires everywhere. He could have gone up like a Roman candle at any moment!'

'But your luck was in ... '

'I should say so. And I was even luckier to work with Humphrey. Why, I'd never have had the confidence to go it alone if it weren't for him. The things he taught me, not just about film but about art and music and poetry – we'd be sitting there drinking tea or smoking and out of nowhere he'd start quoting from John Donne, or Shakespeare. Reams and reams of it! I think he knew the whole of *Henry V* by heart.'

'So you've struck out on your own?'

Teddy made a comical grimace. 'I've taken a few nervous steps. Last year I did a short promotional film for this lot – Cunard – to drum up passenger business now that the war's over. It's just a day in the life of a cruise like this one – the brief was to make it look glamorous, you know, the Captain's table, dressing for dinner and all that. Part of the payment was a first-class return from Blighty to New York . . . so here I am!'

'Will you look for work over there?'

'That's the idea. Eventually I'd like to make a drama. Maybe a war film.'

'Ah, the new Humphrey Jennings . . .'

Teddy frowned, disowning the idea. 'I could never get near to what Humphrey's done.'

'I'm sure you've got your own style. Or else you'll learn to acquire one.'

'But what about your time in the Army? Surely you have stories to tell.'

Key stared off, pondering. He did have a story, though he couldn't imagine Teddy Absolom or anyone else making a film of it.

'I served in France, then in Flanders. But you won't get much out of this old soldier. I've forgotten most of it.'

'Really?' He looked disappointed. Key asked him if he knew anyone on board, and on hearing he was alone told him about his new friends, the Tarrants. 'I'm having dinner with them tonight. Perhaps you'd care to join us?'

Teddy was all for it, and they had another round of drinks before he returned to the gambling room, Key to his cabin and notebook.

Yes, he had a story all right, one that would make Teddy's

insides run cold. What he had said about forgetting most of his war experience wasn't true; it was more like he'd buried it. In those immediate after-years you felt a kind of collective resistance to remembering the war. People wanted rid of it, were sick to death of it, and *pace* Sassoon –

Have you forgotten yet? . . .
Look down and swear by the slain of the War that
you'll never forget

– you would not make yourself popular by talking about it. To quote another poet, humankind cannot bear very much reality. Key was a year out of university and enlisted in the spring of 1915; he did basic training at Litherland Camp a few miles out of town. He had a commission in the Second Battalion of the Royal Welch Fusiliers, and was shipped out to France as a lieutenant that November. By the time of the Somme offensive he had been promoted to captain, not through any conspicuous gallantry but on account of the rapid turnover of officers in the British Expeditionary Force. He read years later that the average life expectancy of a subaltern on the front line was six weeks, though he didn't know for sure if it was true. He did know that the broken ankle he got jumping from a parapet saved him from the worst at Mametz. He remembered lying in a hospital bed in London, relieved and terrified at the same time: he would be returning to the Front with all his luck used up.

How to convey the unimaginable? Even those who served out there found it a conundrum to describe, for while the pity and terror of it were bottomless the day-to-day reality was mundane. You might be posted in a sector that was quiet for days, even for weeks, and instead of action the mechanical duties of soldiering were your entire world. Among the men you felt the resentment and discomfort, but also the boredom, and the spirit-crushing sense that there might be no end to this awful life of cold and filth and homesickness. One of the greatest strains was the lack of sleep. You were always exhausted, but if a man happened to fall asleep on sentry duty he could be had up on a court martial. You were alive, but in the way that an animal was alive, reflexes primed for the slightest noise, the smallest movement. You learnt from others' carelessness. A man might duck into a shell-hole for 'a spit and a drag' – a smoke – and strike a match. A hundred yards away an enemy sniper might spot that tiny flame and next thing you were lying dead with a bullet through your eye.

You lived on your nerves, because you were never safe. It does something to you, that tension. If you were on the move you at least had a purpose and could pretend you were master of your fate. But waiting in a front-line trench before 'a show' you felt the entire precariousness of your little life. The perilous moment awaited out there.

On the Ypres Salient in the summer of 1917 the mood was always nervous, for they were surrounded on three sides by the enemy. Death could come from almost any direction. As an officer Key felt the responsibility of setting an example to the men. However depressed or anxious, he feigned the appearance of calm so as to reassure them, and at times could even fool himself into a sort of nonchalance. It was a mask – one that he wore so determinedly it became his other self.

The only man who saw through it, he felt, was a fellow

officer named Endall – Hugh Endall – whose sang-froid didn't seem a put-on at all. He was an attractive presence, blue-eyed, with light-brown hair, and his easy manner allowed him to make friends in a way Key never could. In Hugh's company he felt able to unburden himself and talk truthfully, as far as he knew how. He always called Key 'old man', though he was the younger of the two. In civilian life he ran a riding stables in Chester; he loved horses and could draw them quite wonderfully. Key had a couple of his sketches still, done on rough butcher's paper while they were at the Front. Hugh was also a Roman, but had kept his faith and still attended Mass; before an action Key saw him with rosary beads in his hand, silently intoning a prayer. If he wasn't on about horses or racing he was yarning over a pipe with the chaplain about the Trinity and the catechism.

When the rains swept down on Passchendaele that August and the ground turned to a quagmire, horses became especially vulnerable, and even among all that slaughter one could see how deeply it excruciated Hugh to see a horse stumble and drown in the liquid mud.

That mud ... you could never cross the ground with any confidence. Key's battalion had been ordered to take part in an attack on Glencorse Wood, scene of unspeakable carnage in the previous weeks. They had come upon a trench broken up by shell-fire and were proceeding up the slope. The noise of the artillery was so loud you couldn't hear yourself speak, but they kept going, one wave after another. The ground up there seemed firm, or what passed for firm at the time. He was running full pelt when he put his foot down and went plunging into the earth; all of a sudden he was up to his armpits in a bog. No one else had seen him go in, so fast were they moving. The shock of it winded him, and as he tried to pull clear he found himself being sucked deeper and deeper. He must have shouted, but who would have heard him above that racket? Then two runners from the next wave – they were London Fusiliers – saw him struggling and stopped; they held out their rifles and he grabbed at them, held on for dear life and hauled himself out. A little later he realised how lucky he'd been. They had *happened* to pass that way, and happened to spot him, otherwise in another minute or so he would have gone under, vanished into the earth. As so many did.

He never discovered who those two fellows were, because they had to catch up with their own lot. But he thought about them still, and wondered if they had got through.

Reading down the lists of casualties in *The Times*, people back home might have assumed one soldier's death to be pretty much like another. At some point the scale of slaughter becomes so overwhelming that how an individual dies seems neither here nor there. A corpse is a corpse. Yet to the man in the trench or the shell-hole, or legging it through no-man's-land, the manner of his death remains a matter of significance. There are many ways to die, some more terrible than others. He talked with Hugh about this and they agreed that to be shot dead was far preferable to being drowned, or mauled by an explosion. He had once come across a man sitting bolt upright in a field, apparently gazing out to the horizon. He approached, began to speak to him – What was he doing out here, not seeking cover? – when he discovered the problem. A mortar fragment had obliterated his mouth, making a terrible surprised 'O' of it, as if he had been interrupted, mid-shout.

No sound would issue from him again. Those mangled bits of burnt flesh, the charred black holes of death, these were things you tried to blank from your mind; but they would come back to you later, if only in a nightmare.

By late September Glencorse Wood, what remained of it, had been taken. The pitted ground of the salient was now like a gigantic sponge, sodden with mud and water. The objective was to push on to the ridge of Passchendaele village, over the swamps of liquid mud, the shell craters stinking of gas, and the numberless dead who had fallen into the morass. If you planted your foot and the ground held firm likely as not you were treading on a corpse. The smell was indescribable.

They had begun the attack on the ridge just after 5 a.m., and had run into trouble immediately. The machine-gun fire from the German positions was prodigious. Soon they were being scattered, bullets spitting busily around them. Along the line he saw Hugh's company being strafed, men collapsing into the mud. A wave would hurry forward, and those who weren't hit would seek a shell-hole for cover. The air itself keened with the sound of whistling metal. A break came, and Key took five or six men with him at a crawl along the slope to see if he could relieve Hugh's lot. Before they could reach them an almighty explosion shook the ground and they fell back. When the smoke cleared there was no one in sight; all the men he'd seen two minutes before had disappeared.

Not quite all. He found a shell-hole, smoking with fumes, and there lay Hugh, his face roasted, in a supplicant posture. *Alive, thank God.* He jumped down and got on his knees beside him. Hugh looked up, frowning, and said, 'Afraid I got one, old man.' Don't worry, Key said, I'll get you back. He checked to see what damage had been sustained; aside from cuts to his arms and face Hugh seemed all right. He unbuttoned Hugh's tunic, but the injuries he dreaded were not there. Can you move? he asked. Hugh didn't seem to hear. (The guns shredded the sound from your mouth.) Key moved crabwise around him, thinking he could get his shoulder under Hugh's arm, and saw that the back of his helmet had buckled. Key lifted it slightly and nearly cried out: a piece of shell had ruptured his skull, just above the ear, and a glistening black mush seeped crimson and white. He could see Hugh trying to speak, and pointing to the breast pocket on his tunic – he unbuttoned the flap and inside found his rosary. He held it in his hand and clasped Hugh's inside it, he didn't know why.

The enemy fire kept pattering away. Having sent a runner to get a stretcher he waited while Hugh's breathing became laboured; he said something to Key, it sounded like 'I'm finished.' By the time the stretcher-bearers arrived he was dead.

Key never felt the same after that day. He went through the motions, did what he had to do, managed to get to the end of the war intact. Except that he wasn't intact, not really. A vital flame had been doused in him, never to be relit. His life turned savourless, mechanical, blank. It was an impersonation of living, efficient enough but bereft of any kind of pleasure or interest. For years he looked at mugshots of certain criminals and would see something dead behind their eyes. But what did people see behind his? Slowly, he made a sort of recovery. Police work helped him back. The camaraderie among the force, the challenges of detective work, the bloody ordinary everyday. The colour seemed to return to the trees, food tasted of something again.

Thirty years after, he no longer dwelt on the war. You could drive yourself mad with remembering – he'd seen it happen. But he still thought of Hugh Endall, those lovely drawings of his, and what a dear man he was.

10

A jolly evening ensued once he had introduced Teddy to Lydia and Mrs Tarrant. In the enclosed spaces of a cruise liner one quickly becomes used to the same faces, the same rooms and corridors, the same conversations. Habit blunts the gaiety. Tedium ghosts around. To discover a new companion in your midst gives an invigorating jolt to the routine – to think that this person has been on board all along, awaiting your pleasure. And to see how Teddy comported himself before the ladies was gratifying to Key, who felt as though he'd been overseeing a young nephew's first eager steps into society.

Not that he really needed any help. Whatever subject was broached Teddy had an opinion to offer; he was like the boy in the class who always had his hand up first. But he also possessed manners enough to draw out the less forthright – Lydia, in this case. 'Ah, the lady in the pool,' he said on greeting her. 'I saw you swimming lengths there yesterday afternoon.'

'My forty a day.'

'Good Lord! I'm always impressed by people at ease in the water ... Not being a swimmer myself.'

'You mean you can't swim? Didn't they teach you at school?'

'I didn't take to it for some reason. Funny, since I'm quite sporty otherwise – tennis, cricket, squash, bit of golf.'

'Perhaps Lydia could teach you ...' Key suggested.

'To swim? That's a good idea!' Teddy looked at her.

'We only have three more days here,' she said, doubtfully.

'Oh, I'm a quick learner. And you're probably a much better instructor than any PE teacher I had.'

The arrival of their egg mayonnaise excused Lydia from any immediate decision. Mrs Tarrant, trying to place the new-comer, asked him where he'd been at school, and gave a little *moue* of approval on hearing it was Uppingham. 'I couldn't wait to leave, quite honestly. All I wanted to do was get to London and work for a film studio.'

'Teddy was an assistant to Humphrey Jennings in the war,' Key supplied, though from their expressions he could tell the name was not familiar to them.

'So you're going to New York on business?'

'No, on purpose,' Teddy fired back, to laughter, not letting on that he was quoting from a play (Key couldn't remember which). 'Actually I'm going to scout around for work. My friend Chris has recommended some people. Who knows, I may even make it to Hollywood.'

'How exciting!' Lydia cried. 'Will you perhaps get to meet Joseph Cotten?'

'I shouldn't think so,' Teddy laughed. 'He's a big star and I'm just ... a rude mechanical.'

'You're a fan of his?' Key asked her.

'Rather. The first time I ever saw him was in a film

called – would you believe – *Lydia*. Then of course there was *Citizen Kane* and *The Magnificent Ambersons*.'

'And you must have seen him in *Shadow of a Doubt*?'

Lydia wrinkled her nose at that. 'No. Someone told me that wasn't very good.'

Teddy and Key glanced at one another. 'I'm afraid you were misinformed, my dear,' said Key. 'It's Mr Hitchcock's greatest, and your man has never been better in it.'

'True,' Teddy chimed. 'May I tell you about it, Miss Tarrant? Joseph Cotten plays this genial fellow, Charlie, who comes to stay with his sister and his niece in Santa Rosa. There's a great sympathy between uncle Charlie and the niece, and yet she begins to suspect he's a bad'un – that he's the "Merry Widow Murderer", in fact. All this is played out against a background of perfect American ordinariness, which somehow makes it more sinister. And it's heightened by Charlie's creeping realisation that he's given away his secret to the niece. She knows, and *he knows* she knows ...'

'It sounds rather disturbing,' Lydia said.

'And horrible,' Mrs Tarrant added, with a little shudder.

'Oh, definitely!' Teddy happily agreed. 'Mr Key is right, it's Hitch's greatest.'

'"Hitch"? Do you know him?'

Teddy blushed. 'No, not at all ... I just wanted to sound as if I did.'

Key smiled at him. 'I think you and Hollywood will get on very well together.'

The serving of the main course – fried fillet of sole *avec pommes vapeur* – punched a brief hole in the conversation through which Mrs Tarrant darted, eager to talk of the things dear to her heart. She was keen to hear, for instance, what they thought of the forthcoming wedding of Princess Elizabeth and Philip Mountbatten, and would they be watching it on the television? Key sensed that Teddy had about as little enthusiasm for the royal nuptials as he did, and once it emerged that neither of them actually owned a television set Mrs Tarrant had the field to herself. Oh, you simply must have one, she continued, it would quite transform your life. As she enlarged on the wonders of the medium Key noticed Lydia quietly retreat into her shell; her mother's holding forth was plainly one of the fixtures of home life in East Sheen. He wanted to bring her back into the dinner chat but Mrs Tarrant's monologue hardly admitted of interruption, she was that practised in 'having her say'. He tried to compensate by keeping their wine glasses topped up, but it was heavy going nonetheless.

He was resigned to her continuing dominance as they repaired to the lounge, but a little miracle intervened when the Captain sidled up to ask Mrs Tarrant if she cared to make a fourth at bridge. Why, of course! The mood among the remaining trio lifted instantly once they had bidden her goodnight and settled down to coffee and cognac, with the pianist's noodling cocktail tunes as background. They reverted to the subject of film. Lydia, restored to her bright-eyed self, was quizzing Teddy about his ambitions.

'So do you intend to write films or direct them?'

'Why not both?' (He was a cocky so-and-so underneath it all.) 'What I need is to find a good story. Something with juice in it.'

'Well, I know one you could make,' she said. 'Do you

remember the Wallace murder case in Liverpool? Mr Key's writing a memoir about it.'

Teddy's mouth fell open in shock. 'Do I remember?! I was *obsessed* with it as a schoolboy. You worked on that?'

He nodded. 'Memoir sounds a little grand. It's just something to occupy me in retirement. Not intended for publication.'

Teddy was incredulous. 'Not intended for – My dear fellow, the Wallace case is the crime of the century! The perfect murder, still unsolved. And here I am with a police detective who worked on it.'

Lydia turned her gaze on him. 'Has anyone ever made a film about it?'

'Not that I know of,' he replied.

Teddy brought his hands together in a single *eureka* thunderclap. 'Well, if this isn't the hand of fate at work I don't know what is. The Wallace Case . . . A Motion Picture. The story of a brutal killing, a police force baffled, a man condemned to hang. It's got the lot!'

'Not quite,' Key said. 'There's no ending, don't forget.'

'Oh, that's no trouble,' cried Teddy, his voice rising in excitement. 'It would be a drama, in any case, not a documentary. Between us we could invent a solution. You know that Hitch – I mean, Hitchcock – is making a film of *Rope*, the Hamilton play? That's a true crime story. Why shouldn't we make one?'

Lydia was looking at him. 'What d'you think, Mr Key? Wouldn't it make an awfully good film?'

He umm-ed and ah-ed for a while, considering the possibilities. Teddy was so enthused by the idea he felt it would be curmudgeonly to turn him down flat. But which version of the story should he tell? The Wallace case was still boobytrapped with secrets; he would be obliged to omit certain aspects that might not reflect well on the official investigation. Not for him to undermine the public's trust in the police force, or to damage the reputation of Liverpool CID.

They talked it over long past the midnight hour. Lydia eventually left them to their cigars, though not before securing an agreement that she could 'make a third' in their discussions. In fact Teddy suggested she might take notes – 'We'll put you on the payroll, of course,' he said, as if he were already a producer, recruiting staff. Key found himself smiling. The boy was suddenly all pep and purpose. They were to begin first thing tomorrow morning, though he laid down certain conditions regarding their 'project'. First, he would insist upon anonymity. Aside from a feeling of loyalty to his old employers he had his police pension to consider; it would be imprudent to put that at risk. Second, he would retain a veto on any part of what went into the script. Having known Teddy all of twenty-four hours, he didn't yet have the measure of the man. It was wise to proceed with caution until then.

Even the nightbirds had quit the bar by the time the two of them turned in. As they headed down the hushed corridors Teddy was full of beans about the prospective collaboration, and Key put a finger to his lips to quieten him. On glimpsing the state of the young man's room he almost reared back. Orderliness was not his forte. Empty coffee cups, loaded ashtrays, a rumpled bed, clothes in disarray on the floor, a paperback splayed on his bedside table next to dead flowers in a vase. It was so unlike the house-proud severity of his own quarters that he gave out a laugh.

'Doesn't the maid come to your room?'

Teddy looked at him, puzzled. 'I think so. Why?'

'Just wondering. I'll see you at eight tomorrow.'

The next morning brought a freshening breeze and an uncertain pale sunlight. The ocean tilted and glittered before them. They had arranged, the three of them, to take breakfast at a table overlooking the swimming pool. Teddy said that scriptwriters in Hollywood tended to eat and work around pools, 'so we should too'. How he knew that, having never been there himself, was mysterious, but Lydia and Key had no objection to perching on their loungers while eating grapefruit and drinking iced tea. Teddy drank black coffee and smoked Lucky Strikes, an American affectation to go with his wide-cuffed trousers and diamond-patterned sweater.

Before they started Key had a question for Lydia. He had got up for his usual stroll before breakfast and had run into Mrs Leverton. 'She's the widow, isn't she?'

'No. That's her sister, Mrs Orme – Gertrude. Her husband died in Italy in 1944.'

'Oh dear. I fear I've been getting them the wrong way round. I've been offering my sincere-condolences smile to Mrs Leverton, and my isn't-life-jolly smile to Mrs Orme. She must think me rather heartless.'

He obliged Lydia with a demonstration of each, and she said, 'I shouldn't worry, if I were you. The smiles look identical.'

Teddy had his pad and pencil at the ready. Of a sudden Key felt the oddity of agreeing to make a drama of the Wallace case. He sensed that other self of his at work, the stranger within he barely knew, acting without permission, prompting, goading him on. It was vital not to let him have the upper hand.

They were just getting underway when Lydia raised a practical question it hadn't occurred to him to clarify.

'What about William Wallace? Isn't it likely he'll want a say in this? It's his story after all.'

Teddy stifled an indecorous laugh, and Key returned a reproving look: she wasn't to know.

'I'm afraid it's too late for Wallace to have a say,' he replied. 'He died two years after he was acquitted. The kidney ailment finished him.'

'*Oh*. Poor man.'

'I should make something else clear. I knew Wallace rather better than I've led people to presume ...' Teddy and Lydia stared at him. This was not the angle of approach they were expecting. 'We first met in 1928, the spring, I think ...' Yes, it must have been the spring, he could remember the light of evening as they came out of the chess club and walked up to the Pier Head. It was Caird who had introduced them. They had a few games; it soon became evident Wallace was not a good player. 'My lack of practice keeps me in a state of mediocrity,' he said, with a small sad laugh. The self-deprecation was, as he discovered, characteristic. They abandoned the board and decided to stretch their legs instead. It was that violet hour just before dusk descended. The odd boat plying across the Mersey, steam curling grey in the air. Across the water the lights of the Wirral winked through the gloaming.

He made an intriguing study. He was about fifty but seemed older; the dark suit was of an old-fashioned cut. His gaunt, beaky face and the hang of his shoulders reminded Key of a large famished vulture. His eyes seemed to swim behind his steel-rimmed spectacles, which he often took off to clean – a habit of his. It was hard to place his accent. Cumberland, he said.

He had seemed reserved on first acquaintance, but once the talk turned to his early life he became quite voluble.

He'd left school aged fourteen and was apprenticed to a draper's up in Barrow. Then a move to Manchester to work for Whiteway, Laidlaw, outfitters to the British Army and the Colonial Services. In the early years of the century he transferred to the company's outpost in Calcutta, and later moved to Shanghai where his brother Joseph lived. He was in the East for two years, and would have stayed but for a recurrent health problem. He returned to England, and for a long time was convalescent after an operation to remove his kidney. So even then it became clear that he was far from well.

'Have you travelled much yourself, Mr Key?' Wallace had asked.

'No, very little, aside from the '14–'18 war. And that was enough to put me off for life.'

'You were in France?'

'And Belgium.'

He nodded, and seemed embarrassed to admit he had not been fit for service in '14. 'That was also the year I married. In Harrogate.'

He had lived up there for a few years, working as an agent for the Liberal Party. On the outbreak of war the post became obsolete, and he eventually moved to Liverpool to take up a job at the Prudential, on Dale Street. His job was collecting insurance premiums around the Clubmoor district. That single bald allusion to his marriage inclined Key to wonder if it had lasted. Only by roundabout questioning did he discover that he and his wife – Julia – had settled in Anfield.

They must have been talking an hour or more when Wallace said, abruptly, 'I'm so glad to talk with you, Mr Key. I can tell you're a police detective. You listen so carefully.'

He said this in a tone of sincerity that took Key by surprise. He had known many police detectives in his time, and 'careful listening' was by no means a universal characteristic of the profession. The majority, he thought, preferred being listened *to*. They walked back towards Lord Street, where they shook hands and Wallace boarded a tram.

'He sounds rather a melancholy fellow,' said Lydia, 'the way you describe him.'

'I think he was. Troubled at heart.'

'Because he was ill?' asked Teddy.

'That, and other reasons . . . I should also say he was a great autodidact. He had studied botany and chemistry, and taught part-time at the Liverpool Technical College. He had learnt to speak Bengali when he was out in India. He read a lot of philosophy – the Stoics, Marcus Aurelius. He was musical, too. When I met him he had just begun learning to play the violin.'

A silence briefly intervened. All that could be heard was the faint movement of Lydia's hand across the page as she made notes. After a moment she looked up. 'May I ask you a question, Mr Key. Did you like him – Wallace? Was he a personable type?'

'I suppose . . . I couldn't help liking him. But he wasn't personable, no. He was too shy – too recessive – to make himself popular. In another life he might have joined a religious order.

I can imagine him as a monk, at prayer in his cell, or illuminating a manuscript, or whatever.'

'But in his diaries Wallace professes not to believe in an afterlife,' Teddy interposed. 'He wasn't a Christian, was he?'

'No. Unlike Julia.'

'He left diaries?' Lydia asked.

'A few fragments. Most of them were lost, allegedly, by his editor. The stuff about the investigation and his trial were written up afterwards. There are some rather poignant entries after he was cleared – shunned by his neighbours, abused in the street and so on. That's why he moved out of Anfield. He bought a bungalow on the Wirral, hoping for some peace.'

Teddy said, 'Doesn't he also write about how much he misses his wife, and how she would have loved to have a house with a garden?'

'There's quite a lot of that, yes. She was still much on his mind.'

And so they peeled back the onion, little by little, getting closer. Teddy and Lydia were a good audience, he found, carefully attentive, ready with pertinent questions. But did they really have any clue of what was to come? Teddy was so convinced of the story's potential as cinema that he even speculated as to who should be cast in the role of Wallace. Alec Guinness was his pitch. 'Not bad,' Key said. 'He would suit the diffident side of the man.' But he preferred Michael Redgrave, who had the right mixture of wariness and absence. Smiling, Lydia asked him who he'd like to see play the detective (there must be a detective, of course). 'This is your role, Mr Key.' Well, he admired Trevor Howard, though the choice would flatter him. 'That's what casting is,' said Teddy. 'We find actors to play much better-looking versions of ordinary people.' 'Thank you,' Key replied, and they all laughed.

Sandwiches were brought to them for lunch. The sun had recovered from its early-morning wanness and pasted their limbs with its warmth. Lydia did her forty lengths while Teddy and Key looked on. She returned to her lounger, sleek like a seal, and wrapped a towel around herself, shivering a little. Eventually they were ready to resume.

11

Though they had first made acquaintance with one another at the City Café they played chess there quite seldom. If Wallace was an indifferent player Key hardly considered himself much better; they found long walks around town more congenial than the smoke and chatter of the café. Wallace read extensively, and regarded the Jesuit-educated copper as a useful sounding-board for his concerns. He was impressed – envious – that Key had Latin and Greek. 'What a thing it must be to read Plato in the original,' he said. Key shrugged, sensing that Wallace understood *The Republic* in translation far better than he did in Greek. He would quote wise sayings from Seneca, whose stoical philosophy attracted him. '"What is freedom? To be the slave of nothing, of no necessity, of no accident, and to make fortune face you on the level."'

It's a nice idea, Key replied, but how to be the slave of nothing? We have to work, after all. 'Yes, and more besides,' Wallace said, and went on to explain. 'We are slave to our obligations – to our nearest and dearest, for example.' 'You sound rather mournful about it,' Key replied, lightly. Wallace stared off, in a sudden reverie – this was another of his tics. It was like watching someone dip into a trance, where an invisible screen came down and shut out the light.

It dawned on Key after some weeks in his company that Wallace was neurasthenic. He suffered from headaches, colds, fatigue, and he often seemed 'low'. The kidney operation of years before had not much alleviated his condition. He bore his ill-health uncomplainingly, though his Senecan stoicism didn't prevent him from talking about it a good deal. Much as he enjoyed a Latin tag there was one Key didn't quote in his hearing: *solamen miseris socios habuisse doloris*. In short, misery loves company. He would sometimes ask Key about his war experiences – the Great War, that is – as if the hardships and sorrows of a soldier's life might put his own in perspective. Was he a hypochondriac? Key thought not; his ailments were real. But they dominated his life. The ill are a race apart; they have crossed into a land from which most realise there's no return. He sometimes caught Wallace looking at him as though from a distance. It was the gaze of a man in long exile.

Of course one formed a picture of married life even before one might make the acquaintance of a man's wife. From his references to Julia he gathered Wallace was quite happy with his helpmeet, or at least not unhappy. She was Yorkshire-born, from a farming family, could read French and played the piano with some accomplishment. It was interesting to hear his accounts of their musical evenings, when they had visitors round to hear Julia sing and play, while he sawed away on his violin. Key wondered who these visitors were, since she kept much at home and Wallace himself was far from gregarious. He had a feeling they might continue their association for years without his ever being invited to the house. It was not that he craved further intimacy; only that Julia, and her husband's apparent reluctance to introduce her, piqued his curiosity.

In the end it was by accident – 'the magic hand of chance' – that they did meet, and he could at last put a face to the name. It was a Saturday afternoon, he had been in town on some errand or other and stopped at the Kardomah on Dale Street for a cup of tea. The room was quite full, and looking about for a spot he saw Wallace at a table talking to someone whose back was turned to him. Wallace caught his eye, and with a quick word to his companion he waved Key over. As he approached, the woman turned her face to him and he knew instinctively who she was. Wallace rose to his feet, and introduced his wife.

He lifted his hat to her, and they asked him to join them at their table. His first impression was of a slight figure, Victorian (like him) and somewhat dowdy in her dress, small-featured, nervous dark eyes. The hand he shook felt light, cool, papery. His next impression, following quickly after, was that she seemed a good deal older than her husband, himself prematurely aged. Her hair beneath her wide-brimmed, feathered hat was clearly dyed, and he marked a paradoxical quirk of the beautician's craft – the tricks deployed to make oneself look younger tended to have the opposite effect.

He joked with Wallace that even on his day off he couldn't resist the lure of the Prudential, whose offices were a few doors down from the café. Wallace acknowledged this with a pale smile and said it was mere coincidence; he and Julia had been shopping at the Bon Marché and Cooper's on Church Street. Backing him up Julia explained she had ordered antimacassars and some material she needed for a dress repair. She also had a carrier from Rushworth's, where she had bought sheet music. Key replied that Wallace had told him about her talents as a pianist ... She gave a little smile at that.

'Are you a musician yourself, Mr Key?'

He shook his head. 'But I live very near the Philharmonic, and I often go to concerts there. Yourself?'

Her eyes briefly shifted to him. 'We'd like to, but the expense is – William thinks the ticket prices are scandalous.'

Wallace frowned at this remark. 'I'm not sure I called them that –'

'Oh but you did, dear. There was an evening of Chopin recently ...'

Key decided to play the peace-keeper. 'Well, I dare say if it were in my power to entertain friends with music at home I would be inclined not to bother with the Philharmonic.'

They both looked mollified by this little intervention, and the talk reverted to genteel inconsequence. They shared another pot of tea; Mrs Wallace told him about helping at her local church bazaar, Wallace listened quietly. When it came to settling the bill Key paid for the whole thing over the objections of them both. It seemed Wallace was embarrassed at not having put his hand in his pocket, which seemed to confirm the tendency that Mrs Wallace had mildly reproved in him earlier. It didn't bother Key, since his paying the bill had been tactical: he was hoping to ingratiate himself with them.

The scheme paid off, for a few weeks later when he was out with Wallace on one of their philosophical strolls he mentioned that he and Julia were planning to have an evening at home. 'It's quite a modest affair, just for our friends. I wondered ...' He was looking at Key uncertainly.

'. . . whether I'd like to come?' It seemed he was almost too diffident to articulate the invitation himself. 'Of course. I'd be delighted.'

He baulked at this show of mild enthusiasm. 'It's really nothing grand. That is, Julia plays and sings very nicely. But I'm afraid the violinist is a duffer.'

Key laughed, and assured him of his acceptance.

Outside the Kardomah that day they had said their good-byes. He watched them as they disappeared together into the crowds on Dale Street, her arm discreetly linked in his. What was his fascination with them? They looked for all the world like any other Darby and Joan, only more old-fashioned, and out of step with the hurrying times. He couldn't quite put them together, she seeming that much older than he; one might have taken her for his aunt, or some other elderly distant relative. He sensed between them a kind of muted affection that stopped short of love. The marital minimum. Perhaps that was enough to sustain them, just as it had marriages from time immemo-rial. But he discerned some unreachable grievance in him, if not in her. That line from Chekhov came to him: 'If you are afraid of loneliness, don't marry.'

The evening of the musical entertainment came round. He took the tram to Anfield, and made his way towards Wolverton Street. It was summer, and the neighbouring roads were full of children out playing; their shrieks and laughter carried over the air. He had heard that Julia was fond of flower arranging, and had taken along a bunch of peonies as a gift. Wallace greeted him on the doorstep with that spiritless welcome of his. It seemed he liked Key's company (he was a 'good listener', after all) but he was awkward in showing it. He hadn't much in the way of social grace, and to feign charm was quite beyond him. Key followed him down a hall smelling of camphor and into the parlour, where a handful of people were already standing about talking. Wallace handed him a glass; it was sherry, a small one, and clouded.

Julia Wallace entered moments later carrying a tray of fish-paste sandwiches. She offered a vague smile as she began handing around these dainties. Wallace introduced him around the room, to his next-door neighbours the Johnstons, to a trio of his colleagues from the Prudential, to a couple of ladies Julia knew from the parish. It was all very 'respectable', from the dark, heavy furnishings to the mantelpiece gew-gaws to the huge aspidistra blocking the light at the window. Framed photographs and gas brackets on the wall, a carved Welsh dresser with an inlaid mirror, a chaise longue with a patterned throw. The piano crouched in wait, a violin stand with the sheet music bought from Rushworth's. It was a curious scene, a simulacrum of social gaiety, as if the Wallaces had organised it without any firm idea of who their friends were, or what indeed friends were for.

He chatted about nothing very much with one of the Prudential fellows. When he learnt that Key was a policeman his back straightened in reflex. He overheard Wallace and Julia in frowning confabulation about a guest who'd not yet arrived. 'We'll give him another five minutes,' Julia muttered, but it was nearer to fifteen by the time Wallace brought the room to order with a formal cough. He invited them to take their seats, and made a half-hearted effort to fill the glasses of the sherry drinkers. Once settled, Julia looked around the room as if to greet them officially, then seated herself at the piano. With a businesslike nod to her husband, the violin now cradled under his chin, she set off on an aria from Gluck, hands purling along the keys, voice modulated just so.

Wallace had been right on both counts: she played very nicely, and he could just about keep up. His bow arm moved without ease or grace, and whenever he hit an occasional wrong note his jaw twitched in frustration. A Bach air followed; a couple of Chopin études; and then another aria, from Handel, which Julia delivered with a confident flourish.

The applause came with a touch of relief. The couple had got through it, and so had they all. Julia gave a little bow; he stood by, as tall and stiff as an old wardrobe. The room relaxed, and for something to do Key collected the sandwich plates and carried them out to the scullery. As he was stacking them in the sink he heard footsteps behind him.

'Thank you for the flowers, Mr Key,' said Julia, setting down a tray of her own. She looked less careworn, more animated than she had at the Kardomah; perhaps she had derived energy from her playing.

'Congratulations,' he said, sincerely. 'Your husband told me you were accomplished, and he was right.'

She gave a modest, closed-mouth smile, and said in her high, lilting voice, 'I've had years of practice – from when I was a girl.' And he ungallantly wondered how long ago that had been. The creases around her neck were hidden this evening by a velvet choker, and her sheep's eyes had a youthful gleam in them. He had started to inquire about the early years when a knock distantly sounded at the front door. She cocked an ear, and a faint blush of pleasure suffused her features.

'That'll be Gordon,' she said, rolling her eyes. 'Just leave these dishes, Mr Key. Come and meet our friend.'

He followed her out of the scullery and back along to the parlour, where a young man was in drawling conversation with Wallace. He was thickset, dapper in dress, with dark brilliantined hair and a spiv's moustache.

'So you made it after all,' Julia called to him, with a little half-laugh.

'Ah, Mrs W., my apologies,' he replied. 'I was unavoidably detained.' He smirked at her, as if he knew the excuse was feeble but could rely on her indulgence. 'I've brought you some beers as a peace offering,' he added with a wink. He had already got started on one.

'She doesn't *drink* beer,' said Wallace, with a sighing reproof. He turned to Key. 'This is our friend Gordon Parry. He's with us at the Pru. Gordon, this is Detective Inspector Key.'

Parry bugged his eyes, then tugged at an invisible forelock in a playful gesture of respect. 'Inspector. I hope you're not here on official business.'

He shook his head. 'I know Mr Wallace from the Central Chess Club.'

'Oh, I go there. And we meet at that café on Thursdays – for the Mersey Amateur Dramatic Society.'

'Gordon's quite a talented actor,' said Julia, beaming at him.

But Parry waved a disowning hand at this acclaim. 'You're pulling me leg, aren't yer? Just a lot of mummers prancing around –'

'And he's a very good mimic,' she continued, determined to pay him his due.

Parry ignored her, and squinted at Key. 'So which nick are you at, Inspector?'

He told him, and Wallace added, 'You'd better watch yourself, Gordon. The detective's with the CID. He won't stand for any of your nonsense.'

Parry gave a laugh, acknowledging some in-joke between them. He looked to Wallace to explain his remark, but nothing followed. Even on this short acquaintance it was clear the young man had a strange relationship with the Wallaces. He seemed an unlikely character to be their friend – a dandyish charmer, youthful, insolent – though it could have been the flamboyance that captivated them; there seemed so little else of it in their life. The way they talked together was almost familial; he might have been the errant son dropping in on his fond but exasperated parents. They listened to him gas on, mostly about his hectic social life – it seemed he had a girlfriend, who hadn't been included in this evening's invitation. He was entertaining, and uncouth; Key was saying good-night to the hosts when he noticed him turn his head away to belch, quietly, and without apology.

Outside a motor car was parked in front of the house. He had a strong intuition it belonged to Parry; he had talked about taking his girlfriend out on trips to North Wales. Key wondered how he was able to afford it on a clerk's salary. Unless the vehicle had been borrowed, or – just as likely – stolen.

After that evening he didn't see Wallace for about six months. He was too busy to play chess at the Central, and work had taken him to Southport on a case. He might well have let their acquaintance slide into neglect had he not received a note through the post, early in the new year. It was written in an unfamiliar hand:

Dear Mr Key, I wonder if you would mind calling at the house one day soon? William has been ill in bed and I am sure he would appreciate a visit. He is troubled you know I think by a kidney condition. Sincerely yours, Julia Wallace.

She had appended their address, in case he'd forgotten it.

Truthfully, he felt a stab of guilt. Of course he had no obligation to Wallace, or to his wife, but he had pegged Wallace for a lonely man and ought to have kept the association in some kind of repair. He wondered if he had asked his wife to write, being too proud to do so himself. He dropped Mrs Wallace a line to say that he'd be sure to visit them one day the following week.

When Key presented himself at Wolverton Street one morning he found the door of number 29 open and a char on her knees, washing the step. On inquiring if Wallace was at home the girl got to her feet and said, 'He's upstairs in bed. A friend, are yer?' He assured her that he was and she stood aside.

As he walked in he remembered the camphor smell in the hall from last time. Ascending the stairs he detected a strong whiff of chemicals when he reached the landing. Not knowing which was Wallace's room he tried the first door back and found a sort of laboratory, shelves of glass jars and a desk cluttered with papers and paraphernalia – this was where the smell was coming from. He tracked back up the landing and from the middle room a voice croaked, 'In here.'

He opened the door and found Wallace in bed, propped up on pillows. He looked terrible. His sallow complexion was corpse-like, his eyes darkly shrunken into his skull. Grey bristles patched his chin. He raised a hand in feeble salute. Key hoped the friendly greeting he made would conceal the dismay he felt.

'Sorry to drag you out here,' Wallace said, the voice cracked and froggy.

'My dear fellow, it's no trouble at all. I should have visited you before but I've been out of town with work, I'm sorry . . .'

'I told Julia not to write, but she insisted.'

'I'm glad she did. If I'd known you were – You've had the doctor in?'

He nodded. 'I've had a bout of pneumonia, then this bronchitis. He's given me all sorts of medication.'

It was only now he took a proper look around the room. The heavy Victorian furniture sulked in the gloom. The bed next to Wallace was neatly made. On the bedside table stood two brown jars of pills, a tin of Vick's, and a water glass, inside which grinned a set of false teeth. Spares, he supposed.

By Wallace's own bedside was an armchair, which he invited Key to take.

'Is your wife at home?' he asked.

Wallace shook his head: she was out on parish work. She had been very good to him during his illness, 'all that one could ask of a wife', he added, as if he were offering a character witness.

'One becomes quite frustrated, cooped up like this. I long to go for a walk . . .' He let the plaintive note hang in the air.

A book lay on his counterpane. Key picked it up and read its spine. *Thus Spake Zarathustra* by Nietzsche. He said lightly, 'At least you've been keeping your mind active.' Wallace replied, with an earnest look, 'Yes, I've been reading all about the theory of eternal recurrence, and the will to power. His idea is that time is circular, and all things recur eternally. So we live our life over and over, every pain repeated alongside every joy. The same pattern, into eternity.'

Key looked at him. 'Sounds very bleak. Some lives seem hardly bearable once. To repeat them eternally would signify a pretty cruel universe.'

Wallace stared off distantly. 'True. Nietzsche calls it "the heaviest of burdens". But maybe, if life does come round again, we could correct the mistakes we made the first time?' He still had the book in his hand, idly turning its pages. 'Is it something you'd like to borrow?' he asked. He smiled and replaced it on his bed.

'Too deep for me. Believe it or not I prefer detective stories.'

'Rather a busman's holiday for you, I'd have thought.'

He shrugged. 'There's a lot of trash out there, certainly. But you find the odd diversion ... I like the ones where you can't guess the ending.'

They talked about work. He assumed the Prudential had granted Wallace sick leave. Yes, they'd been very decent about it, Wallace said, although he'd brought trouble on himself in recent weeks. 'You remember meeting Gordon Parry?' The story emerged: in December, when he was first incapacitated, Wallace had asked Parry if he'd do his rounds in Clubmoor for a few weeks. When he came to do the books he noticed some discrepancies in the amounts Parry was collecting and paying in. 'I spoke to Gordon about it, and he admitted that he'd been careless and would make up the deficit. He knocks around with another young chap, Marsden, who came here a few times.'

'Also from the Pru?'

He nodded. 'I thought that would be the end of it, but just after Christmas the same problem recurred. It's embarrassing more than anything, since I have to explain it to my boss. I haven't seen Gordon since, so I can't say whether it's a genuine mistake or if he's up to his tricks again.'

He now understood why Wallace had asked to see him. 'You'd like me to have a word with him?'

'No, no.' He shrank at the suggestion. 'If he thought I'd brought the police in he'd never speak to me again.'

Key privately wondered if that would qualify as a misfortune. But the invalid was plainly exasperated by what Parry had been 'up to'. 'I wouldn't need to talk to him as an officer of the law,' he said. 'I'd just give him a warning – friendly, like.'

'He'd know it was me,' he said, shaking his head.

'Would that be so disloyal? He knows you could land him in real trouble. Instead you've had a quiet word with a friend in the force ...'

Wallace blinked in a reflex of gratitude. 'You'd do that – for me?'

'It's no big favour. Once Parry knows I've got his number he'll be extra careful. My guess is you won't get another peep out of him.'

At that moment the sound of the front door opening alerted them to the return of his wife. She could be heard moving about downstairs, talking to the char. He saw a shadow pass over Wallace's face as they listened.

'Whatever happens,' he said, quietly, 'don't let Julia know we've spoken about this. She's very fond of Gordon, and if it gets out I've been making complaints ...'

He didn't enlarge on that scenario, but Key took his meaning.

It was time for him to leave. They briefly shook hands, and he told Wallace not to worry about his errant colleague – he'd take care of things. At the foot of the stairs he stopped to gaze at a framed photograph of the Wallaces, arms linked, in front of a church. Their wedding day, 1914. They looked old even then. Julia's faint smile was not that of a blushing bride, but it *was* a smile, at least, unlike the noncommittal expression her husband presented to the camera. He rationed his smiles like a miser with his coins.

He heard a light step behind him, and turned to find Mrs Wallace.

'Mr Key. So good of you to visit. How did you think William looked?'

'Rather frail, but improving, I hope. He said he had a very good nurse.'

She returned a short laugh. 'I think he gets restless at home all the time. But we do have someone to cover for him at work.'

He hesitated a moment. 'You mean – Parry?'

She nodded. 'Gordon's been doing the rounds for a few weeks, with Mr Marsden. They drop in sometimes for tea. Much better than having a stranger fill in.'

He offered no comment. They chatted briefly – he asked her about her church work – before he made his excuses. On his way back to the tram stop all he could think of was the glass on the bedside, and the pink rictus of those false teeth.

12

Laughter woke him from a doze. The sun had continued its descent on the horizon. The wind, shifting about in the vaulted sky, ruffled the glinting sea with tones of silver, green, aquamarine. He sat up on the lounger to see Lydia and Teddy in a giggling commotion at the shallow end. She had at last yielded to his request for a swimming lesson, and was drawing him by the hands through the water, like a child, his legs paddling furiously behind. Attendants were collecting discarded towels and languidly restoring order to the poolside scene. He had run out of cigarettes, and reached over for Teddy's pack of Lucky Strikes. He couldn't exactly make out Lydia's coaxing instructions, though whatever they were the pupil was not good at following them; every so often would come a loud thrashing of water and hoots of laughter. They looked as happy as dolphins.

An hour previously they had concluded the 'script meeting' for the day. Teddy had been drawing storyboards as they went. He would interrupt the narrative to ask about a particular room or interior – he was fanatical about the Wallaces' house, and the exact disposition of each room – of which he then made a little sketch. (He turned out to be a quite talented draughtsman.) He also asked for a description of every person mentioned, and made a profile of them. Whatever shape his projected film might take, it would not be found wanting for historical accuracy.

There was an impatience in him nonetheless. Teddy knew the big scenes were coming up – the murder itself, the arrest, the trial – and wanted to hurry it along. Key told him early on that the solution he had devised required a steady build-up, each piece put in place. He understood this, and yet betrayed his restlessness in manner and mood. Perhaps that was what made him a film-maker. He had scented blood. Lydia, on the other hand, was more comfortable with the pace; she enjoyed the unfolding of narrative, savoured the intricacy of character, understood that an audience had to be teased. Those nights she had spent at her local cinema had not gone to waste. When he spotted her notebook on the lounger opposite his first thought was: here is temptation. His second thought: resist it.

His third thought was an irrelevance, for the book was in his hands and, while Lydia frolicked at the far end of the pool, he stealthily riffled its pages. Her responsible schoolgirl cursive was all too easy to read. She had already filled about twenty pages with notes, some of them direct quotations from Teddy or himself.

K. emphatic on atmosphere chez Wallace: 'The whole house reeked of illness'.

An attentive listener, it was clear. Behind him he heard them returning, wet footsteps slapping on the tiles, and without any sudden movement he closed the notebook and replaced it on the lounger.

'Teddy, I'm sorry, I just nicked one of your cigarettes.'

He spoke while towelling his hair dry. 'What's mine is yours, sir. Lydia and I have been thinking – might we continue our little project this evening after dinner? What with the Farewell Ball tomorrow night there won't be much free time, so perhaps we should, you know, *carpe diem*.'

'Or in this case, *carpe noctem*. Yes, of course, I'm at your service.'

'Good. Then let's go straight to the bar after dinner.'

'How's the swimming coming along?'

Lydia laughed. 'He's not a natural, I have to say. But we'll have another try tomorrow.'

Teddy shook his head good-humouredly. 'Another work in progress, Mr Key. In the meantime I must pray this boat doesn't go down – else it's Davy Jones's locker for me!'

His cheerfulness was endearing. Key could see its effect on Lydia, who had begun the cruise in her mother's shadow but had now emerged into the light, transformed. She seemed to stand taller, and spoke in a more confident voice. It was evident to him on his rejoining her and Mrs Tarrant in the dining room. They were rather late sitting down, and he saw that Lydia was placed between the ship's chaplain (a dry old stick) and an American lawyer (dryer, and older). He'd had his penance with them at table earlier that week. He feared for her, and yet she behaved quite beautifully, smoothing the feathers of these old birds and charming them with her attention. She was wearing an amber-coloured silk sleeveless dress with tiny buttons up the back. He noticed Teddy watching her from across the table, admiration glittering in his gaze. Key imagined a scenario where they had to fight one another for her . . . and he laughed to himself. *I grow old*, he thought . . . It would not become him to play the lothario.

The scheme to pick up the script after dinner was scuppered when Mrs Tarrant insisted on her daughter's company for a music concert. The Captain himself would be playing. Lydia's forlorn glance amply reflected his own disappointment. Deprived of their able amanuensis he and Teddy went off to the casino where they played blackjack for an hour. Neither of them won anything.

Back in the bar they consoled themselves with Old-Fashioneds and Romeo y Julieta coronas. Teddy became expansive amid the clouds of smoke. He had turned thirty in the summer, he said, which to a young man of ambition had sounded a hurry-up. Key laughed at the idea of feeling old at thirty.

'You don't look old enough to be retired,' said Teddy.

'I didn't take retirement voluntarily. They – my superiors – decided I didn't fit there any more.'

He considered this for a moment. 'You never know when you're going to be moved on, I suppose. That's why I want to make this film.'

'Teddy, let's not – we only *started* this morning.'

A small ridge creased his brow. He looked at Key curiously. 'What were you doing at thirty, Mr Key?'

'Oh, I'd just made Detective Sergeant, I think. Our generation had been rather shaken up, you may recall. It took me a while to get used to civilian life again.'

'I can imagine. But tell me, you didn't always mean to be a copper, surely? What was your dream as a boy?'

He blew on the tip of his cigar. 'I probably imagined myself playing cricket for Lancashire.'

Teddy's face lit up. 'I wanted to be a cricketer, too! Denis Compton, preferably. You know I saw him last month make a marvellous hundred at Lord's?'

'He's had quite the season, hasn't he? My ambitions were less grand. I played a bit for the school, opened the batting. Had a decent defence, but . . .'

'Did you ever score a hundred?'

He laughed, and shook his head. When Teddy asked eager questions like that you could still see the boy in him. 'You?'

'Heavens, no. I was terribly keen, but I never batted higher than ten in our second eleven. Funny thing, I had a great-uncle Charlie, a Cambridge man. He once played for England. I mean *literally* once, in Australia, eighteen-seventy-something. And he made a fifty, too! My father told me about him. Said he was a useful bowler, ten years with Kent.'

'He's in *Wisden*, then?'

'Oh yes, he's there. Quite a popular chap, by all accounts. But for some reason he quit after that Test and emigrated to America. No one in the family ever saw him again. Died in Trinidad about ten years later.'

'Interesting. Maybe you should make your first film about him.'

'No, no, no, it's got to be Wallace. Fate has thrown us together, Mr Key. I'm not going to pass up an opportunity like this.'

He paused, before saying, 'You know, Teddy, this mightn't turn out to be exactly what you think it is.'

Another frown drew Teddy's brows together. 'Why would

you say that? I told you, the story's got everything. All we have to do is get it down properly.'

'You think it's that simple?'

'Look, if we don't do it someone else will. Hitchcock, for instance.'

He had to admire the young man's self-belief. Midnight found them still talking. Their cigars had burnt to the stub. Teddy looked wan and bleary-eyed, and the knot of his tie was askew. He was about to call an end to their evening when he said, 'She's a lovely girl, isn't she? Don't you think?'

'You mean – Lydia?'

Yes, he did mean Lydia, and he proceeded to deliver a slurring but heartfelt tribute to their companion of the day. 'So sharp and capable. D'you know, I really would hire her if I get this film off the ground. Make her the script editor. Or the script *writer*. Or the producer!'

'I think you're getting ahead of yourself, my boy. Let's see if she can teach you to swim first.'

At that he bared his teeth in a silent guffaw. 'Wise words, sir. Wise words.'

Key rose to his feet and – *whoa* – almost fell over. Not the booze, but a sudden swell below had rocked the ship.

'Looks like we might be in for a storm,' said Teddy, now looking the worse for wear. Key realised he should help him back to his bed while he was able to stand. They said goodnight to the waiter and tottered out of the bar. Their progress down the stairs and corridors to his room was halting as the floor rolled them this way and that. 'Didn't know a ship this size could pitch so,' he muttered as they approached his cabin door.

Key began to say good-night, but Teddy's mind was still stuck on their previous conversation. He was halfway across the threshold when he stopped and turned. 'D'you know, if it came down to it I could even put up with the mother.'

'Sweet dreams, Teddy,' he said, turning back along the swaying corridor.

13

Sometimes you don't know what you're after until it presents itself and you realise, *Ah, so that's what I came for.* It was a trick of the unconscious, and a handy one if your job involved looking for clues. As a copper you set out on an inquiry thinking it was X, but somehow you ended up with Y, which might be more interesting, or more useful: the thing you didn't even know you wanted.

Key's motive in sitting down with Gordon Parry was ostensibly altruistic. Wallace, if not an actual friend, was someone he felt friendly towards. His awkwardness and eccentricity were his ball and chain, and they stirred a sympathy in Key. He cut such a lonely, frustrated figure, a man who found solace in intellectual pursuits but no companionship. Key was touched by the regard in which Wallace seemed to hold him – perhaps it was his fellow feeling with another loner, albeit one who'd not made the mistake of getting married. That Wallace was also vulnerable and in poor health put Key on guard against someone who might take advantage of him – someone he trusted.

A week or so after he had visited Wallace on his sick bed

he was waiting across the road from the Prudential building. It was about 5.30, the lights were coming on and the traffic thickening towards rush hour. A tram heaved along, and stopped briefly in front of him. By the time it continued on its way a number of office people had come down the steps and dispersed along Dale Street. His quarry was among them. Key crossed the street and fell into step with him. The young man looked around, frowning, wondering if it was a face he knew.

'Mr Parry?' he introduced himself. 'We met last summer at the Wallaces' house.'

His expression cleared. 'Oh, yeah. The chess club. I'm off to the Central tonight, matter of fact – drama society.'

'I wonder if you'd have time for a quick drink.'

He looked a little surprised, but had no objection. They walked around the corner to the Grapes on Mathew Street. 'I'll have a Higgy's,' Parry said, expansively, leaning against the bar and surveying the room. He was wearing a boxy pinstripe suit, gangsterish, with a burgundy-coloured silk tie. He kept combing his moustache with his fingers, as if to check it was still under his nose.

A couple of young women had come in after them and stood by, waiting to be served. Parry stared at them appraisingly, and took off his hat to smooth down his hair. It was evident that if Key had not been there he would have struck up a conversation with them.

'Mind if we talk over there?' Parry followed him with his ale to a table by the window. Key offered him a cigarette and they both lit up. They talked about the Pru, which he had joined as an apprentice last year. It seemed that he'd got the job through his father.

'I gather you've been collecting for Wallace while he's been ill.'

'Yeah, poor feller,' Parry confirmed. 'I went to visit him and the missus the other week. Coughing and spluttering like an old horse he was ...'

'He told me you'd called. What did you talk about?'

Parry looked at him from under his brow. 'Oh, you know, business an' that ...'

Key nodded, and let the pause lengthen.

'He regards you as a friend, you know,' he said. 'So he was upset by what you'd been up to.' Parry gave him a blank look, and went back to fingering his moustache. 'He calls them "discrepancies", but we may as well call it what it is – fiddling the books. He said he'd talked to you about it once already.'

'He doesn't need to worry about me –'

'But he does. I've seen the accounts. This isn't the odd bob or two you've been skimming off the top. It all adds up in the end.'

Parry set his jaw insolently. 'So he's snitched on me?'

Key shook his head. 'Wallace doesn't know about us meeting. He told me because he was worried – for *you*. I could have gone straight to your boss – Crewe, is it? – but maybe you could sort it out yourself.'

He brooded in silence for a while. 'Look, I appreciate you not ... Tell Wallace I'm sorry, it won't happen again. I've just been short this last month. I'll make up the deficit, honest. Couple of weeks.'

Key stared at him levelly. He knew this type – not wicked, but weak. He must have realised he'd been done a favour by keeping it on the QT. Another copper might not have been so understanding. To show there were no hard feelings they stayed for another round. Parry lit a cigarette and smoked it cupped inside his hand, in the approved manner of the criminal classes. An affectation, possibly. They talked about the Wallaces, and Key remarked that Mrs Wallace seemed to have taken a shine to him.

He shrugged. 'We get on. Dunno how she puts up with him. "Julia, you left that lamp in the kitchen blazing all night".' A good mimic after all: he had caught the plaintive Wallace bleat to the life.

'Maybe she's no ray of sunshine either. Apart from the music they don't seem to have much in common.'

'No kiddin'! I sometimes get the feeling they can't stand each other.'

'I gather she was a governess once. Maybe if they'd had kids it might have been different.'

Parry made a face in demurral. 'That was never gonna happen.'

He seemed so convinced of this Key had to ask him why. At first he blathered, dismissing their suitability as parents. But then something else occurred to him, and he gave an odd smile. 'It's funny, we were talking in her kitchen once – the missus and me – about their courting days. She said it might have been nice to have kids but by the time she and him were married it was too late. I said to her, weren't you in your thirties when you got hitched, and she looked embarrassed and said, Actually I was a bit older than that – and she blushed! I didn't think anything of it at the time, but when I reminded her of it a few weeks later she got quite shirty and said I'd misunderstood. Well, it didn't make any difference to me. But she asked me not to mention it again ...'

'Odd thing, very first time I met her I thought she looked older than him.'

'What d'you reckon?' he asked. 'Seven, eight years maybe?'

Key nodded, though privately he judged it to be more like ten. A silence intervened between them, and then Parry, with a musing half-laugh, said, 'I dunno. Can't trust anyone, really, can you? Not even yer missus to tell you how old she is!'

So there it was, the one you didn't see coming. He had set out to deal with a 'discrepancy' and had ended up with the tantalising rumour of another. If Parry hadn't stayed for a second drink he might never have let slip that little admission of Julia Wallace's, and Key's suspicions about her would have lain dormant. The following week he took a couple of days off to visit the General Register Office, at Somerset House in London. Why was he pursuing this? He barely knew either of them, and if she had misrepresented her age to him, so what?

The truth was, he couldn't help himself.

Plenty of women lied about their age. Maybe a few men, too, though as a sex they were under less pressure to seem youthful. If Julia Wallace had shaved some years off her age it would hardly rank as a gross falsification. Still, he had to know. From what Parry had told him it was obviously important enough for her to conceal the information from her husband. The hunt was slow going at first, with only her maiden name – Dennis – and an address in North Yorkshire as a guide. But having consulted various censuses he discerned through the long veil of years a tampering sensibility at work. Even her Christian name had been fudged. In one handwritten entry it was 'Juliana'; in another it was 'Jane'. But the pieces finally fell into place. And if what the files disclosed was a surprise to him, he could only imagine its effect upon Wallace.

He might have informed him straight away, but his inclination was otherwise. For one thing, he didn't want to seem to be playing the snoop. Wallace might have wondered, justifiably, why Key had gone to the trouble of digging out his wife's past. There was another, less creditable reason to withhold it. Now that he had Julia Wallace's secret he was doubly curious to observe the couple through its prism. He began inviting them to occasional evening concerts at the Philharmonic. At first there appeared nothing amiss between them; they sat together, attentive listeners, grateful guests. They were both shy in public, and gave little away.

It was in the sphere of domestic relations that he noticed the stamp begin to smudge. Their musical gatherings had become less frequent, but he made sure not to miss one if invited, and latterly he was always invited. Julia was becoming more forgetful, and a little slovenly in her habits; a whiff of physical decay ghosted about her. Wallace was as remote and taciturn as ever, the dogged accompanist on violin, and an ungenial host. (Why *did* he have company, given how little pleasure it afforded him?) Key stayed in the background, watching their interaction, or rather, he watched him watching her, performing, or petting 'Gordon', or gabbling away. Sometimes he sensed an impatience on the husband's part, a suppressed peevishness; more often he looked so lost in thought she might as well have not been there. It was a marriage, with its traditional arrangements of habit and politeness, and boredom held in check.

One evening he dropped by Wolverton Street with a box of cakes he had bought in town. Julia was especially delighted with these dainties (Wallace's tooth was less sweet) and they ate them in the parlour. After a while Wallace asked Key if he minded him putting on the wireless – he wanted to listen to an Ibsen play that he'd read about. Key naturally consented, and the three of them settled down with the cakes, and a sherry. Julia, reclining on the chaise, was less interested in the broadcast than in a brindled cat she had recently adopted. The creature sat in her lap gazing at them while the play unfolded its anguished story of domestic discord somewhere in Scandinavia. The programme was perhaps halfway through its span – was it *A Doll's House?* – when from the chaise a low guttural rumble emanated. At first he thought it was the cat; but then the growl gained a rhythm, and there was Julia, mouth hanging open, snoring. He glanced at Wallace, who stared dead ahead, ignoring her.

Distracted, he began to lose the thread of the drama, its different voices now indistinguishable. Almost as mortifying as her snoring was his monkish, impassive silence. Key gave a dry cough, and gestured at her slumbering form. 'Should I ...?' Without answering him Wallace rose from his chair and crossed to the chaise. For a moment he stood over her, looking down. His expression couldn't be seen from where the visitor sat, but he guessed it wasn't a friendly or indulgent one. 'Julia,' he said, quite sharply. She woke with a start, and the cat jumped in fright off her lap. 'Go to bed, dear.' She looked around dozily, blinked, and brushed crumbs from her cardigan. He didn't offer her his hand as she rose, merely stood there, waiting. With a quiet 'good-night' to them she left the room.

Wallace mumbled an apology and returned to his chair.

They listened to the remainder of the broadcast, though Key's concentration had been shot by the little scene he had just witnessed. He estimated that he'd probably taken in less of that play than Julia had – or the cat.

After that all contact appeared to cease. They didn't have a telephone in the house, so he dropped them an occasional card. No reply came. He had a sense of Wallace withdrawing ever deeper into privacy, wary of allowing further witness to sad scenes from his marriage. It was no hardship to stay away, in truth. One never entered that house in a mood of hope, or left it feeling uplifted. And the reserves of his curiosity about the couple had run low. They were two people living under a long black cloud. Ibsen in Anfield.

It must have been the autumn of 1930 when a telephone call was put through to his desk at Cheapside, and he heard the voice for the first time in months. Wallace apologised for his long silence; he had been unwell, and was 'not fit company'. Key offered expressions of sympathy and hoped that his health was on the mend. He asked after Julia: she continued much the same, he replied in an offhand way. They talked about the chess club; it transpired neither of them had frequented it of late. Key sensed his hesitation, so he came to the point – they should meet. Wallace seemed relieved, and they agreed upon an evening the following week.

He might have known that Wallace was not familiar with city drinking holes, and when asked to appoint a rendezvous he suggested the Vines on Lime Street – a grand old palace whose interiors of polished mahogany and patterned glass screens breathed an air of old-world charm. As he carried drinks to their corner table Wallace seemed bemused by the place.

145

Key said to him, chaffing, 'I wonder how you could live here for fifteen years and not set foot in one of its greatest pubs.'

He gave a pained shrug at that. 'There's a lot in this town that's still unfamiliar to me. Julia doesn't like pubs, I'm afraid, so I'm a stranger to most of them.' Key inferred from this that his companionship was not much sought after by colleagues at the Pru. Wallace was still staring at the fancy carvings that adorned the walls and ceiling. 'The workmanship that's gone into this . . .'

Key followed his gaze, nodding. 'A mate of mine at the station, his old man knew the architect, a feller called Thomas. He also designed the Phil on Hardman Street.'

Wallace absorbed this information in his dispassionate way. A twitch of his chin, but no thought of meeting one's eye, no social effort to match or mirror. One sometimes wondered if he was bored by people, even by Key, despite his early estimation of him being a good listener. The latter decided to hold his tongue, let Wallace make the running for once.

It took a while, but they eventually got round to what was on his mind. 'I often think back to one of the first conversations we ever had – about Seneca's definition of freedom, to be "a slave of nothing". D'you remember?'

'I do. We agreed that it was a fine principle but impractical in day-to-day life – obligations being as they are.'

Wallace squinted over the rim of his glass, thoughtful. 'Lately I've . . .' He paused, and his gaze dropped. 'I've wondered what it might be like to live an absolutely free life. Nothing, and no one, to constrain you.'

'What would that involve?' Key asked.

'Disappearing,' Wallace said, with a shrug. 'Just . . . chuck the whole lot in and get as far away from here as I can.'

But where would he go? 'I don't know. Somewhere they wouldn't find me. Australia. South America?'

'You can get a passage from here to Valparaiso, you know.'

It was spoken lightly, and Wallace half-smiled at the whimsicality of the idea. Then he said, in a changed voice, 'There's no chance of me going anywhere, Mr Key. Not now.' Key stared at him, and his silence asked the question. 'I'm dying, you see.'

He'd had an appointment at the Royal the previous week with a specialist, who had put him through tests. His kidney was diseased beyond help. He was told he might have another year, possibly two, but in the longer term his prospects were nil. Around them the life of the pub maintained its banal, anonymous hum – a distant laugh from the saloon, a glass clinking on a marble top.

Key took out his cigarettes and offered him one. The condemned man. 'I'm sorry,' he said. He struck a match and they lit up.

'How did your wife take it?' But he knew the answer before he'd spoken.

'I haven't told her. She would only fret and make it more difficult for both of us. I dread to imagine how she'll cope once I –'

For some minutes the disclosure of his doom seemed to have a tonic effect on him. He spoke animatedly of all that he wanted to do before his time was up; to travel – no, not as far as Valparaiso, but Paris, Italy, Greece – the Parthenon! To see those places he'd only visited in his imagination . . .

'Why shouldn't you?' Key said, moved by this unwonted confession of longing.

But the question seemed to puncture his bubble, and the

light in his eyes dulled abruptly. 'She would never agree to it,' he said, with a sigh. 'I'm not sure she's capable of it.'

Now he began to understand Wallace's earlier musings on escape. It wasn't just an awareness of responsibility that imprisoned him. It was her. His partner in life had become his jailer. Key knew he would have to proceed carefully with what he said next. The information he held on Julia Wallace felt like a deadly weapon in his pocket. He couldn't decide which was more callous, to show it him or to withhold it. Some dark other was goading him on to speak, and he cleared his throat.

'Given the prognosis, you should use your time as fully as you can. Might that not necessitate striking out on your own?'

He looked at Key dubiously. 'You mean – leave her? No, I couldn't do that. It would be – no.'

'Why not? The day's coming when you'll have to leave her anyway. You could use the time that remains doing the things you've always wanted – visiting the places you've longed to. I'm not suggesting you leave her destitute! You could make a legal settlement, put aside some money ...'

He shook his head. 'It can't be done. It would be the end of her.'

'We're all going to die, my friend. And your wife may not be that much further from the grave than you are.'

He stared at Key queerly. 'What d'you mean?'

Key paused: here it came, his moment of truth. The *anagnorisis*, as his sacred Aristotle called it. 'Let me tell you a story. I came by some information not long ago, pertaining to a certain party. A woman. In her younger years she had perpetrated a deception. She had lied about her age, on census forms, on her marriage certificate. The year she was wed she claimed to be thirty-seven. In fact she was in her mid-fifties. Nobody thought to question her, probably because it seemed quite plausible. So she got away with it, for years. One day she let her guard down to a friend – admitted the lie she had been living. By my reckoning, she's now close to seventy.'

Wallace stared at him. 'Why are you telling me this?'

'I think you know why, Mr Wallace. This woman – this woman I'm talking about – is your wife.'

He was still staring. Then his features contorted into a mask of incredulity. From somewhere he found his voice again. 'Julia? You're saying Julia is – No, that can't be.' Key said nothing, only watched him struggle with the idea, with the inconceivable, and perhaps his own unconscious collusion in it. 'Mr Key, are you making sport with me?'

The old-fashioned locution might have made him smile at another time. But not now. He shook his head gravely. 'When I first heard of it I wondered. She had seemed to me ... older. So I checked. It's incontrovertible. There's a record of her aged nine, from the census of 1871. You can find it in the General Register Office at Somerset House.'

'You – you checked?' It felt as if he were being accused of something.

'Forgive me. I'm afraid one of the occupational hazards of being a police detective is an inconvenient curiosity. It's difficult to keep in hand, even when it trespasses into the personal life of a friend.' He could have said *especially* when.

Wallace was still shaking his head. He looked shrunken; his gaze seemed lost. Around them voices and footsteps rose and fell. Life continued – it would always continue – oblivious to suffering. He took out his cigarettes again, opened the pack to him, but Wallace didn't notice. He was elsewhere, searching dimly through the dead leaves of the past, wondering what wilfulness had shielded him from the truth. Seventeen years. That was the remarkable trick his wife had played. When they had met, some time in 1911, she had given him to understand she was thirty-three. But she was fifty – just old enough to be his mother. He had been deceived. Worse, he had been fooled.

At last he spoke. 'How did you – you said she told a friend. Was it Parry?'

'Who else? She once let slip she'd not been honest about her age, but even Parry doesn't know exactly. He guessed she'd taken seven or eight years off.'

His eyes narrowed in confusion. 'Why on earth did she tell him? He's the least ... She told him and yet she didn't –'

'Tell you? Maybe she wanted to, and couldn't. And then it must have got harder, every year adding to the lie. In the end she was probably too scared to tell you.'

He didn't know why he was making excuses for her. Perhaps he meant to soften the blow, as he watched Wallace across the table struggling with his bewilderment. A husband might feel humiliated in all kinds of ways – by the disclosure of an infidelity, or the realisation that his wife no longer loved him. Or that she had never loved him in the first place. But to discover that your wife had lied about her age, to the point of becoming, unbeknownst to you, a pensioner, that was surely grotesque? It had an element of black farce to it, like a ribald song from the music hall – *Oh! – dear! Say it isn't true/ I thought me wife was thirty-five/ But she's damn near fifty-two!*

Their glasses stood empty. Wallace appeared not to understand the tradition of buying rounds. Key pushed to his feet and asked him if he'd have another, but received only that uncomprehending blindfold look, as if he'd just interrupted a deep train of thought – which he probably had.

Wallace had risen from his chair, and said, 'I'm sorry, Mr Key, I have to go home' – *and murder my wife*. That was the detective's macabre thought, never to be repeated. He didn't suppose for a moment that Wallace had murder in his mind. Not then, anyway.

14

'Poor Wallace,' said Lydia, with a little shiver. She gazed out beyond the pool to the wide swell of the ocean. The morning sky had gone a gunmetal shade, and a sturdy little breeze had got up, blowing her hair attractively across her face. The gulls wheeling overhead were in raucous voice.

'Hmm. I didn't see that one coming,' said Teddy, a thumb pressed against his chin. 'Could you ever imagine being fooled like that, Mr Key?'

'We tend to be more suspicious, as coppers. But the mind plays tricks on all of us. Human beings have a strange capacity for knowing and yet *not* knowing at the same time.'

Lydia, still thoughtful, said, 'One must also bear in mind the possibility that he was very much in love with her. When they first met, Julia might have appeared to him as fresh and young as the May blossom.'

Key made a conceding expression at her, though his feeling was less gallant: she had forgotten he had seen Julia in her wedding photograph. No one would have mistaken her for a fresh young anything, or Wallace for a besotted suitor. He was a scientist, a rationalist, and even in the early days of courtship he must have suspected that something didn't sit right. How do you make seventeen years of your life disappear? With a single-minded determination in her case. Somehow she must have secured the silence of those who were in a position to know – her sister, for example – and to the rest of the world had simply brazened it out.

'I don't remember this deception being mentioned at the time of the trial,' said Teddy.

'It wasn't,' Key replied. 'Nobody knew about it apart from Wallace and myself. If anyone had got wind of it Wallace would have been even more deeply implicated as prime suspect.'

'What a terrible thing, though. To trick a fellow like that into marrying her. I should have been furious myself.'

Lydia, kindly to a fault, said, 'But Teddy, think of it from her point of view. A spinster who believed she had missed her chance of marriage. Living in a Harrogate boarding-house, probably with few friends and a job she disliked. She meets someone as lonely as herself, who's not badly off, seems to enjoy her company . . . it was probably desperation that hatched the plan in her mind. I can't help feeling sorry for her. Mr Key, you understand, don't you?'

He shrugged. 'To a degree. I see the unhappiness of her plight. But to risk that imposture – to deceive someone so flagrantly? I don't know.'

'She might have got away with it, too, if Parry had kept his trap shut.'

There was a silence, and he could tell what they were thinking – *And she would have been safe if his policeman friend had kept his trap shut.* But neither of them said anything. Lydia put down her pencil and notebook, and looked over at Teddy.

'Are you ready for your swimming lesson?'

He smiled, rose from his lounger. She was already hurrying towards the diving board, and Key watched as she took the ladder up to the white stage. She paused for a moment to tie up her hair, then set herself at the board's edge. A tiny hop, and she sprang and arched herself into the water with barely a splash – like an envelope posted through a letter-box. The blue and white hoops of her swimsuit were a sudden blur beneath the wobbling surface until, halfway up the pool, her dark head jerked up with a breathy gasp.

Teddy, at the shallow end, minced down the safety ladder to join her.

He left them to it, and set off on a stroll around the ship. Inside, stewards and bar staff were carrying tables and flowers into the ballroom in preparation for this evening's gala entertainment. He stopped to say hello to Mrs Leverton, the happily unwidowed sister, then moved on to the bar where he bought cigarettes. A bevy of musicians were lugging their instruments down the corridor: rehearsal time.

He came out on deck again in time to see the back of a familiar capped figure at the taffrail. Captain Jarrett turned on hearing his steps and took the pipe from his mouth. 'Mr Key,' he said, with a sideways tilt of his head. 'I trust you'll be joining us for the Farewell Ball later?'

'Of course,' he replied. There would be many more ladies than gentlemen in attendance, Jarrett continued, so they should prepare for a busy night. Key replied that his name was already pencilled on the dance cards of the Tarrant ladies.

'Yes ... I've noticed you ensconced with Miss Tarrant and Mr Absolom down at the swimming pool.' He left a suggestive

154

little pause. 'You have the air of plotters. I've wondered what you could be talking about.'

He had narrowed his eyes. His tone was half amused, half curious, as if he might really be expecting to be let in on the secret.

'Oh, just an old case I worked, years ago.'

'The Liverpool murder case, you mean? The unsolved one?' So he had remembered. Suddenly Key didn't feel quite at ease with his questions: the Captain seemed to have sharpened his focus on him in an insinuating way.

'Yes. Teddy – Mr Absolom – has a particular interest in the Wallace case. He believes it might make a feature film.'

Jarrett absorbed this. 'And your role is to be – what – the inside man?'

'Something like that,' he replied, bristling at the thin note of scepticism in the Captain's voice. Abruptly he changed the subject. 'I think you told us a storm was on the way?'

Jarrett looked out over the horizon, his antennae on alert to the shifting weather fronts. 'It might get up lively,' he said, from the corner of his mouth. The other corner held the stem of his pipe.

'In that case I might cut along to the infirmary and get something for my *mal de mer*,' said Key, and wished him good morning. He felt Jarrett's eyes still on him as he walked off.

On returning to the pool he had expected to find Lydia and Teddy in their usual state of gay hilarity, her patient encouragement against his floundering efforts to stay afloat. But instead he found them in murmuring stillness, heads close together, hugging the edge of the pool. They were so deeply preoccupied in talk that they didn't notice him padding by and pausing to listen. He couldn't make it out exactly, though from small fragments – *I think he would . . . when he found out . . . that's more plausible* – he inferred that they were raking over the intricacies of his story.

They stayed in this huddle for another ten minutes. He began to wonder if the mood was not so much conspiratorial as romantic. Then Lydia happened to raise her head and caught sight of him, silent on the lounger.

'Mr Key!' she called, then disappeared for another mumbled confab before they hauled themselves out of the pool. They came back to the table, feet slapping on the tiles, their voices just a shade too loud to be mistaken for unselfconscious innocence.

After the revelatory evening at the Vines he didn't hear from Wallace for some weeks. It didn't require much psychological acuity to imagine what was going on inside him. The audacity of his wife's deception must have preyed on his mind to a tormenting degree. Key reasoned that two reactions would have been foremost. Anger the first, anger at the way she had fooled him, mocked him for not guessing . . . and yet he wondered if any of it had found an outlet in the dismal domestic quiet of 29 Wolverton Street. Would he confront his wife with her lie? From what Key knew of him it seemed unlikely. Wallace was a brooder, not an accuser. The wrong she had done him would be festering, but he would not take her to task. It was not his way.

The other reaction would be as intense, though its fibres more difficult to unpick. It was humiliation. This would cut more deeply, for the awareness of his predicament now involved an outsider – the person who had brought it to his notice. Key had assured Wallace of his confidentiality, and that he could be trusted to remain as close-mouthed as he was. Still, he *knew*, and the idea of someone else being privy to the wretched secret would harrow Wallace's waking hours. Did Key feel guilt as the messenger? Certainly he did, but his sympathy for Wallace's situation – marital and mortal – was such that to have let sleeping dogs lie was out of the question. He couldn't have forgiven himself for keeping that secret in the vault.

He next encountered Wallace on a late November evening at the chess club. They had both neglected it that year, and the coincidence of their being there seemed to tighten the invisible bond between them. Key felt himself being watched as they progressed around the tables, match by match, until they sat facing one another. They shook hands, exchanged formal pleasantries, as if they were being overheard. Of the three games they played Key had almost no memory, except that he won them all. No satisfaction in that (there never was). They both had something else preoccupying them, and fetched their coats.

In silence they walked around the dark streets, looking for a quiet pub. The rain had started, shining the cobbles and making the street lamps glimmer – a Liverpool nocturne, like something by Atkinson Grimshaw. The city never looked more beautiful than in the rain, at night. Eventually Key decided on the White Star, which had a secretive back room where they might talk uninterrupted. A fire had been lit in the grate, and their coats steamed as they settled there, with pale ales and chasers. Under the pub's antique illumination Wallace looked sickly, ghastly even, and the brave face he had presented at the chess club began to crumble, piteously.

He had been to the doctor to seek stronger medication, he said, so the pain had become manageable again. But the sickness at his heart had found no relief at all. The obvious question hung in the air, and his answer was as Key had expected.

'I can't talk to her about it, Mr Key. It's impossible. Whether she admits it or denies it makes no difference.' He stared at the fire for a moment. 'The truth is, I can hardly bear to look at her.'

His eyes had moistened, and Key put a hand to his shoulder. 'Would you rather I hadn't told you?'

He shook his head in a muddling denial. He blamed himself for having allowed her to get away with it. He'd supposed she had taken 'a few years' off her age when they were married, but had never guessed the real extent. Who could have?

Life at home dragged on, he said. Gordon Parry had called a couple of times; even he seemed daunted by the lowering atmosphere.

'These last few days I've wondered to myself – what's the use in going on? I have no love for her. I have nothing to live for.'

'You mustn't think that.'

He didn't seem to hear. 'I believe I'd be better off dead. You know what Seneca said? "Life itself is slavery when one lacks the courage to die".'

'Really? It seems to me that it takes more courage to live than to die. When we last met you told me what the doctors had said. Wouldn't it be better to use what time you have than let it go to waste?'

Wallace's gaze dropped, and he said quietly, 'I am aware of what little is left to me. But how can I enjoy it when the whole tenor of life is blighted by –' He shook his head sadly. 'For a long time, before all of this, I used to imagine an existence without her. If she were one day just *gone*, vanished from the earth . . . '

'You mean, if she was dead?'

'Well, not exactly. That is, I didn't wish death on her – I simply envisaged her as an absence from life. From my life. A nothing. D'you understand?'

Key gave a slow nod. How grimly characteristic of Wallace that his fantasy should involve the annihilation of the woman he had chosen for a wife. Given that Julia Wallace was unlikely to vaporise at any minute it seemed he was resigned to sharing the remainder of his days with her. Or was he? It was possible to wonder if, behind the recessive manner, behind those poached, deep-sunken eyes, there lurked some darker instinct.

'If it came down to it, how far would you be willing to go?'

Wallace looked at him, puzzled. 'What do you mean?'

'It boils down to this. We talked last time of your "disappearing". I could secure for you a passage to South America, say, and ensure that your traces were covered. No one would ever know where you've gone. But in your condition establishing a new life thousands of miles from here may not appeal. I can understand that. In which case – what if she disappeared instead?'

He blinked, sudden alarm in his eyes. 'How – how could she?'

'It's merely a philosophical speculation.' Wallace was making to protest when Key raised a calming hand. 'Just humour me a moment. What if you could choose to make someone vanish – *phut!* – and yet no suspicion of guilt would attach itself to you? Think! A moment's decisiveness, and in the blink of an eye that person – that burden on your soul – was gone, for ever. Would you do it?'

'This is a rum sort of conversation …' He realised that an answer was expected. 'No. However much I might hope for that person's … *demise*, I couldn't have it on my conscience. You're asking me if I would commit wilful murder, and the answer is no.'

Key held his gaze, and he looked away. 'Well, we understand each other. But one more question, if you will. What if circumstances were different, and a third party, hypothetically, could deliver you from your predicament – if the liability was not yours, but someone else's? How would that sit with your conscience?'

Wallace squinted, seemingly uncertain as to what, if anything, was being proposed. He had accused Key before of 'making sport'; now he knew better.

'I'm not sure I understand, Mr Key. This hypothesis you present seems to me, well, macabre. Who is this "third party" that might save me – the angel of death? I can't believe in such an entity.'

Key wondered if he did understand, at a deeper level; only it might take him longer to accept. Wallace had admitted to dreaming of an existence without her. But a dream it might have to remain.

Teddy and Lydia had fallen silent at this point. They briefly glanced at one another. Both of them were seized in expressions of such fearful incredulity that Key burst out laughing.

'I haven't seen such terror-struck faces since *I Walked with a Zombie.*'

'What *were* you proposing to him, Mr Key?' Lydia finally said.

'A second chance,' he said. 'He was desperate, and dying, and I wanted to help him. I would have paid to send him to the other side of the world, if he'd been willing. The alternative was to send his wife off somewhere, from which there would be no return. I didn't think for a moment he'd entertain the possibility.'

'You mean – to eliminate her?' said Teddy.

He shook his head. 'Killing isn't in my line. Not since I served on the Front at any rate. But if Wallace had asked me to arrange some permanent exile for his wife, who knows what might have happened?'

'Permanent exile . . . you mean a sort of banishment?'

'Why not? We used to send whole shiploads of people off to Australia. Would it be so difficult to arrange the disappearance of an old lady?'

'Mr Key!' Lydia exclaimed. 'You, a policeman? I don't believe it.'

'You'd be surprised, my dear. If you'd been in the job as long as I was you'd know exactly what a policeman was capable of.'

At that moment a steward came to their table with a note for Lydia. She opened it to read, and let out a groan of exasperation. 'From my mother. She wants me urgently – running repairs on her ballgown for tonight.'

'There's a seamstress on board. She can put it on account.'

But Lydia was pulling a face. 'That won't wash. If I don't offer to help there'll be an almighty row.'

'For crying out loud,' said Teddy. 'We're just getting to the denouement! Can't she at least *wait*?'

She had risen from her lounger and was pulling on her towelling robe. 'You two can work it out together. That way it'll be a surprise for me!'

Teddy blew out his cheeks in disappointment. Key gave Lydia a farewell salute.

'See you at the ball.'

'Yes, and get there early. You're both on my dance card, don't forget.'

She walked off, hugging her notebook to her chest. It was nearing four in the afternoon. They had left behind the fitful sunshine hours ago and were heading towards fields of grey cloud.

'Pretty unprofessional of her to dash off like that,' Teddy muttered. Yet the little setback seemed to lend him a jolt of energy. 'All right, Mr Key, let's cut to the chase. We need an ending, and that rather sinister conversation you had with Wallace in the pub has given me an idea.'

'Oh yes?'

'Wallace, enraged by his wife's deceit, plots her murder. What if – what if he set it up to look like a burglary that's gone wrong? Let's imagine: he tells some shady friend of his that there's a cashbox at the house. And the best time to break in is on the Tuesday evening, when it's full to the brim with his collection money.'

Key shook his head. 'But there was only four pounds. And if he was an opportunist thief why did he end up beating his victim's brains out?'

'But that's it. The man he's hired turns out to be a killer, not just a thief. In the meantime Wallace has to make sure he's got an alibi on the night.'

'Hmm. So how would Wallace, of all people, know of a killer for hire? Parry was the only man of his acquaintance who might have links with the underworld, and he was never going to be an accomplice. He and Julia were friends.'

'Ah, but listen to this. Let's assume Wallace *does* have killing in mind. He would need an intermediary to find him the man. Think about it. Who did he meet regularly through the Prudential, on a professional and a personal basis?' Teddy splayed his hands, as if the answer was obvious.

He considered, and then looked at him. 'The police?'

'Exactly! He dealt with coppers all the time – insurance investigations, life policies, frauds. This was his world. Who understood the mechanics of murder better than a policeman, and who would be more likely to know a killer?'

'But what would motivate a policeman to plot the murder of a defenceless old lady?'

'It's a crime drama we're writing, Mr Key. We invent his motivation. Maybe Wallace has something on him. Maybe the copper has got into debt and needs a lot of cash quickly. Desperation might be driving him. It happens.' Teddy was by now quite inflamed by his own morbid inventiveness. A light danced in his eyes. 'Right then. We have to put together a scene in which Wallace and his copper form a plan. We should have them meet at a famous location in the city, a landmark, but where they can speak without being eavesdropped. Like ... the top of the Liver Building?'

Key considered for a moment. 'I think it would seem more realistic out of doors. By the river, perhaps.'

'Yes! We could film them in long shot, two figures on a ferry.' Teddy, palms facing out, smoothed an imaginary line across the air. 'Twilight on the Mersey. The gas lamps just coming on. A deadly plan being hatched.'

'That's good ... but I have a more windswept scene in mind. How would it be if the two met on a lonely strand, with nothing to distract the eye but miles and miles of sea. Do you know Crosby Beach? It's about half an hour north of the city ...'

15

Crosby Beach. In that blank, hungover week between Christmas and the new year it looks like the end of the earth. You take a train from Central Station up to Blundellsands, where you cross the road down to the shore. It's blowy, of course, and the salt wind cuts like a whip on your face; but if you arrive early afternoon you may catch that pearly light and one of those vast cathedral skies.

He was already there when you arrived at Blundellsands. In the distance his tall, lean figure was unmistakable; in his black overcoat and bowler he could have been taken for a harbinger of Death himself. No one else was about as you approached him across the sand. You greeted each other, and talked briefly of Christmas. He and his wife had spent a couple of days with his sister-in-law and nephew at Ullet Road – a blessed escape from the atmosphere at Wolverton Street.

You stood for a while looking out at the sea, its cold grey distances seeming to reflect the sombre occasion of your meeting. The waves fidgeting, tottering, breaking on the shingle. You turned to walk, and long silences kept in step with you. He had succumbed to a new habit of gnawing his cheek from inside, a nervous tic of which he was quite unconscious. Presently you halted, and said,

'Did I ever tell you about the time I nearly drowned? In Belgium, that summer of '17. We were in the first wave of an attack and somehow I stepped into a quagmire. Stuck in it up to my armpits. Two lads from another regiment happened to run past and dragged me out. Another half a minute and I would have sunk right under.'

'How terrifying,' said Wallace.

'It was. It happened a lot out there. Men just vanishing into the mud. Most you didn't see. You'd get back to base and there'd be a roll-call. A name was read out, with no reply. Then another, and another. They were strange, those unanswered calls. It wasn't like seeing a man die from a mortar fragment or a bullet wound – that was death, right there in your face. But those men who disappeared . . . they seemed posthumous before we'd even taken in the manner of their dying –'

Wallace had heard enough. 'I've been thinking about what you said. What time remains to me . . . I should make use of. I've known weariness, and futility, but I didn't realise I'd also been deluding myself. I've come to the end with her. If I still had my health I would leave, but I don't have the will to start again somewhere else. And I don't have the courage to –'

'To remove the stone from your shoe. I understand. You already know I'm willing to help you. But the way is long, Mr Wallace, and fraught with danger – for both of us. You must be prepared to grant me absolute control in this . . . undertaking. If not, we shake hands here and never mention it again. You should decide now.'

Wallace, ashen-faced, returned a level, unillusioned stare. 'I'm ready to do whatever you propose. Only, grant me one thing. Don't – please don't let her suffer unnecessarily.'

It was the despairing proviso of a man prepared to gamble for his life. 'She won't have to suffer. The man I have in mind is a professional. He deals in abductions, kidnappings. People go missing every day, every year, thousands of them, and very few get found again. This man does disappearances for a job.'

'But – how? Where does he dispose of them?'

'Asylums, mostly. Mental institutions. In Ireland they have devised an entire system to keep women prisoner for a lifetime. If you pay people enough they can secure silence for you.'

'And how will I explain – Julia, gone? To her sister, her family? She couldn't just vanish into thin air.'

'People do. All the time. Husbands, wives. Whole armies of missing people. Some do the disappearing act by themselves. And some have it done for them.'

It starts on the evening you return to the chess club. Your name will be up on the fixtures board. You arrive at the Central at around 7.45. A telephone message will have been left for you. The message will be handed over and you'll read it there. It is from a client who intends to put some business your way. He will have left his name, his address, and a time for you to call on him the following night. But this client is a hoaxer who has lured you from the house. While you are gone, he will pay a call on your wife. Do you understand?

Wallace said, Who is this man? A friend of yours?

That doesn't concern you. All you need is his name. Think of it as our codeword. Once you hear it you will know the plan is underway. But on receiving his message at the Central there is something vital you must do – you must convince those present you have never heard of this man before.

His name?

The sound of the sea beat in your ears. You stood facing one another *on the beach. You picked up a thin stick of driftwood and drew letters across the wet sand.*

QUALTROUGH

Teddy, seated opposite, put down the storyboard he had been drawing and stared at Key. The name had sounded like a knell. Here it was at last, the dark heart of the Wallace story.

'Qualtrough,' he said. 'Why would he – why write his name in the sand? Does he fear to speak it out loud – like saying "Macbeth" in a theatre?'

Key laughed, in spite of the moment. 'Perhaps, a little. Wallace has to remember the name, without writing it down, or hearing it spoken. The name in the sand would make it memorable. A few minutes later it's gone, washed away on the tide.'

'So ...' Uncertainties chased back and forth over Teddy's boyish features. 'Are you saying Qualtrough wasn't an invention of Wallace's after all? Were you – was he an associate of *yours?*'

'No. But I'd heard of him. Seen photographs. He was a professional. And he was the man they called on when certain ... arrangements had to be made.' He looked at his young companion – the film-maker. 'Your face, my Thane, is as a book, where men may read strange matters.'

Teddy smiled at the quotation, and his eyes narrowed. 'What do you suppose he was like? Could we – would you have a go at describing him?' He had taken up his pencil and sketchpad.

'Oh, Teddy ...'

'Please? You've at least seen a photograph of him.'

So they went through the details, and Teddy made marks on

his pad – a square face or oval? Straight nose or crooked? Eyes prominent or deep-set? It was like collaborating with a police artist, only this time Key was on the other side of the desk, helping out. He took pains over it, and as the minutes passed the late afternoon darkened, and they felt an early warning roll of the ship. They asked a passing steward about the forecast. He said the weather was closing in quicker than they'd thought, and that the Captain might have to make a decision about the Farewell Ball. 'It's the safety of the passengers that's concerning him.'

'Oh dear,' Key said, after he'd gone. 'Lydia will be heartbroken if it's cancelled.'

Teddy, however, wasn't listening. He had put the finishing touches to his artist's impression, and held up Qualtrough's face for his inspection. Key stared at it for a few moments.

'Not bad,' he said. 'That's as close as you'll probably get.'

He rose to his feet. As usual they had seen off every other poolside loiterer and sunbather – but Teddy stayed his movement.

'Why, you're not going?'

'Time to dress for dinner, dear boy. And from the look of that sky it's about to tip down.'

'Oh, but we're so close! And we promised Lydia the denouement, don't forget.'

It was true. A certain recklessness seemed to have infected both of them. Key felt that other self pushing him on, prodding him to walk the plank. Teddy's face was alight, and in his bright gaze darted an animal excitement.

'I have a murder scene to write, Mr Key, and I can't do it without you. You said before that Qualtrough was a professional. You must have imagined how he went about it. Let's get the thing done, right now.'

He gave Teddy a long look, and felt an exhilarated resignation as he sat back down.

16

FADE IN:

EXT. A DESERTED STREET. NIGHT

The sound of a bell, and out of the fog comes the rumble of a tram. It stops, briefly, then moves out of shot. The street is the same except for a single figure, his back to us. Dark overcoat, hat, a man of medium build. The camera follows him as he begins walking, his footsteps clicking on the pavement. He enters the back entry of another street, cobbled. He steps into a recessed doorway, and waits.

EXT. BACK YARD OF A HOUSE. NIGHT

The door opens and Wallace emerges, followed by Julia Wallace. Low, muttered exchanges between them. He is on his way out for the evening, and as he leaves by the yard door he turns and gently pats his wife's shoulder. The door closes, and Wallace sets off. He stops for a moment, seeming to wonder if he's heard something, then continues to the corner and disappears.

EXT. A DESERTED STREET. NIGHT

The footsteps have faded. From a nearby church a bell rings, announcing the quarter hour. The man, seen again from behind, steps out from the shadows and makes his way to the back door of the Wallace house.

EXT. BACK DOOR OF THE WALLACE HOUSE. NIGHT

From here all the action unfolds from POV of the man. His hand knocks on the door. A light comes on in the back kitchen. A shadow looms behind the frosted half-window, and the door opens. Julia Wallace stands there, surprised. Her greeting is muffled beneath a steady throb on the soundtrack – a heartbeat.

INT. THE WALLACE HOUSE. NIGHT

The man follows her inside, through the back kitchen into the hallway. We see Julia turn and say something over her shoulder as she enters the parlour.

INT. PARLOUR. NIGHT

JULIA: I'm afraid you've just missed him.

A knock at the front door. Julia exits the room. He listens as she talks to someone on the step. He has taken off his hat and overcoat and hung them in the hallway. When she returns, moments later, she has her husband's mackintosh thrown over her shoulders.

JULIA: Just the milk boy. It's cold in here, isn't it? I'll get
         some matches.

She exits. The camera pans around the room, at the curtained window, the piano, the violin stand with its sheet music, the mirror, the prints, the rug. The heartbeat is louder now, drowning out whatever it is Julia says as she returns to the room. He is standing near to the fire as she bends down to light it. A little pop as the flame catches. Unseen by her he takes out a pair of gloves and pulls them on. She is adjusting the heat, still crouching, as he approaches. POV shows him take from a holster beneath his jacket a policeman's truncheon. Heartbeat now a monstrous pulse in our ears.

Just as she turns to speak he brings down the truncheon on the side of her head, the sound like a bat hitting a cricket ball. A damp thunk. Blood spatters the camera's POV. Julia's body topples over across the rug, right by the fire. For a minute he seems in a daze, his victim crumpled and prone on the floor. He smells something burning. Julia Wallace groans. Alarmed that he hasn't made a fatal strike he swings the truncheon against the back of her head, once, twice, three times, then a flurry, a frenzy of blows, pulping the flesh and bone. He catches his breath, looks away, and looks back. Dead. She is dead.

Something is burning still. The edge of the mackintosh has caught fire, and he stamps it out. He takes hold of the mac, folds it and places it beneath her shoulder, as respectful as an undertaker. He breathes out, collects himself.

INT. KITCHEN. NIGHT

He goes into the back kitchen, takes the jar of money from the shelf, empties it. Replaces the jar.

INT. BATHROOM. NIGHT

He goes upstairs to the bathroom, where he cleans blood from the truncheon. And fails to notice a drop he spills on the rim of the toilet bowl. He takes out a piece of cloth and wipes down his face and neck. From below a noise at the front door. He freezes. And waits.

INT. LANDING. NIGHT

Moving silently to the top of the stairs he looks down, and sees a newspaper on the door mat.

INT. HALLWAY. NIGHT

He descends the stairs, picks up the Echo *and takes it into the kitchen, where he spreads it open on the table.*

INT. PARLOUR. NIGHT

Slow pan around the room, walls and carpet spattered with blood. He drags her dead body onto the rug. He kneels to switch off the gas fire. He is about to get up when he notices a small object on the floor. It glistens, pinkly, and he squints at it. Julia Wallace's false teeth. They must have jumped from her mouth when he struck the first blow.

CLOSE SHOT *of the false teeth on the carpet, and beyond them, Julia Wallace's face, her mouth a slackened 'O', yawning out empty. Shadow of the man on the other side of the corpse.*

He picks up the teeth, hesitates for a moment, then kneels down. Twisting her head slightly his gloved hand inserts the teeth back into the dead woman's mouth. They are not properly fitted, and protrude, eerily. He steps over the corpse and exits the room.

EXT. BACK YARD. NIGHT

He emerges from the darkened house in hat and overcoat, but-
toned to conceal his bloody clothes. He walks down the path to
the yard door and exits.

EXT. DESERTED STREET. NIGHT

The same scene we began with. The glimmer of a street lamp picks
out the man's shadowy form as he walks away from the house,
unseen, unheard.

'And cut!' said Teddy, gazing at him. 'My hat off to you, sir.
If I ever get to film this it'll be a corker. Tell me, though, what
made you think of the false teeth? They weren't mentioned in
the police report.'

'It was something I once saw at another murder scene. The
force of the blow to the head caused the teeth to fly out the
victim's mouth.'

'Nice! That should have them screaming at the Gaumont
in Lewisham,' he said. 'And I like the idea of keeping
Qualtrough's face hidden. I wonder what history relates of
him ... still living, do you think?'

'I couldn't say. We never met, and I wasn't privy to his ...
dealings.'

'Fancy, though, the Wallace killer, still out there ...'

The sky had gone leaden. Key felt the air almost crackle with
the charge that precedes a downpour.

Teddy was sorting through his loose sketchpad, and looked
rather pleased with his recent handiwork. 'I must show these
to my friend Chris when I get back to London. I dare say he'll
have tips on how to shoot it.'

Key smiled fondly at him. 'Have you got a title yet?' He spoke lightly, humouringly, because he knew the thing would never get made. But Teddy was all in earnest when he replied, 'Well, my first thought was "The Anfield Murder". But that's rather dull. "The Mysterious Mr Qualtrough" won't do, either – too Agatha Christie, hmm? I want something that intrigues, but doesn't give too much away.'

'Why not call it – I don't know – "Menlove Gardens East". The mythic address, the *chimera* at the heart of the hoax.'

Teddy narrowed his eyes, and made a little note on his pad. 'That might work. You're full of ideas, sir. I'll make sure you get proper credit for it, whatever happens.'

Key looked at him. '"Whatever happens"? That sounds rather fatalistic.'

'I – I'm afraid we'll have to call it a day, Mr Key.' His tone had changed to something sorrowful, and tense. Key took out his cigarettes and offered him one; struck a match and lit them both.

'May I ask why?'

Confusion clouded his face. 'You must surely understand ...'

'Something you doubt in the story?'

He shook his head. 'The story is an excellent one. I wouldn't have missed it for the world. But if what you've told me this afternoon is true, well, it's plain you're an accessory to murder.'

'But it's *not* true. I thought that was clear ...'

Now he looked at Key as if he were insane. 'But the conversations you had with Wallace. The way you insinuated you could get rid of his wife. If I hadn't been so mesmerised by the story I'd be knocking at the Captain's door right now urging him to put you under arrest.'

Key took a drag on his cigarette and expelled a long stream of smoke. 'I strongly advise you not to do that.'

'Why not?'

'Because it will cause embarrassment, and you'll probably end up making an ass of yourself.'

Teddy paused, at a loss for words. 'I believe the charge of accessory to murder is generally received in a spirit of mortal dread, not ... *embarrassment*.'

'Teddy. Listen to me. I've had the most wonderful time these last days, talking with you and Lydia, imagining our film. So don't go and spoil it. I helped you with this story because I thought it would be diverting, and possibly useful to your career. And because, well, I *like* you. But for some reason you've suddenly decided the entire thing is my personal confession.'

'Believe me, I'm grateful to you. You're right, it has been wonderful, and I wish it could have lasted. But Mr Key, we're talking about your involvement in a *murder*. You, a policeman, sworn to uphold the law and keep the public safe, connived in doing away with an old lady.'

'On what evidence do you make such a charge?'

Teddy narrowed his eyes. 'For one thing, I don't believe you invented that detail of her false teeth. I think someone told you – someone who was there. The man who killed her, in fact.'

'That's not much to base an accusation on, Teddy. Like I said, I'd been at murder scenes before. I'd seen false teeth coughed up on the carpet.'

He scowled. 'I think you got it from Qualtrough. The mere fact you knew about him is enough for them to haul you in.'

Rain had begun spitting. Teddy had got to his feet, pulled

on his sweater, refusing to make eye contact. 'Oh dear,' said Key. 'Could this be the end of a beautiful friendship?'

When at last he lifted his gaze it was filmy. 'I'm sorry, sir. Really I am.'

He was about to walk away when Key made a parting shot. 'There's a Latin proverb, *quod gratis asseritur, gratis negatur.* Maybe you've heard of it. "What can be asserted without proof can be dismissed without proof." Bear it in mind when you call on the Captain.'

He watched Teddy as he climbed the steps to the main deck. The rain was coming down thick now, and he scooped up his cigarettes before hurrying off to dress.

17

Half an hour later the storm had fallen full on their bows. Captain Jarrett had decided that the ball should proceed, the danger notwithstanding. His crew had gone all-in with the preparations. The corridor to the ballroom had been fitted with fairy lights, awnings and a red velvet rope, the latter a decorative accoutrement in normal circumstances but this evening a veritable safety measure as the floor swayed from the roll and pitch of the ship. Dressed in their finery the revellers would have preferred a stately amble to the entrance, but were instead obliged to grasp at the rope to hold themselves upright. Some moved like staggering drunks before they'd even reached the bar.

Inside the chandeliers shivered glassily under the tilt, and the gleaming dancefloor itself seemed to undulate. Party balloons wobbled from all sides in mad profusion. Stewards steered about the tables with trays of drinks, and the occasional sound of tinkling glass provoked whoops from the guests. Among the low-lit crowd Key searched for Lydia, but the first faces he encountered were those of Mrs Leverton and Mrs Orme; once again he'd forgotten which sister was the war widow, so he played safe with a smile halfway between gladness and sympathy. He fetched them drinks and they talked about what a wonderful cruise it had been, and what a shame it was nearly over.

The orchestra looked, and sounded, remarkably unfazed by the storm-tossed conditions. Their conductor kept the music coming – 'Smoke Gets in Your Eyes', 'Begin the Beguine', 'Embraceable You' – and his beatific smile seemed to encourage couples to venture out onto the dancefloor. Their sliding collisions spiked the mood with an awkward hilarity. Cries of 'Oops, excuse me!' and 'Sorry, my fault' were accompanied by peals of laughter. He made another circuit of the room and found Mrs Tarrant, resplendent in a bosomy, teal-coloured gown and a daring little tiara perched on her head.

'Mrs Tarrant, you look absolutely splendid,' he said.

She took the compliment with a coquettish smirk and suggested he might ask her to dance. He held out his hand in invitation and they stepped forward onto the floor. 'Don't let me fall, Mr Key,' she laughed in a muddle of fear and excitement – possibly at the idea of his having to catch her. As they swayed about the room a look of incandescent pleasure settled over Mrs Tarrant's features which he flattered himself to think he had somehow induced. She *did* look splendid, in her unseductive matronly way, and he hesitated for as long as he could to spoil the illusion of her being the single thing on his mind.

'I haven't seen Lydia this evening,' he said to her with as much nonchalance as he could muster.

A petulant frown creased her forehead. 'Oh, she had to dash off suddenly to see Mr Absolom – said he was very out of sorts.'

'Really?'

'I wonder, Mr Key. Have you noticed a *tendresse* between them?'

'Well, Lydia's been teaching him to swim, and they obviously like one another. All quite innocent, as far as I can tell.'

Mrs Tarrant looked dubious. 'She tends to get spoony about certain men. I'm afraid she's easily led – and hurt.'

It occurred to him that this maternal solicitude might be disingenuous – that her real fear was of Lydia flying the nest and thus leaving no one for her to pester. He replied, with every look of innocence, 'I think it more likely that men get spoony about her.'

It had been obvious to him that Teddy was enamoured of her. But it was dismaying that she might have fallen for him. Not in her class *at all*, he thought.

They had just withdrawn from the fray when a steward approached and told him the Captain wished to have a word. At his side Mrs Tarrant looked quizzical, and with a quick shrug he turned to follow the man out of the room. They made their way down unsteady corridors and up a flight of stairs to the bridge. A knock on the door, and he was ushered through. Jarrett sat on a bench, alone and pensive with his pipe. Great gouts of seawater kept flinging themselves at the large windows.

'Apologies for dragging you from the fun, Mr Key, but I've just had a conversation with young Mr Absolom. He's in a terrible way.' He gestured for Key to take a seat.

'Oh dear. Seasick?'

'A little. But that's not what concerns me. He came to my office an hour ago in a state of extreme agitation. He asked me whether I had the power to make an arrest on the ship. Of course I told him I did, and there's a brig for confining offenders. You spent most of the day with Mr Absolom, didn't you?'

'That's right. And most of yesterday, too.'

'Did you have some sort of falling out – an argument?'

'With Teddy? No. Quite the reverse. We parted on very friendly terms. You say he was agitated – about what?'

'Apparently it has come to his notice that someone on board is, in his words, psychopathically disturbed.'

'That's a bit harsh on the chaplain, I would have thought . . .'

His face didn't twitch. 'This is no joking matter, Mr Key. I pressed him to tell me who it was but he wouldn't – just claimed that this man –'

'*Is* it a man? You said just now it was "someone on board". Mightn't this "psychopathic" person be a woman?'

Jarrett gave him a narrow-eyed stare. 'I understood him to indicate a man. He said – this person was a killer, or at any rate had implicated himself in a murder case. Now you and Mr Absolom have been almost exclusively in one another's company –'

'I'm not sure I like where this is going –'

'– and your discussions, as you told me, concerned the Wallace murder case. Not wishing to jump to conclusions, but that would suggest the person Mr Absolom has in mind is you.'

'And there, in one leap, you have reached your undesirable conclusion. You're also forgetting that Miss Tarrant has been with us the whole time. Perhaps you should ask her how things stand between us. And whether she suspects me of being psychopathically disturbed.'

'I intend to,' he replied. 'In the meantime I think it advisable that you stay away from Mr Absolom.'

Key gave him a surprised look. 'Is that at his request, or yours?'

Jarrett had stood up. 'We can resume this discussion tomorrow morning. Thank you for your co-operation.' His voice was as cold as ashes. Key was dismissed, it seemed.

Back in the ballroom the mood of jollity had been only slightly deflated by an injury. Two stewards were stretchering out a young lady, crumpled and white-faced, apparently a victim of the dancefloor's treacherous movement (Key overheard a woman saying not-so-*sotto voce*, 'she was quite tipsy already'). A forest of couples remained swaying on the floor, defiant of the toppling peril. He shouldered his way to the bar, and just as he caught the barman's eye another huge roll upended a steward and his tray. An almighty crash of glass silenced the room, for about five seconds – then laughter and the hum of conversation came roaring back. It reminded him a little of the Blitz. Creeping fear, sudden alarums, a boom or a crash . . . and, if you were still standing, relief and joking and the immediate need for a drink. It really wasn't so long ago.

He was sipping a large whisky and soda at the bar when across the room Lydia appeared, in a ruched blue silk dress, pinned with a boutonnière of gardenias. Her hair was up, tenderly exposing her swan neck. He waved, though she was already making a determined beeline towards him, the dress shimmering around her legs as she moved. He had barely got out a 'good evening' before she was urgently at his ear, her voice competing with the din.

'Mr Key, I've just been with Teddy . . . He seems to be having some kind of nervous breakdown! What on earth did you say to him?'

'I can't imagine. He was fine a couple of hours ago. What's happened?'

She shook her head, worriedly. 'He came to my cabin, about six, straight after seeing you. I couldn't get any sense out of him at first, and he'd just been awfully sick – he's no sailor. He said that you'd both gone through the murder scene (which sounded horrible, by the way), but then something you'd said – about a set of false teeth? – gave him the creeps and made him think you were actually there, *in the room when it happened*! I told him he must be mistaken, you couldn't possibly have been there, but he seems to believe you and Qualtrough were somehow in cahoots!' Her gaze had turned pleading. 'You weren't, were you?'

'Of course not. That boy's got it all mixed up. I was trying to draw as realistic a picture as I could of Mrs Wallace's last moments. For Teddy's film! Of course it was Grand Guignol, pretty gruesome stuff, I admit ... but he's got the wrong end of the stick. And now I've just had a *mauvais quart d'heure* with the Captain, who's practically accused me of being a psychopath!'

She still stared at him, as if making some private calculation of her own. Could the mild-mannered former police detective secretly be a brutal killer? He gurned in a hapless, comical way, and something cleared in her expression. She could see that the idea was preposterous, and that they were friends just as before.

'Where is he now?' he asked her.

'Still in his cabin. He looked like death! I should go and check on him.'

'Poor old Teddy.'

'You're not cross with him, then?'

'No, not at all. Just a misunderstanding.'

The orchestra had struck up 'Good Night, Sweetheart', and

184

he caught hold of Lydia's hand. 'Before you go, may we have a dance?'

Her smile came, diffident, then beaming, and she allowed him to lead her on to the floor. She was wearing an unfamiliar perfume that had a cedarish note beneath; it carried him back meltingly through the years to that night at the Wellington Rooms. He was once more the smitten swain, holding her in a dancer's clinch, the space between them quivering and electric, yearning to be closed. The future seemed to be calling him on, and its name was Esmé. *Time was away and somewhere else . . .* Useless to dwell on it now, another lifetime and two world wars away. Just at that moment Lydia lifted her face to him, and his heart dropped a curtsey. Before he could stop himself he dipped his head to her ear. 'You're a lovely girl,' he muttered, wistfulness almost choking his voice. 'I do hope you find some nice fellow to marry.'

Her answer was giggly, brief, and innocent: 'You're very sweet to say so!'

They swayed to the end of the song, and as they drew apart she gave him a little round of applause, as if he'd been – what? – 'marvellous for your age'.

Another sudden lurch beneath their feet gave her a prompt. 'I'd better go and see how Teddy's doing, Mr Key.'

He offered to accompany her, and she had no objection. They made their way out and, half holding on to one another, climbed the stairs towards the first-class cabins. At the turn of a corridor a steward was toting mop and pail where someone had been sick. The stench of vomit was evil.

They arrived at Teddy's cabin. Lydia knocked at the door, without reply. Over her shoulder she made a grimacing face at him before gently calling out, 'Teddy? It's Lydia. I'm with Mr Key. Can you let us in?' She gave another rap, louder this time, and they heard muffled movement within. The door opened, and there was Teddy, his face pinched and pale, so pale he might have been his own ghost. His bleared gaze lifted beyond Lydia to her companion.

'Mr Key. I hope you've not come to punch me. Because I'm in no condition to fight.'

'Of course not, my dear fellow. Lydia told me you're not well, that's all.'

He turned away, and staggered back to his bed. They followed in after; with the curtains drawn the cabin was dim and brown. Teddy was in quite a state, dinner suit crumpled, hair in disarray. The room, always untidy, now looked as if it had been burgled: clothes, blankets, papers lay scattered around. Lydia had gone to sit next to him on the bed, where he groaned piteously. She patted him like a sick old dog.

'Should we get a doctor?' she asked him.

Key nodded; he would call for one. He picked up the bedside telephone and asked for the infirmary. They connected him, but there was no one picking up.

'I suppose it's a busy night for him.'

Then he remembered the medicine he'd collected for his own *mal de mer* earlier that day. About half was still unused, so he told Lydia he'd fetch it. Back down the corridors he went, tipped this way and that; the sentimental refrain of 'Good Night, Sweetheart' crooned maddeningly in his head. And that in turn made him think of Lydia's nonchalant, devastating *You're very sweet to say so!* Her smile betrayed not a trace of understanding, or even suspecting. He walked blunderingly on until he gained his cabin and found the little envelope of powder on the table.

On returning he mixed the draught with a tumbler of water and handed it to Lydia. She got Teddy to sit upright, and, like a kindly matron with a schoolboy, brought it coaxingly to his lips.

He swallowed the mixture, and his expression closed into a wince. Slowly, he unbuttoned his collar and pulled loose his dickie-bow. 'I'm afraid, unlike Cinderella, I shall not be going to the ball.'

'I think you should get yourself to bed, darling,' Lydia said. 'That medicine should help you sleep.'

Key pushed to his feet, and said, 'You'll feel better in the morning. The Captain told me the storm should have blown itself out by then.'

Lydia had also got up to leave, but Teddy stayed her with a hand. 'Would you mind awfully – staying here – until I drop off?'

'No, of course not,' she said softly. She exchanged a look with Key, who nodded, and wished them both good-night.

Back in his cabin he drank another whisky and soda before turning in. He could still hear ghostly distant strains coming from the ballroom. But they were not for him. Sleep was a long while coming, and when it did the dream of the strange tram ride reared up again. The same faces, the same rain coursing in fat runnels down the windows, his own vaguely responsible role – and the shrouded figure in black at the head of the car, her face averted. He moved towards her, closer now, until the figure slowly turned to face him, and he knew her: it was Julia Wallace. Her eyes were open, but her mouth had disappeared into a wide black maw, like that dead soldier mangled in the field.

The tram driver must have gone crazy, because he kept ramming the vehicle against the buffers, over and over again. Key woke to realise it was the sea pounding against the bows, just as it had on the first night – *whump . . . whump . . . whump.*

It was just before sunrise when he heard a tap at his door. He assumed that it was a steward who'd got the wrong cabin, and ignored it. But the caller persisted, and wearily he dragged on his dressing-gown to answer the knock.

Teddy stood there, bedraggled in his dinner suit, a green polka-dotted kerchief incongruously poking from his breast pocket. His face was still drawn, but he no longer looked half dead.

'Teddy. What are you doing here?' he croaked.

'Sorry, sir, but I wondered if you were awake . . .'

'Well, I am *now*. What time is it?'

He glanced at his watch. 'Quarter to six. The storm's passed, thank heaven, but I can't get to sleep and I wanted to apologise for – you know –'

'It's fine, Teddy –'

'You told me I'd make an ass of myself, and you were right.' He blew out his cheeks. 'I was just going for a turn on the deck. I need some fresh air.'

'Probably a good idea.'

'. . . I was hoping you might join me. It's pretty lonely up there at this hour.'

Key stared at him. After what had happened it sccmcd a bit rich to be presuming on his company, but Teddy's wan, hollow-eyed look and the chastened note in his voice weren't easy to resist. He asked Teddy to wait a minute, and he loitered outside while Key threw on some clothes. His eyes stung with fatigue. He knew he didn't look much fresher than Teddy did.

They headed up to the open deck, blinking against the half-light of dawn. The sky had a dazed grey pallor, as though it were in shock. The wind was still up, no longer at storm force but jousting with the sea. It piled high, the waves barging into one another and sending up plumes of froth. He shivered, and felt glad to have put on an overcoat. They met not another soul as they made a halting, geriatric progress from stern to bow. Arriving at the pool – the 'outdoor script-room', as Teddy had called it – they found it denuded of loungers and tables; it was even too early for the staff to have set up. They sat on the edge of the diving board and smoked his Lucky Strikes.

He wondered about Teddy's change of heart, whether it had more to do with expediency than regret. An ending was required for the script, and as his collaborator Key was best placed to provide one. Ambition stirred deep in the young man. If he had gone public with a denunciation it would only have acted as a spoiler for the film. He needed to set aside questions of criminality for later. For now it was the film he meant to devote himself to.

18

In the early days of January, just before the die was cast, you had to make sure Wallace was prepared for what lay ahead. You warned him he would be chief suspect in the event of his wife's disappearance. He would probably be arrested, and their marriage investigated. His name would be smeared across the papers. The pressure on him would be intense – nearly intolerable. Was he ready for this ordeal? By the merest dip of his chin he indicated that he was.

In the immediate aftermath of what happened you had kept your distance, as you had arranged. If you happened to see one another at Cheapside you talked briefly and impersonally. The chief fear was that Wallace might break down and blow the story. But he kept up his end to the last. A more phlegmatic character you had never known. That you had admitted to your colleagues a slight acquaintance became in a way the perfect screen; the minor coincidence of it felt authentic. No one would suspect your connection went any deeper, and so it proved.

The only time you saw Wallace give way to emotion was on the occasion you talked in the prison grounds at Walton, just prior to his trial. By unspoken consent what had happened at Wolverton Street that night was taboo. But you knew Wallace had been reading the papers, with their explicit accounts of the brutality visited upon his wife. He must have realised by now that almost everyone – every copper, every neighbour, every saloon-bar know-all – took it for granted that he had murdered Julia. He had been given warning of this public obloquy, and he had been acquiescent. Yet the force of it had shocked him.

You told him he would not recover his peace of mind as long as he continued poring over the newspapers.

'I don't expect peace of mind. Ever.'

'Then what was the point of –' You stopped yourself. It was guilt that had hold of him, and the accompanying realisation that he could never make atonement for what he had done.

'I asked you – you remember – when we talked, I asked you to make sure she wouldn't suffer unnecessarily. Did you not tell him that?'

'Of course I did. I don't know what happened. We didn't talk about it.'

'You said he would arrange her disappearance, not her – How could it have happened?' He stared at you. 'Eleven blows to the head. What sort of man is he, this Qualtrough?'

'An unpredictable one. Even professionals get panicked.'

'Panicked? He must have gone berserk. When I think of her lying there –'

You gripped his wrist. 'Don't think of it. For your own sake. The thing is done. You have to ready yourself for the trial.'

He stared off, his cheek twitching where he gnawed at it. 'May God forgive me for what I've done,' he muttered.

'You don't believe in God. Remember what you told me – that you'd come to the end with her, that you wanted the rest of your life free of her. You said you couldn't do it yourself . . .'

'No, I couldn't,' he said, brokenly.

'So – it was taken care of. It's over. Hold your nerve, and you will be acquitted. There isn't enough evidence to convict you.'

'In the court of public opinion I'm already guilty.'

'Fortunately it's the court of law that will decide. The public is a giant idiot that stuffs itself with scandal and outrage. Once it has sickened of your case it will forget you and move onto the next victim.'

But Wallace didn't appear to be listening; his mind had wandered off to some lost place where perhaps he was harangued by the ghost of his wife, bloodied from her wounds. He had swapped one tormenting burden for another, the difference being that he now paid in guilt what had previously been levied with boredom and discontent.

You made a tactical decision not to visit him again. It was plain that your very presence troubled him. You had been the agent of his deliverance, but also of the dark deed that enabled it. You were the goad to his bad conscience.

Meanwhile the official investigation had run up against a brick wall. It had become the impossible case. Wallace couldn't have murdered his wife, but neither could anyone else. Of the debate that raged around the city, that fascinated every crime reporter, you have already heard. The case had taken on a perplexing life of its own, and all that could resolve it was a trial. Of course you believed the verdict would be a formality. It was inconceivable that a jury could convict him on the evidence available. But it was your hubris to have reckoned without the human factor.

'That's the problem with juries, isn't it?' said Teddy, at his side. 'All too human. The Wallace jurors would have read all about the case as soon as it was in the papers. So they'd probably have made up their minds before they'd even entered the courtroom.'

'I'm afraid so. And this despite the judge carefully explaining to them their role in the proceedings. He'd told them – it's there in the transcript – "whatever your surmises or suspicions or prejudices may be", if Wallace's guilt hadn't been established as *a matter of evidence* then they should find him not guilty. The evidence wasn't strong enough. But suspicions and prejudices will have their way.'

'What did Wallace say to you – I mean, once the verdict was out?'

'He was calm. I told him it would go to appeal, and that it'd be quashed. You know Doctor Johnson's line – when a man knows he's to be hanged it concentrates his mind wonderfully – well, that was Wallace.'

And yet he was sure it agonised him all the same. Wallace was naturally prey to low spirits, and his illness nagged away at him. He was aware of his time narrowing, and Key believed that even if the Appeal Court had upheld the verdict he would have gone without demur.

Teddy said, wonderingly, 'But once the gallows threatened didn't he try to pin it all on Parry?'

'That would never have stuck. Parry had an alibi. But later Wallace thought about putting a detective on his trail. He wrote in his diary, "Parry must realise I suspect him of the terrible crime".'

Teddy looked thoughtful. 'When I first read about the case I was convinced Wallace *must* have done it. The precision of the plan, the detail in it, the whole balancing act. He knew the case against him would be strong, just not strong enough to put him at the murder scene. He was betting on a jury to find him not guilty. But it was such a gamble!'

A verdict of 'Not guilty', however, is not a certificate of innocence. With the case still unsolved the suspicion around him lingered. Someone had murdered Julia Wallace, but with no plausible suspect beyond her husband a vacuum was created. Into it seeped a toxic gas mixed of rumour and hostility. Wallace went against the advice of his family and returned to Wolverton Street. It was a mistake: the case had made him a pariah. Out on his rounds in Anfield he was jeered at, or shunned. Letters of accusation were sent to him from all parts of the country. His employers at the Prudential eventually transferred him to an office job at Dale Street. The newspapers continued to speculate, and several times he sued for libel.

In the end he did leave Anfield and moved to a bungalow on the Wirral. He lived there in quiet anonymity, though notoriety pursued him. Key was at the chess club one evening when he walked in. Key greeted him, of course. No one else did. He took the cold shoulder with his usual stoicism, but it hurt him.

'It wasn't a long penance, though. He was dead the following year.'

Teddy said, 'So he lived, what, two years longer than his wife. I wonder if, secretly, he felt he was better off without her.'

'Impossible to know . . .'

'You never asked him?'

'Hardly a question you *can* ask. His curse was always loneliness. It's not uncommon. He tried to solve it, as people do, by getting married. Seventeen years later he saw the mistake he had made. But Julia's death didn't settle anything either. His loneliness was an affliction of the self – there's no escaping that. You see, Teddy, character is destiny.'

Key looked around at him. In the half-hour they'd been

talking the ship hadn't stirred. The only sound was the ponderous sea, still moaning after its bad night. Teddy was silent,
deep in thought. He didn't have his sketchpad with him, so his
attention had been undivided. Key could tell he was wrestling
inwardly with some problem or other.

'Still thinking about the film?' he asked him.

Teddy blinked, seeming to emerge from a reverie. 'No, no.
I think I've got that worked out quite satisfactorily.'

'Well, I'm glad of that.'

Teddy's frown was deeply grooved. 'I'm sorry, Mr Key. I
made rather a mess of things last night. I went into a panic –'

'My dear fellow. Just forget about it.'

But this magnanimity didn't clear his brow. 'That's awfully
good of you, sir. But the truth is, the Captain, you see, he called
on me last night, wanting a name. I feel terrible about this . . .'

'Go on.'

'He's a stickler for form, and radioed ahead to New York. I
think there'll be, um, officers of the law waiting for you when
we disembark.'

He sighed. 'What else did you tell him?'

'Oh, only that you seem to have known Qualtrough. I left
it quite vague.'

'So they're going to take me in for questioning?' He put
heavy irony on the criminal phrase. Teddy looked suddenly
mortified.

'They'll interview both of us,' he said, trying to make it
seem friendlier. 'But don't worry, I'll clear it up. We've been
writing a script, knocking round a few ideas. I talked a rare lot
of nonsense, that's all.'

'But you did mention Qualtrough . . . that's unfortunate. I

fear you've given them a peep behind the curtain. And they'll want to know more.'

'Well, they won't get anything. Not even if they arrest me.'

His tone had taken on a martyrish defiance, and Key couldn't help but laugh. Only when he looked closer did he see that tears were bulging at Teddy's eyes. From guilt – or relief at having confessed? Teddy got to his feet and stood on the lip of the board, plucking the polka-dot hankie from his breast pocket to dab his eyes. He looked rather desolate, standing there, and Key rose to join him.

'Teddy, you mustn't upset yourself,' he said, patting him on the shoulder. 'We've had some fun, haven't we?'

He lifted his sad spaniel gaze, and smiled.

19

Key got back to his cabin, itchy with tiredness, and lay upon his rumpled cot. He must have been sparko within seconds. He had calculated on missing breakfast and rising again in time for lunch, but that plan was disrupted when a peremptory rap sounded on his door.

'Mr Key? Are you there?'

He got up to answer in his dressing-gown. Standing there was the First Mate, a man named Rogers, his expression unreadable. Key was asked to accompany him to the Captain's quarters. He glanced at his watch – nearly 7.30.

'What's this about?'

'I'll wait here, sir, while you get dressed.'

So for the second time in a couple of hours he got into his clothes and padded after Rogers. He supposed the Captain had decided to make an early start following the commotion of the previous night. Entering the room, he found Jarrett sitting at his desk in a pose of deep preoccupation, chin resting on his fist. When he lifted his face it was pale, sharply focused and yet evasively inward; there was a lot going on behind his eyes.

He gestured for Key to sit. The First Mate stood covering the door, arms folded as if anticipating violence.

'Mr Key,' Jarrett began, 'you know why I've asked to see you.'

'I presume it's about that business with Teddy last night.'

The Captain stared hard at him. 'The officer of the watch spotted you with Mr Absolom earlier this morning. This in spite of my asking you to stay away from him.'

'And I did. It was Teddy who called on *me*. I wasn't going to turn him away.'

'When was this?'

'Just before dawn. I was still half-asleep, but he wanted company. So I agreed to take a walk with him outside.'

The Captain's eyes flicked to Rogers, behind his shoulder. 'Whereabouts did you walk?'

'Around the main deck. Then we stopped at the swimming pool and talked for half an hour or so.'

'About what?'

'He was upset about his behaviour last night. He said he'd talked "a rare lot of nonsense" and wanted to apologise. I told him not to worry, we'd obviously had a misunderstanding. No harm done.'

Jarrett was silent for a moment, considering. 'No harm done . . .' he said in echo.

'I hope not. Why? Has Teddy been to see you?' He held his gaze on me. 'What – he hasn't changed his story again, surely?'

'No. He hasn't changed his story.'

Something in his voice sounded off. 'Then what's this about?'

A beat, then Jarrett said, 'We found Mr Absolom's body in the pool an hour ago. Dead.'

Key looked at him, open-mouthed. 'What? No. *No*. I only saw him – How?'

'He drowned. As you know, he couldn't swim.'

He bowed his head, and didn't look up. He could hear Jarrett talking to the First Mate but he wasn't listening to them. Teddy. Oh, that poor boy . . . The image of his face, tears pricking his eyes, loomed before Key. He felt dangerously close to tears himself, but he didn't want to give them the satisfaction.

At length, his mind swam back into focus. The Captain was telling him that he was under his arrest, on suspicion of wilful murder. He stood while Jarrett quoted a long screed of maritime law to seal it. Then the Mate was at his elbow, leading him out of the office and down into the bowels of the ship – to the brig.

The cell was basic – a bunk, a toilet, no window – though not much less comfortable than his cabin. It might have been used as a storeroom. Down there you could hear the ship's mysterious creaking and clanking, the massive vibration of its engines; the belly of the beast.

They had taken away his belt and shoelaces, as they might have done with a common criminal. He supposed they weren't going to take any chances. At about midday a steward brought tea and a sandwich. An hour or so later the Captain came down to interview him again. He wanted to establish precisely the time Teddy had visited Key's cabin, how long they had been talking, which of them left the poolside first. On being asked about Teddy's state of mind Key replied that he was somewhat low – he suspected his blabbering the previous night had caused him a certain contrition.

'How long are you planning to hold me here?' he asked him.

'We arrive in New York in about six hours.'

'May I be allowed to return to my cabin at some point? I need to pack my things, get a wash and brush-up.'

Jarrett rose to his feet. 'You'll be allowed ten minutes before we dock.' He eyed the prisoner with cool disdain. 'I'm sorry that young man ever got mixed up with you. He said that you were dangerous.'

He left the room. Key lay back on his cot and pictured the scandalised mood of the ship. By now everyone would know that a passenger had drowned in the swimming pool that morning. But would anyone know that an arrest had been made in connection with the death?

He had a visitor midway through the afternoon. The man posted outside the door knocked and admitted her. Lydia's face was dreadfully pale but composed, her eyes swollen from weeping. A handkerchief was balled in her hand. She took the chair, while he sat opposite on the bunk. For some moments she looked at him, pleadingly, as if he might be able to explain it all as a mistake, and that Teddy was fine. He would like to have done, for her sake as much as his.

'I'm surprised the Captain allowed you down here.'

'He was very reluctant. I had to beg him.' She shook her head hopelessly. 'What happened? I left Teddy sleeping in his room. The next thing I hear . . .'

'He came to my cabin around six. Said he wanted to talk. We wandered on deck for a while. He was very sorry about – everything.'

'Of course he was! That's what he told me. It was all just a horrible mistake, wasn't it? He didn't mean to –'

'No, he didn't. We agreed it had been a crazy misunderstanding.'

'But you didn't go back inside at the same time?'

'No, I was dead beat. I told him I needed to sleep, so I left him there, smoking.'

Again, a plaintive appeal creased her face. 'So why has the Captain – he believes you meant to – you wouldn't have done anything to Teddy, would you, Mr Key?'

'Lydia. Come on. All those hours we spent talking – the three of us. I thought we'd become *friends* . . . '

At that her eyes welled up, she choked out a sob, and hid her face in her sleeve. He leaned across to pat her arm, but that only made it worse. Her shoulders twitched, then convulsed under her silent sobbing. He held her hands in his, and murmured words that might soften her grief.

Minutes later a knock came, and the guard put his head around the door. Their time was nearly up. Lydia, calmer now, made a quick repair to her face. He was always impressed by women who could put on a brave front. She asked him what would happen when they got to New York.

'I gather they're going to take me into custody.'

'Not the police?'

'Unlikely. The New York Police Department has no jurisdiction over this ship. I dare say I'll find out soon enough.'

She looked at him earnestly. 'Is there anything I can do? Mummy's cousin is a KC in London. Very eminent. We can call him if needs be.'

She was already imagining a trial. 'I hope it won't come to that. But thank you.'

They had stood to say goodbye; to his surprise she threw her arms around him, and they held one another for a moment. She gave him another searching look, then turned and left the room.

It was not the way he had hoped to greet New York for the first time. He'd had visions of his arrival, having heard so much about the waterfront, the Statue of Liberty, the glittering citadel of Manhattan. Alas, these landmarks were lost to him, confined in the troglodytic and windowless gloom of the brig. It appeared that every single passenger had disembarked by the time the First Mate came down with two crew members to conduct him – in handcuffs – down the gangway and into a waiting van. He had packed his suitcase in the presence of the Captain, who was possibly on the look-out for an offensive weapon in Key's luggage.

From the pier he was driven down the length of Manhattan island to the financial district at its tip. As he emerged from the van he looked about and felt the newcomer's awe at the stone canyons dwarfing them on all sides. An insect in the land of shadows. His new berth was as plush as his previous one was poky. The Cunard Building on Lower Broadway was a vast limestone edifice of the 1920s, imposing without, majestic within. Its vaulted lobby was a rococo dream of bronze and gilt and marble tricked out with maritime decorations and wrought-iron screens. It reminded him of a Liverpool banking house, only appointed on a scale that defied any moderation and scorned any budget.

The building was not equipped with a holding cell, of course, so makeshift accommodation was found for him in one of Cunard's wood-panelled offices. While it was a form of house arrest, the inconvenience of being under guard was offset by the grandeur of his surroundings. There was a 'bathroom' on hand, with brass taps and marbled sinks, though no actual bath in it. He was permitted to eat in the company canteen, use the telephones, wander the premises at leisure. The building's many lifts – elevators – were sleek Art Deco boxes of ebony and gold. He made friends with one of the janitors, a black man named Albert, with whom he played poker last thing at night. Albert had elegant long hands, and a wheezing laugh which Key feared might indicate emphysema. He was respectful as well as genial, and called Key 'sir' until he asked him not to. (The last person to address him that way had been Teddy.)

As to how long he'd be detained he heard nothing for forty-eight hours. Then Jarrett called by to inform him there would be an inquest into Mr Absolom's death. Surely not over here? he said. Jarrett shook his head. Legal proceedings following disembarkation depended on the jurisdiction where the alleged crime had occurred. If it was committed in international waters, the inquest would be held in the country where the ship was registered. So they'd be returning to London. He ought to have been dismayed at the curtailment of his stay, but he met the news with equanimity. Maybe the poet was right – the only thing you changed on crossing the seas was the sky.

He was guest of the Cunard company for six days while his return to England was being arranged. On the last day he was allowed to go out, under escort, and he walked the neighbourhood around Lower Broadway for the one and only time. He had breakfast in a diner, ate hash browns and eggs over easy, drank some repulsive coffee. He read the *New York Times* in a bar on Third Avenue, which he visited in tribute to Ray Milland's alcoholic from *The Lost Weekend*. Strange that the story of a man's spiritual degradation should have brought out the tourist in him. But he had accepted by now that his personality was not of the common run. Then he walked to one of the bridges – Brooklyn, or Williamsburg? – and watched the boats tacking up and down the river.

He returned to his quarters on Broadway early evening, and packed. Albert, who'd taken a shine to him, had smuggled in beers and pretzels to mark their last night. Key told him about his day, where he'd walked and what he'd seen. His minder told him that next time he should take a boat trip around the island. And that he should visit him and his family up in Harlem. He discovered that Albert was a few years older than himself, had married just after the First War and had three grown-up kids. He had worked all different jobs, as garage hand, road-sweeper, waiter, hotel porter; he said that his present position was the best-paid he'd ever had. It was plain he didn't get much, yet he was contented. And perhaps he knew not to complain.

He asked Key what he'd liked best about the city, and Key confessed it was the river. Almost as great as the Mersey, he added, near where he lived. Albert looked at him to see if he was joking, then laughed his agonising laugh. He couldn't believe there was a river finer than the Hudson. Come to Liverpool, Key said, and you'll see.

20

Teddy's death made a brief paragraph in *The Times* a couple of weeks later. The story of a passenger drowning in the swimming pool of a cruise liner was not, at first sight, very remarkable. It was noted that another passenger (unnamed) was interviewed by police on his return to England, but no arrest was made. It seemed that Captain Jarrett had misinterpreted a story told to him by the deceased. Charges had been dropped on grounds of insufficient evidence.

The City of London medical examiner had carried out a post-mortem on the deceased, and an inquest had been ordered. Key received a letter from Lydia, who told him she had been to Teddy's funeral, near Uppingham. She had met his parents, and his younger sister: '. . . all terribly upsetting, as you can imagine. They knew about our meeting one another on the cruise and I told them what a wonderful companion he'd been, and so on. They know it was just a tragic accident. Of course I couldn't bring myself to tell them about the swimming lessons. It's been rather haunting me, to be honest. Do you think if I'd been a better teacher he might perhaps have survived?' He wrote back, reassuring her. It had been kind of her to go to the funeral, and he could imagine the comfort she had given Teddy's parents, anxious for a last report on their son. As for his drowning, she must know there was nothing she could have done.

He had found himself brooding on Lydia and her becalmed life in East Sheen. He wondered if she would ever break out from the domestic servitude her mother had quietly imposed. There were times on the cruise when he imagined the girl had looked at him with an appeal in her eyes. Did she want to be rescued? An idea sparked in him one evening when he happened to be on the telephone to an old university friend, Lawrence Haydon, a widower who for years had been at the Foreign Office in London. They were debating whether to attend a reunion dinner a few weeks hence. The talk later turned to the government's work in Germany on the plans for national reconstruction, and Lawrence mentioned in passing the recruitment of good translators. Key, hearing this, said that he knew of a talented young linguist who was looking for exactly that opportunity, and offered a brief profile of her. His friend told him they had a full complement at present but added there were occasional openings: he would bear Miss Tarrant in mind.

The next day Key wrote to Lydia recounting this conversation in cautious terms; he wanted to offer encouragement without raising her hopes prematurely. She replied straight away, thanking him for his trouble: she would be thrilled even to be asked for an interview. 'What a dear man you are!' she wrote, words which he read again with a little glow.

But there followed a postscript in her letter that was less agreeable. At the funeral she had also met an old friend of Teddy's from London, one Christopher Beadnell, who'd been in correspondence with him almost to the end. He'd heard about their discussion of the Wallace case and the film Teddy was eager to make of it. 'He wrote asking me to lend him the notes I'd made on the cruise – and could he also have your address? I hope you don't mind that I gave it to him. Should I also give him my notebook, do you think?'

A thin siren of alarm started within him. He'd hoped that the notes Lydia had kept on their 'script' had been forgotten, or discarded. He guessed they would contain information on the case that might be ticklish if they ever surfaced in court. Adopting a quite reasonable tone about it, he wrote back to Lydia asking her *not* to hand over the notebook – 'I'm sure you understand the trouble it might get me into!' – and left it at that, trusting to her discretion.

What concerned him was the nature of Teddy's relationship with this friend of his. Christopher Beadnell ... He recalled the name had cropped up in conversation, more than once. He had an idea this was the fellow who had introduced Teddy to Humphrey Jennings, therefore likely to be someone in the film world. And perhaps influential? He found it inexplicably galling that Teddy hadn't bothered to mention this correspondence of his, kept up 'almost to the end'.

At the end of that week another letter arrived for him. Mr Beadnell was no slouch, it seemed, and had written without delay.

Clissold 3003   Highbury Studios
                                          96 Highbury New Park, N5
                                              November 27th, 1947

Dear Mr Key,
    I beg your pardon for writing out of the blue. Lydia

Tarrant kindly passed on your address to me after we met at Teddy's funeral. As you may know he was a dear friend of mine, and his death has been the most dreadful shock. In truth I have barely come to terms with it.

I'm not sure if you're aware that Teddy had written his very last letter to me from the liner. It was found in his luggage and forwarded to me some weeks later. Among the effects handed on to his parents was a large sketchbook, apparently of storyboards for a feature film. This is now in my possession.

In that letter he explained it was your involvement in the Wallace case that initiated the project. The storyboards, though provisional, indicate that his planning was quite thorough. I would be most interested in discussing this with you in greater detail. I am in the office Monday to Friday if you care to telephone.

Yours sincerely,
Christopher Beadnell

Key, staring at the text, heard his own dry laugh. He had no inclination *at all* for a discussion with Mr Beadnell. On board ship in the company of two lively young people he had been flattered into playing along with the notion of a film. He had been under no illusion that it would ever be made. But here came an unwelcome renewal of interest, from a stranger, and what was more one who might have an influence in taking it forward. The consequences did not bear thinking about.

Clearly he was obliged to answer, if only to commiserate with the man for his loss. But another, more threatening spectre hovered in the shadows. How much had Teddy disclosed to his friend back in London? If he had been anything like as indiscreet as he was with Jarrett some firefighting would be required. He decided to adopt an innocent tone in replying; any display of vehemence might arouse suspicion. He offered him his condolences, professed great admiration of Teddy on their (regrettably) short acquaintance, and lightly dismissed the idea of pursuing the film any further. He must understand, given Key's professional background, he was obliged to exercise discretion, etc., etc. He managed to convey a subtle hint of disappointment that the 'project' was a non-starter.

In the meantime he felt ominous reverberations on a different front. He should have known that Jarrett, having been thwarted in bringing charges, was not so easily shaken off the scent. Beware the tenacity of an old sea dog. One afternoon in early December he happened to drop in at his club to catch up on some reading. The sallow winter light on Church Street was just beginning to darken, and he could hear the gates clang shut at Bluecoat Chambers down below. A couple of ancient members were chunnering away in a far corner, and he was undisturbed – or so he thought.

A youngish fellow in a demob suit had sidled in and, surveying the almost-empty room, approached. 'Mind if I ...?' he asked, pointing to the armchair facing Key's. He gestured unconcernedly, and the man sat down, fixing him with an ingratiating smirk. Key wondered if they knew one another.

'It's Mr Key, isn't it? Gordon Tulloch.' He thrust out a hand, moistly eager to the touch. His accent wasn't from here. 'From the *Middle*. I'm following up a story, about a murder case –'

'Sorry, how did you know to find me here?'

'Oh, I telephoned your old station at Cheapside. I told them I had urgent business with you.'

'Urgent?'

'Well, I laid that on a bit. But I know that you worked on the Wallace case, and I was hoping you might supply me with some information.'

Key looked at him more closely. Sandy hair, slightly pudgy face, the insincere friendliness of his expression a dead give-away.

'I'm retired, Mr Tulloch, and I always had a rule not to talk to the press unless it was official business.' He turned back to his newspaper.

'This *is* sort of official,' Tulloch continued, evenly. 'It's about your friendship with William Wallace. There's a rumour that you were more deeply involved in the case than was known at the time.'

Key stared at him, put the paper aside. 'Where did you get hold of that?'

He made a regretful moue. 'I can't tell you, I'm afraid. But my source is convinced that you knew Mr Qualtrough.' It was as he thought: Jarrett had been bending his ear.

'Tell your source from me he's a joker. There's no evidence that Qualtrough ever existed. You must know that.'

'Well, that was the assumption at the time. Tell me, how well did you know Teddy Absolom?'

He glanced at his watch. 'I'm sorry, Mr Tulloch, I don't take kindly to being badgered. Especially not in a private members' club. Who let you in here?'

'It appears that Mr Absolom made certain allegations on the basis of a testimony. Your testimony, I hear.'

'Testimony?! We were tossing around ideas for a film on a cruise liner. This is preposterous. And disrespectful to my late friend.' He rose from his chair. 'If you're going to pursue a story you'll need a more reliable informant than Captain Jarrett.'

'So you reject the charge that you and William Wallace connived in the murder of his wife?'

That tore it. He grabbed Tulloch's collar and dragged him from his chair. 'Choose a window,' he snarled in his ear. 'You're leaving.'

'Steady on. Just doing my job,' he said, trying to wriggle free of Key's grasp. Key marched him to the door, and more or less shoved him through it. Tulloch stumbled onto the landing, where a balustrade curved invitingly towards the ground floor. He backed up against the wall, in case his adversary was tempted to hurry his descent with a boot to his backside. He muttered something about being uncivil, and Key cut him short.

'Try running any of this and your editor's going to be up in court. And you'll end up in a back alley searching for what's left of your teeth.'

Tulloch reversed his way down the staircase, eyes on him. Key feinted suddenly to fly at him and he jumped, hurrying off – and the phrase came to him, 'with my laughter ringing in his ears'. But he didn't feel like laughing. If he really intended to scare off Jarrett he would have to talk to his lawyer, which in turn meant recounting the conversations he'd had with Teddy.

He returned to his armchair, and brooded. Vanity had got him into this mess. For sixteen years his story had lain in the vault – where it ought to have stayed. Only vanity could have tempted him to unlock it. He had underestimated Teddy, who had sensed his willingness to talk, even brag a little. Early on he remembered him referring to it as 'the crime of the century'. He was clever to have set up the pretext of writing a script. It had encouraged him to be expansive. But Teddy must have been amazed at the catch he had landed. Whether the film were made or not, he had got something close to the story – the *real* story.

21

Things went quiet over Christmas, which he spent as usual with his parents in Calderstones. They attended Mass on Christmas Day, and walked in the park. On the way back he took a short detour and wandered around Menlove Gardens. The address Wallace had made famous. Or infamous. It struck him now, all these years later, as the weakest part of his plan. Why had he given Qualtrough a bogus address when he could have named an actual road that was a little further away but equally suited to the purpose of an alibi? The good liar invents details. The best liar does not. As it was, suspicion would naturally fall on Wallace for not checking the address beforehand. He had advertised his ignorance of the place much too obviously – to the tram driver, the copper on Green Lane, the newsagent – when he ought simply to have consulted a map and realised that no Menlove Gardens East existed. Hemmerde had made this point at the trial, had practically accused Wallace of the fakery. But it didn't stick.

The new year was a few days old when his telephone rang one morning.

'Mr Key? Hullo, this is Christopher Beadnell. Teddy

Absolom's friend. We exchanged letters a few weeks ago, you remember?'

Of course he remembered, and his heart sank. 'Indeed. Happy new year. What can I do for you?'

'Well, I'd very much like to talk – in person – about Teddy's film project. It would be very useful to have your perspective, as his co-writer.'

He wasn't falling for that. 'As I said in my letter, Mr Beadnell, I'm not in a position to help you with that. My loyalty is to Liverpool CID. Releasing more information about the case would be a breach of trust.'

'Yes, I understand that,' he replied smoothly. 'I don't wish to put you on the spot. It's just these storyboards of Teddy's I want to discuss. One or two points you could clarify, that's all.'

'Alas, I very rarely get down to London –'

'Ah, no need! You see, I'm here in Liverpool. Just booked into a room at the Adelphi. So we could meet at your convenience.'

Key was briefly reduced to silence. He was here? Either this man was an aficionado of the Wallace case or else Teddy's sketchbook contained some unsuspected dynamite. Or both. This was potentially far more dangerous than anything the fellow from the *Middle* might throw at him. He told himself to stay calm. Hold your nerve, wait until he makes his move.

He told Beadnell he had some time free later in the week. He could call on him at the Adelphi, if that was agreeable.

Feeling somewhat on the rack, Key telephoned the offices of a lawyer he knew from his time in the force and made an appointment. It would be as well to be forearmed in the event of a story coming out.

He had found himself restless in those early months of

retirement. There seemed many more hours in the day to fill now that he was at leisure. Liverpool was a mournful shadow of itself, still raw with the scars of its near-destruction but bereft of the siege spirit that had got them through. He drifted about town like a revenant among ruins; two years after VE Day the place was a bombsite necropolis. Whole streets pulverised, buildings burnt out, open spaces gaping at the magnitude of the loss. The air itself carried the wartime smell of cinders. Or did he only imagine it? At Canning Place, they had hired teams of men to tear down the damaged Custom House – noble landmark of the port – finishing the job the Luftwaffe failed to complete. The excuse the Corporation gave was that it created 'employment'.

Impossible to forget those days after the raids, when the air swarmed so thick with dust people wore masks. It got into your throat and made your eyes stream. As a copper you were better off than most civilians. You were still allowed to run a car (if you could find petrol), and you got plenty of overtime. And policemen didn't take anything like the risks that Heavy Rescue teams did in those half-collapsed buildings with their floods and gas leaks. But they were kept busy all the same. Crime didn't take a break during the war, and in some ways it thrived. What greater opportunities for the burglar than a city in moonless blackout? Looting was a huge problem. If a shop's premises took a hit you had to be quick, otherwise the place could be stripped bare by the time you arrived.

With shortages as severe as they were the black market had a field day. People who might never have broken a law in peacetime now found themselves linked, however distantly or reluctantly, to the thief, the counterfeiter and the racketeer.

Stolen ration books and clothing coupons would change hands for exorbitant fees. False compensation claims and billeting forms for non-existent evacuees became a lucrative swindle. Gangs of thieves were always on the look-out for valuables to lift in air-raid shelters. People who took refuge underground with their life savings hidden on their person might wake up the next morning without a penny. Or else they might return home to find their houses not just damaged by bombs but cleaned out by looters. Though they mounted patrols it was hard to deter the thieves during bombing hours, when the sound of breaking glass or gelignite blowing open a safe would be lost in the din of the ack-ack guns. It being Liverpool there was always an element of black comedy. He recalled one chancer being collared after helping himself from a shop to hair oil, cough medicine and a pair of slippers. When charged he pleaded that he was drunk at the time.

Most wartime robberies and frauds were reported, if not always prosecuted. But there was one type of crime which stood a better chance of escaping detection. The number of people being killed in air raids made it impossible to conduct a post-mortem in every instance. Fire and falling masonry sometimes meant that the remains of a victim were beyond identification. To how many did it occur that this would be the perfect time to do away with someone? The dark deed impossible to conceal before the war might pass unnoticed in the present chaos. A corpse charred to anonymity wouldn't warrant such close attention.

There were no police statistics compiled on opportunistic murders during wartime. Successful murders, that is. Unlike a successful robbery, those who got away with such a crime would not be known to have committed it. Only the killer who blundered would be a statistic. He recalled going with Ged McMahon one night into the cellar of a blast-damaged pub and finding amid the rubble a man's dead body; neck broken, head covered in blood. Had falling debris killed him? Or had he been attacked – pushed down the stairs? There were no other fatalities in the building, just this one man, lying dead. They talked about it afterwards, he and Ged, and agreed that they would probably never know what, or who, had done for him.

It made another question difficult to avoid. How many other Wallaces were out there, wishing their spouse dead? How many Qualtroughs, willing to carry out the job? It has been rightly said that many behaved heroically during the war, in circumstances of unimaginable hardship. The conflict tested the limits of bravery and self-sacrifice; it brought out the best in people, revealed in them depths of fellow-feeling hitherto unsuspected. But one cannot deny that it also provoked the baser instincts, of greed, of meanness and wanton cruelty. And the basest of all. Murder has never had a more convincing disguise than in war.

On his way home through town he happened to be passing the Adelphi, and stopped by. At reception they told him Mr Beadnell was out, so he left a message asking him to call.

He rang about an hour later. Key had decided to play the host and invited him to visit the house at Falkner Street that evening. He had just laid a fire when a knock sounded, and on the step stood a tall fellow, of medium build, with raffishly tousled dark hair. He took him through to the living room, where Beadnell dispensed with his hat and overcoat. Key recognised the black boards and trailing ribbon of the sketchbook he set on the table.

'A cold night,' he said, warming his hands at the fire. He told Key it was his first time in Liverpool. 'Taken quite a lot of bomb damage, I see. People told me it was quite a handsome city.'

Christopher Beadnell was a few years older than Teddy. His manner was self-assured, patrician, with a languid entitlement. He looked about the room as if sizing it up for a scene. He smoked untipped Turkish cigarettes. Key offered him whisky, and poured each of them a good two fingers.

'I'm sorry about Teddy. You were old friends?'

'Our fathers knew each other from school. Teddy was a great enthusiast, and once I knew Humphrey was looking for an assistant ... I was glad it all worked out, and the film was a success.'

'Yes, he told me how thrilled he was to be part of it.'

Beadnell gave a slow meditative nod. 'I gather from his letters you and Teddy got on pretty well. How did he seem to you?'

He hesitated. 'Seem?'

'Well, was there something troubling him? I know they said it was an accident but one wonders ... '

Key saw where his thoughts were tending. 'He didn't seem to me in any way depressed, let alone – You know there was a storm that night, the ship was still tipping about the next morning.'

'There's the inquest, of course. You'll be there?'

Key nodded. 'I've been asked to attend.'

Beadnell was silent for a few moments, staring into the fire.

Presently he drifted to the table and opened the sketchbook. 'As I said, Teddy's storyboards are pretty interesting. Would you care to have a look?'

Key joined him at the table as he flicked over the pages one at a time. The Wallace case, as narrated by DI Key (ret). A fluent hand had sketched scenes of Wallace with his wife, of Wallace playing chess, walking alone on a street, drinking in a pub opposite another man. He had caught the man's lean, cadaverous figure very adroitly. 'Teddy really wasn't a bad draughtsman,' Beadnell drawled, and Key had to agree. That boy had been a quick study. More or less everything he'd described to him was here, each scene enclosed in a numbered box, some with a comment appended beneath.

'I'm afraid Lydia Tarrant has lost the notes she took, but thanks to Teddy it's no matter,' Beadnell continued. 'He's got the story almost entire.'

He was right, it *was* pretty interesting. Perhaps too interesting.

'You said you wanted to clarify something.' He'd guessed what Beadnell meant to ask about, and he wasn't wrong.

'Yes, it's about the murder scene.' He turned each page, a light in his eyes like a votary with a sacred text. 'You see, the sequence opens on the street, the camera shadowing Qualtrough as he waits for Wallace to leave the house. Now, when he knocks on the door and Julia Wallace admits him, the camera takes on the killer's point of view.'

'Well, I suppose that was Teddy's idea. A sort of switch from the third person to the first person.'

'That's what I thought,' said Beadnell, reaching into his pocket. 'But in this last letter Teddy wrote it seems it wasn't

so straightforward.' He had unfolded the letter and was looking for the passage in Teddy's rapid staccato hand. 'Here, he
writes: "there's a note of ambiguity once we're inside. You see,
after he's killed her it seems that someone else is in the room
with him – someone who spots the victim's false teeth on the
carpet. I'm not sure what K meant to imply, but the killer can't
be standing over the corpse and stuffing the teeth back in her
mouth *at the same time*".'

'That was Teddy's interpretation,' Key said in a level tone.

'But you did know there were two men in the room?'

'How could I have known that?'

'You were part of the investigation. Surely the question came
up?' His voice had assumed a slight hectoring edge Key didn't
like. The man was shrewd, but he didn't have Teddy's amiability, or any of his charm. There was not that instant sympathy
of strangers between them, as had united him and Teddy.

'We considered many theories, Mr Beadnell. No one could
say for certain whether the killer was alone or not. Some still
believe that Wallace was there.'

He squinted at him. 'But what is *your* conviction?'

'Conviction is the wrong word. My version of the story is a
hypothesis, based on what emerged from the investigation. It
may be true. It may not. But you must understand, I was simply
helping to put a script together. As a film-maker you know that
it's not truth that counts – it's plausibility.'

'That's questionable,' he said, rather sulkily. He continued
to flick through the pages, pausing now and again to query
something. Key could tell that Beadnell was frustrated by his
non-committal answers, but he ought not to have been surprised: his letter had forewarned him.

They appeared to have reached a conclusion, and noticing the fire had dwindled he fed it more coal. Beadnell had lit another cigarette; he wasn't finished yet. He had returned to Teddy's last letter.

'One more thing. Teddy says he had just made an "artist's impression" of Qualtrough's face, thanks to your description. "This will be, as far as I know, the only portrait of him in existence. Could be valuable in years to come." You remember this?'

'I do.'

'The mysterious thing is – it's not here.' He showed Key the torn edge of a page towards the end of the book. 'Someone's ripped it out.'

Again Beadnell looked to him for an answer, and he shrugged. 'Maybe Teddy showed the sketchbook to Captain Jarrett, that last night of the cruise. Jarrett had some wild idea that he might use it in a prosecution.'

Beadnell was shaking his head. 'No. I checked with Jarrett. He knew nothing about the portrait.'

'Then possibly Teddy himself – hiding it somewhere?'

'It doesn't make sense. He had no reason to separate it from the book. Which makes me think someone else took it – someone who didn't want the picture out there.' He was looking at Key, half-amused.

'I sense you're about to put it on me.'

'Well, who else knew of this thing? I discount Lydia, who's far too nice a girl to take what doesn't belong to her. Which leaves you. My guess is that Teddy had got too close, and pictures of murder suspects belatedly appearing wouldn't reflect well on the police investigation. So please, let's drop the riddling statements and get it straight. You took it, didn't you?'

'Extraordinary. To have come all this way to accuse me of nicking a picture. Sorry to disappoint you, but I haven't got it.'

'So you took it and then destroyed it? Well, of course you'd deny it. Just as you've denied involvement in the murder.'

Key looked at him squarely. 'I don't know who you think you're talking to. I was a senior detective on the force for thirty years. There's not a blemish on my record. You think this' – he picked up the sketches from the table – 'constitutes a case against me?'

'Ask me that again when the film goes into production.'

The intended menace came out as a playground taunt. But it irked him all the same. He weighed the sketchbook in his hand, and with a little wink tossed it onto the fire. Beadnell's face went rigid with shock.

'What the hell are you doing?!' he cried, and made to barge past. Key blocked him off. When he squared up to him Key laughed in his face. Beadnell was tall enough, and might have taken a swing, but he knew he couldn't fight him. 'For pity's sake, man ... that thing is all I've got of Teddy's.'

Key looked around to see the boards start to singe, the paper crinkling brown under the flames. All that care and effort Teddy had invested in them. Up in smoke. He leaned in and snatched the thing off the coals, its pages smouldering but just about intact. Hardly knowing why he thrust it back, smoking, onto the table.

'There. No harm done. Or not much.'

Beadnell was frantically brushing off cinders from its charred edges, muttering to himself (*You swine, you bloody swine*) and looking daggers at him.

Key waited out his little tantrum. Of course there was

nothing he could do to stop him making a film, if he was determined. He might even use Teddy's bequest of the story-boards. It didn't matter one way or the other. He wouldn't be able to pin a thing on him. In the calm following this set-to he thought of offering to top up his drink, but Beadnell looked in no mood to linger. So instead Key handed him his coat, which he took and shrugged on in aggrieved silence. He raked his gaze around the room, and it finally landed on his host.

'I don't suppose we'll ever be sure how Teddy died,' he said, quietly. 'He was an excellent fellow, one of the best I've known. It pains me to think I'll never see him again. As for you ... they ought to lock you up.'

He tucked the sketchbook under his arm and left the room without another word. Key heard the front door open, and shut.

The evening of the university reunion dinner came round. Key arrived late at the Adelphi, and under the glittering illu-minations of the long room he searched out his friends, some of them a little more frayed with age since the last time, some slightly deafer and slower. All of them greyer. He wondered if the awareness of time slipping away put a keener edge on the bonhomie of old boys together, for their drinking had become prodigious. Perhaps in life's saloon bar they could sense the bell about to go for last orders.

Key had arranged to be seated next to Lawrence Haydon. They spent most of the dinner reminiscing on the old days, on the city in those prewar years, on the companions they had lost or who had fallen by the wayside. Lawrence was one friend who had barely changed, still athletic and straight-backed, with a diplomat's suave, low voice and a winning readiness to charm. He had left Liverpool more than twenty years ago, settling with his wife and children in a suburb of southwest London from where he commuted to Whitehall. He had risen through the ranks, travelled widely, made his name. What had seemed to everyone a gilded life had suffered a shocking blow six years earlier when his wife went into hospital for routine surgery; she contracted sepsis, undiagnosed, and it had killed her.

Because it had happened during the war there seemed less opportunity to grieve, and along with all the disruptions and inconveniences of that time he and Lawrence saw one another infrequently. They continued to correspond, in a brisk, non-confessional spirit that apparently suited both of them. Key had felt guilty about neglecting his friend in that early stage of loss, but if Lawrence had noticed he never betrayed any sign of resentment. This evening, in fact, he seemed quite at ease talking about his life as a widower, and about how it had brought him closer to his children.

'They seem rather eager for me to marry again,' he said, musingly, 'which has taken me by surprise. I thought they'd resist any idea of their mother being replaced.'

'Maybe they're worried about you being alone,' said Key. 'Have you taken a fancy to someone?'

Lawrence returned a shake of his head. 'I'm not on the lookout, to be honest. I feel like I've had my go at marriage. It was very happy, while it lasted, and for me that's enough.'

'It's not too late to try again.'

'That's rich, coming from you,' he laughed. 'You're the living embodiment of contented bachelorhood.'

Key looked at him, wondering. 'Is that how I seem? I've

never felt hostile to marriage ... it's just never happened for me.'

'But have you really made the effort? When was the last time you were with a girl?'

Key paused, blushing, as a face flashed before his mind's eye and dissolved just as quickly. 'Not recently. But I'm not philosophically opposed to the idea. You know, *no man is an island ...*'

Lawrence grinned. 'You're as close as I've ever seen. I think you've got your life nicely arranged, you live on your own terms and you don't need a woman getting in the way. Am I right?'

Key merely smiled, though deep down he felt rather stung; affectionate though his friend had sounded, there seemed almost a dismissiveness in his judgement, as if the idea of Key's actually marrying was somehow fantastical – outlandish, even. He couldn't regard himself as such a hopeless case. Why, hadn't a young woman fondly called him a 'dear man' not that long ago?

Later in the evening Lawrence said, 'By the way, that girl you mentioned the other week – Lydia? – there's going to be a vacancy coming up in the department. If she's still interested I could put in a word for her.'

'I think she'd be very grateful. I'll let her know.'

22

In the days following the reunion he interrogated his past self, raking over his lost romances like cold ashes. Yes, there had been women, and some of them had stayed around ... not especially passionate relationships, but fond enough, as he recalled. It had always been their choice to end it, the reason usually some variation on his unsatisfactory commitment – too selfish, too secretive. He accepted it, because it was true. But he had not considered his bachelor state as fixed and immutable, however 'nicely arranged' it felt. Lawrence's estimation of him as an island was a surprise – a disagreeable one.

In the meantime he wrote to Lydia with the news of the opening Lawrence had mentioned. His mission to rescue her from East Sheen was underway.

On the eve of the inquest he went for a long walk. He had taken a train from Lime Street to Euston that afternoon and checked into a small hotel off the Strand, intending to have a quiet night before the drama began. But the room he had been billeted in was cramped and uncongenial; he felt under siege from the institutional drabness of the place, and had to get out. He bent his steps up Chancery Lane, which was in the middle of being rebuilt after bomb damage. London was quicker to fix up its face than Liverpool, which hadn't the money – or possibly the will – to make a priority of repairs. He passed by a bombed church at Holborn Circus and found a tiny pub of medieval origin just off Hatton Garden.

As he sat in the gloomy snug with his ale and a chaser, he took stock of the perversity that had brought him to this pass. That he had taken a transatlantic cruise in the first place, when he had no particular love of travel. That he had conceived of writing a memoir that no one would ever be allowed to read. That he had entrusted a complete stranger with a story that could have fatally compromised him. And still might. It must have been that other self, goading him to play with fire. For what was life without risk? Perhaps you would have had to fight in a war to feel the terrible compulsion of courting doom head-on. You can never be the same person once you have lived in the knowledge that any minute might be your last.

On his way back to the dreary hotel he happened to pass a huge terracotta-brick edifice on High Holborn, and did a double-take. It was the headquarters of the Prudential Assurance, almost a twin of the late-Victorian beast brooding over Dale Street. The Pru! ... It had not struck him before that an organisation conceived as a bulwark against risk would now be associated with its most risk-taking employee: William Herbert Wallace. Another who had taken the gamble of his life. In the early days of their acquaintance Key had thought him about as staid and cautious a character as he'd ever met. But he'd got him wrong. As a young man Wallace had travelled to the Orient for work, dangerous at a time when his health was poor (it didn't improve). And, if one regards all marriage as a lottery, he took another chance in offering Julia his hand. How long was it before he recognised his mistake?

He stood gazing up at the Prudential's façade, the brick a sooty mauve under the street lamp. The company had done right by Wallace in the event, raising the money to pay for his defence, keeping his position open while he awaited trial. They believed in his innocence, even when the outcry was raised against him. 'Those who know him think it inconceivable that he should be capable of such an atrocious murder. No motive has been assigned or suggested, except robbery, which would clear Mr Wallace.' Interesting that the only motive they took seriously was robbery. Did it not occur to any member of the Prudential's executive council or the staff union that their colleague might have been driven to murder by something more complicated than greed?

Key had observed him in his wife's company, had listened to his complaints. He knew that the future held only misery for them. Somehow Wallace persuaded himself that his wife might be safely 'disappeared'. So he agreed to a high-risk plan that would involve her abduction. Did he suspect that it might go wrong? Or did he in fact hope that it would?

Key had set out for the Old Bailey in good time, intending to avoid a crush. But as he turned into the street crowds were swarming around the public entrance to the court-house, eagerly pressing to get inside. The two constables posted there looked in danger of being overwhelmed. He dodged through the scrum and flashed an ID card; the younger of the coppers pointed him off to the witnesses' entrance.

Inside, the lobby was thronged with people awaiting the

start of hearings and trials. He did a quick circuit of the place, already loud with babble. He spotted a number of faces he knew from the cruise – the chaplain, the purser, various stewards. They didn't acknowledge one another, for what was there to say? *Nice to see you again* hardly felt appropriate in the circumstances, still less *Wonderful cruise, wasn't it?* But then he sensed steps detaching themselves from a knot of people and there at his side was Lydia, ethereally pale and dressed in a primly high-necked blouse and navy coat fit for a funeral. Her mouth crinkled in a half smile.

They grasped one another's hands. 'I'm sorry that this should be the place of our reunion,' he said, looking about them.

'I know. It's awful, isn't it?' Anxiously she searched his face. 'I've never been a witness in court before.'

'There's nothing to worry about. Just keep your answers clear and truthful, and you'll be fine.'

She nodded, but her brow still looked clouded. He asked her if Mrs Tarrant had accompanied her, and she nodded. 'She wanted to be here early to get a seat in the gallery.'

She gestured with her eyes at the people she'd been talking to, and identified, in a low voice, Teddy's parents, his sister, a couple of family friends. At that moment he saw Captain Jarrett approach them and gravely introduce himself. If they hadn't known who he was before they certainly would now. Teddy's mother, already in tearful distress, had bowed her head to absorb his condolences. The father threaded his wife's arm protectively with his own. Key looked away before Jarrett could pick him out.

The Coroner's Court was located on an upper floor. He and Lydia entered the wood-panelled chamber together and found a place at one of the pews reserved for witnesses. The family lawyer, a Mr Perrett, was already at his table, arranging documents with the unhurried air of someone playing patience. He was a large man at ease with his bulk, with a jowly pink face and an old-fashioned watch chain that emphasised the girth beneath his waistcoat. His mind, Key had heard from reports, wasn't at all flabby, and in his gaze darted a quick intelligence. Above them could be heard the hum of talk in the public gallery, where the press were also stationed. Key wondered if Tulloch from the *Middle* was among them.

Five minutes later the clerk called the room to order and the coroner entered. He presented an unassuming figure, lanky and bespectacled, dressed in a dark formal suit without any of the trumpery of a judge's robes and wig. He seated himself on a fancily carved chair that might have been lifted from the high table of an Oxford college. He surveyed the room for a moment, in silence, and got down to business. An inquest, he explained, was an inquisitorial process, not an adversarial one. In other words, they were assembled there to establish only the facts concerning a death, not to make accusations regarding guilt.

He felt Lydia shift uncomfortably beside him.

Invited by the coroner, Perrett spoke on behalf of the family to the character of the deceased, Mr Edward Absolom. The court heard about his schooling at Uppingham, his rejection by the conscription board in 1939 and his early employment as a runner for film companies, his stint at the BBC, his fruitful apprenticeship to Humphrey Jennings at the Crown Film Unit. 'Latterly Mr Absolom had undertaken promotional work for the Cunard Shipping Company, which is how he came to be aboard a cruise travelling from Southampton to New York in September of last year.' 'So he was a guest of the Cunard Line – and travelling alone?' asked the coroner. 'Indeed he was. I gather from his family that Mr Absolom was heading for America with a view to gaining employment, possibly on the West Coast.' Perrett went on to highlight Teddy's trustworthy nature, his sense of adventure, his will to succeed. 'In short, sir, this was a young man who had everything to live for.'

The first witness summoned was Lydia, who approached the stand and took the oath. She did her best to look composed, though her eyes would now and then flit nervously towards the public gallery. As Key studied her he wondered how he could ever have thought her plain. It hadn't occurred to him before that suffering could enhance a woman's features – perhaps even ennoble them. Lydia explained the circumstances of meeting Teddy on board, 'introduced by Mr Key', and of how the three of them would meet and have lunch around the swimming pool.

'And what impression did you form of Mr Absolom?' Perrett asked.

'I thought he was delightful, and charming. He made us laugh. I have only fond memories of him.'

'I gather you and Mr Absolom became interested in a story from Mr Key's time on the police force – the Wallace murder case, in point of fact.'

'Yes. We talked about it a lot. Teddy – Mr Absolom – had an idea it could be made into a film, so –'

'You mean a documentary film?'

'No, a feature film. A murder mystery.'

Perrett raised his eyebrows, maiden-auntishly, at that. 'I see. And how far did you get with this ... project?'

'Not far at all,' Lydia replied. 'My small contribution was to make notes. Teddy drew some storyboards.'

There was an interruption while the coroner asked her to explain what storyboards were. Then Perrett resumed his questioning. Was this 'murder mystery' idea of Mr Absolom's quite serious? Lydia coloured a little, and said that she thought it unlikely. Teddy had never made a film before, so they didn't regard it as an imminent possibility. It was more in the spirit of 'what if', she said.

'You said that you made notes of your discussions – detailed?'

'Quite detailed. I wrote in a little notebook, and filled about forty pages.'

'So you have an extensive record of what was said during that time?'

'Yes, that's correct.'

'It sounds like an interesting document. Why has this notebook not been brought forward as evidence?'

Lydia paused, flushed. 'I'm afraid I no longer have it.'

Perrett peered over his spectacles. 'But when I asked you a moment ago you said that you did. I said "you have an extensive record" – *have*, note – and you replied, "Yes, that's correct".'

Key felt a crackle of apprehension shoot through him. He had caught her out. She had indicated that she still had the notebook: everyone had heard it.

Lydia, flustered, replied, 'I'm sorry. I made a mistake.'

'Where, pray, is the notebook now?'

'I must have lost it – while we were travelling,' she added, weakly.

The lawyer allowed a short sceptical silence to follow. Then he cut to the evening of the Farewell Ball, and the story of Teddy's bad night. Lydia recounted his terrible agitation, and then his retirement to his cabin to be sick. Perrett asked her about the last time she had seen the deceased.

'Mr Key and I were in his cabin at about two in the morning. Mr Key fetched him a draught for his seasickness, then he left. Teddy asked me to stay for a while, so I did. I left him asleep at about three.'

'You said he was agitated – about what?'

'Oh . . . I think it was a misunderstanding between him and Mr Key. On a question of authenticity.'

Perrett paused, waiting. When nothing came he said, 'So there was ill-feeling between the two men?'

'No, no, it was all cleared up. That's why Mr Key was on hand to fetch medicine for Teddy.'

The coroner thanked Lydia for her evidence. When she returned to her seat she looked briefly in Key's direction but said nothing. Her testimony about Teddy had taken the heat off him. The next witness was not so obliging. Captain Jarrett's aspect was at its most saturnine as he took his seat in the witness box. One sensed in him a suppressed fury that might not need much provocation to trigger. His pale, cold gaze had already sought Key out, and Key found no pity there. He first became aware of Mr Absolom, he told the court, when he saw Miss Tarrant trying to teach him to swim. Then he noticed Mr Key in their company at the swimming pool.

'Did you have much to do with them?'

He shook his head. 'Not until the evening of the ball. That's when Mr Absolom came to see me. He was in a state of extreme distress.'

'What had happened?' asked the coroner.

'I'm not quite sure. He told me there was a person on board who ought to be placed under arrest. Because he was "dangerous". I asked him who but he wouldn't say, only that he suspected this person was psychopathically deranged. I pressed him for a name but at first he refused.'

'And then what happened?'

'I called on Mr Absolom later, at his cabin. I was certain by this point that he'd been talking about Mr Key. He seemed relieved that I knew.'

'Why did the deceased suspect Mr Key was deranged?'

'On the grounds of some involvement in the Wallace murder case, though he wouldn't say exactly what.'

The coroner frowned, muttered something to himself. So the last time the Captain had seen Teddy was in his cabin, around midnight. What then?

'The officer of the watch woke me around seven in the morning to say that a passenger had been found dead in the swimming pool. I accompanied him to the spot and found Mr Absolom, drowned.'

'Regarding the deceased's agitated frame of mind, do you think it possible he might have taken his own life?'

'I do not,' said the Captain. 'I don't believe he was a danger to himself at all. He expressed regret for telling me about his conversations with Mr Key, and tried to go back on his earlier theory. But by then the cat was out of the bag.'

'Which leads me to suggest,' the coroner said, 'that Mr Absolom fell into the pool by accident.'

'Or he was pushed,' the Captain said crisply.

A shocked *oooh* echoed around the courtroom.

'Do you have any evidence to back up such an allegation?'

The Captain shook his head. 'I am only speculating from the circumstances. Mr Key had good reason to stop Mr Absolom from being interviewed. He also had the opportunity. He knew the man couldn't swim ...'

That had certainly perked up the public gallery. The coroner swung his gaze up at them, and asked for quiet. He called another witness, Mr Andrews, the officer of the watch. He testified that he had seen Teddy and Key at around six in the morning, talking by the side of the pool. Was there any suggestion of hostility, or antagonism? asked the coroner. The man said it was difficult to know, being at a distance, but he judged from their disposition that 'they seemed like friends'.

Then Key was called to take the stand. He noticed Teddy's father leaning forward, a sour challenge in his glare. His wife stared at Key, mesmerised, like a mouse before a cobra. The coroner began with questions about his police service, establishing his blameless record as an officer. When he narrowed his focus to the week of the cruise Key was quite prepared. Yes, Teddy and he had liked one another on sight, and they'd had a marvellous time batting around ideas for films.

'Did you imagine his interest in the Wallace case would lead to anything?'

'No, I didn't. We talked in a speculative way of how a film *might* be made of the case, but it was never a serious proposition. Teddy was great company, and I caught at the thread of his enthusiasm. Unfortunately, we ended up in a muddle where

235

fact and fiction became confused. He reported it in this garbled way to Captain Jarrett, and very quickly regretted it.'

'You were seen together at the pool. In what sort of temper was the deceased?'

'A good one. He'd offered me an apology, which I accepted, and we were back on friendly terms. I was tired, we'd talked ourselves to a standstill . . . so I took my leave of him and went back to bed.'

The coroner craned forward in his chair. 'In your view, then, how did Mr Absolom end up in the swimming pool?'

'I fear it was a simple accident. The ship had been pitching and rolling all night, and it was still unsettled in the morning. I'd left him by the pool . . . Teddy had been exhausted by his seasickness. It's my guess he was not fully aware of the danger. A sudden sharp tilt of the bow and he would have been thrown.'

The coroner then sought a separate verification of the weather that morning, first from the Captain, then from Mr Andrews. The latter, with no axe to grind, gave it as his opinion that the deceased had probably been pitched into the swimming pool and drowned in a matter of seconds. When he stepped down Perrett went into a long whispered confab with Teddy's parents, which was interrupted by the coroner summoning him to the bench. An adjournment was announced, allowing him a short time to consider his verdict.

Key turned to Lydia. As he made to thank her she backed away slightly.

'Don't thank me yet. The verdict isn't in.'

He understood; she was still fielding nerves from her moment in the witness box. To beguile the time as they waited he changed the subject, and asked her whether she had given any thought to the Foreign Office opening. It seemed she had, but hadn't yet written to Lawrence about it.

'Why not?' he asked.

'Mummy's not sure about it. I don't think she's very keen on the idea of me living abroad.'

Key was quietly incredulous. 'First of all, it's a job based in Whitehall. You wouldn't necessarily be sent abroad. Second, what's it got to do with your mother?'

His vehemence seemed to surprise her. 'Well, I had to tell her something. It does concern her.'

'What about your father?'

She rolled her eyes. 'He's hardly around to notice. That's part of the problem. She thinks she's lost Daddy, and she doesn't want to lose me, too.'

'But it's your *life*, for God's sake! Do you want to stay in East Sheen for ever? Don't you want something more?'

Perhaps this was too hectoring, because she looked astonished. 'I don't understand. Why does it bother you?'

'Because . . .' he began, and stopped. Why did it bother him? 'Because I don't like to see a bright young woman sacrifice herself for no reason. You should be out there enjoying yourself instead of playing companion to some devious old –'

Again he stopped, but too late, the words were out. The shock that had seized Lydia's features was slowly changing to a pursed look of hurt – of offence.

He was about to make apology when the coroner re-entered the room and the court came to attention. He had weighed the evidence, he began, taking into account both the naturally sunny and optimistic disposition of the deceased and his

237

erratic behaviour on the night in question. 'This latter appears to have been the result of a misunderstanding between him and Mr Key, which was later settled to their satisfaction. Despite the suspicions of Captain Jarrett there seems no plausible reason why Mr Key might have maliciously conspired in the drowning of Mr Absolom. So I must judge on the balance of probability that the unpredictable motions of the ship caused Mr Absolom's tragic fall. My condolences are with the young man's family and friends in this courtroom. And I duly record that the verdict of the inquest conducted today is accidental death.'

There were no whoops or cheers, no calls of 'Shame!' as one might hear at a trial. The verdict had come, to most, as a matter of relief. He looked at Lydia, whose face was unreadable. He was minded to thank her, but it was clear that his recent out-burst was not forgiven. They joined the press of people as they filed out of the chamber, and thence down the stairs to the lobby. He realised he had to speak before her mother arrived, and as they dawdled on the margins of the crowd he turned to her.

'Lydia, I'm sorry about what I said. About your mother. I only said it out of my regard for you.'

She paused, and addressed a spot just beyond his shoulder. 'There's no need to say anything else.'

He took the implicit rebuke. 'In any event, I wanted to thank you for, well, supporting me back there. Things might have got very unpleasant.'

At last she met his gaze. Something in what he had just said had jolted her. 'You make me feel like I've been complicit in something, but I can't tell what it is.' Her voice dropped to a low tremble. 'Will you tell me, truthfully, did you ...' She couldn't bring herself to say the words.

'Teddy? No, I didn't. He was – we were – why would I?'

He looked for a sign of acceptance, but there remained on that lovely face of hers something dubious, unpersuaded – a sense of pardon withheld. He felt almost driven to beg, to say *Lydia, please believe me*, and he bit it back.

Just then, out of the madding crowd emerged the bustling figure of Mrs Tarrant, whose social antennae not untypically failed to pick up the mood. 'Well, thank goodness that's all over,' she sighed. She had the air of a mourner, but not the feeling – she was simply glad it had all 'passed off' without a hitch. She said to her daughter, 'You did marvellously, dear,' touching her cheek, and added, 'You, too, Mr Key' – as if they'd just come off stage at the Eastbourne Hippodrome.

He had discerned her intention to keep Lydia as her pet, on an invisible leash, and had tried to warn the girl. It had backfired on him.

Outside on the pavement they performed an awkward minuet of farewell. He didn't take seriously Mrs Tarrant's invitation to pole over to East Sheen when he was next in London, there being, in her words, 'so much still to talk about'. He glanced at Lydia's face, distant with preoccupation, and despaired of his belated rescue attempt. He shook their hands, and they parted.

In the weeks that followed he experienced low moods, of regret, and of remorse. He thought about what had happened, and about what Lydia must have been thinking. Did she really believe, in spite of her avowals, that he had pushed Teddy into the pool that morning? He was tempted, increasingly, to write it down, to see if he could bear to tell it. He remembered the dawn sky that morning, the colour of wet flour.

... As Teddy and I talked it over by the swimming pool the ship was still unsteady, not the seesawing of the night we'd just experienced, but pitching enough to keep us on guard. He had told me about Jarrett calling on him, and his eventual admission that I was the person he'd thought 'psychopathically disturbed'. He'd withdrawn that accusation, as you know, though he'd let slip that I'd been associated with Qualtrough. With one hand he giveth ... He didn't mean to land me in trouble, I know, but the idea of us both being questioned on our arrival in New York boded ill. I had no fear of explaining away the obvious confusion. But I doubted that Teddy could do the same; he was likely to give something away just through his own innocence.

There we stood, swaying slightly, both of us bone-tired. Teddy, eyes glinting with tears, remorseful, but not unhappy. I said I might see him at breakfast, and walked off. I'd just reached the staircase up to the deck when the ship listed suddenly. I heard a splash, and a cry. Of course I knew immediately what had happened. I retraced my steps and saw him there, bobbing, plunging, gasping out for help. He didn't see me. I don't think he saw me. If he had I couldn't have stood there, watching him go under, arms flailing, struggling for dear life. Another gargled cry, another grasp at air; and he was gone. In those seconds that I'd witnessed I must have calculated the advantages of his permanent silence, though it didn't feel that way.

So you see, I didn't touch him – didn't even raise my hand to him. Sometimes I wonder, if I had my time over again, would I dive in to the rescue? Here I am, Teddy, don't worry, old chap, you're safe now ... But I honestly don't know if I would ...

The typed sheet remained on his desk all that evening. Before he turned in he read it again, then held a match to it. As it began to crinkle and burn he threw it into the grate.

23

For a while a certain notoriety followed him around. The week after the inquest he had a call from his old nick at Cheapside. The Super there, a youngish man named Shankland, asked him to come in for a chat. His initial assumption was that they meant to lure him out of retirement. He'd heard that they were short of senior detectives, and assumed they were recruiting either from outside or else from the old guard.

Shankland couldn't have been friendlier, asked him how he was getting on, even joked that he was envious of 'you lot with your police pension'. They drank coffee and smoked, all very matey. Key was about to say, *Look, sir, if this is about my coming back to the nick I'm flattered but honestly* ... He was glad he held his tongue, for it soon became clear it wasn't his return Shankland sought at all. 'I've heard that you've been writing a memoir,' he began. Key admitted it, though he was quick to reassure Shankland it wasn't for publication, merely something to keep himself occupied. The man stared at him for a moment, to check that he was on the level. 'It's just that we have to be careful, these days, about releasing information. The Chief

Constable is particularly concerned about the Wallace case. He's aware that there were anomalies in the handling of the investigation at the time, and that it could reflect poorly on us. It's best for all concerned if we keep a lid on what we know.'

Key assured him that he understood. Why, he'd been ambushed by some hack from the *Middle* recently and had to be quite brusque with him. Shankland smiled, and went on to query a few details regarding the inquest down in London. 'There was even a rumour going round – wait till you hear this – that *you knew Qualtrough.*'

They both laughed. 'I don't know where they get this stuff from, sir.'

He continued revising the memoir, he wasn't sure why: even if he finished the thing it would never be published. He felt its tone grow more defensive with each draft. But he had nothing else to occupy him.

Months crept by. He received a letter from Lawrence, with news that Miss Tarrant had impressed them all at her interview and was now doing very well in their Eastern Europe department. 'So this is by way of thanks for your good offices,' he wrote. 'I gather the young lady is thriving. Apparently all she needed was some encouragement ...'

Key was pleased, and only a little saddened that Lydia hadn't bothered to tell him so herself. He contemplated dropping her a line, just to offer his best wishes, but her silence seemed forbidding. He couldn't forget that morning of the inquest, the question she had asked him, and her doubtful expression as he protested his innocence. But if she did believe he was in some way responsible, why on earth had she gone to the trouble of saving him in the witness box?

He might have tormented himself about it indefinitely had it not been for the arrival, weeks later, of another letter. The sight of her upright schoolgirl script brought a smile to his face. He took the letter and placed it carefully on the mantelpiece, drawing out his anticipation before he permitted himself to slit it open.

> 12 Walnut Tree Walk,
> London s.e.
> August 25th, 1948

Dear Mr Key,

I have been feeling very remiss about not writing to you before now. The only excuse I can give is the unlikely, but truthful, one of being rushed off my feet. Since I started at the FO three months ago I have barely had a moment to myself, what with learning the ropes, working long hours and – as you will notice from the address at the top – moving to a rented flat. Quite the change! Your stern words to me back in March had their effect, you see, and I made myself write to Mr Haydon just as you proposed. He set things in motion and before I knew it I found myself with a desk, an office, friendly colleagues and, best of all, a sense of purpose I haven't felt since the war. My mother (as you might have guessed) made rather a fuss about it, but having told her what a marvellous opportunity it was, and that it might not come around again, she at last capitulated – probably realising that it was too late to stop me anyway.

I'm keenly aware of what I owe to you for this. If you

hadn't tried to persuade me I don't think I'd ever have worked up the nerve. Perhaps you'd let me thank you in person? I don't suppose you come down to London very often, but if you did I could host you for a lunch in town. Apart from anything else it would make me happy to see you again. I feel that we have much to discuss, after I made things more awkward between us than they should have been. A truth Teddy's death has brought home to me is the need to live as much as we can while we can. I read something recently to the effect that it doesn't really matter what we do so long as we have had a life – otherwise what has been the point of our being here?

Oh dear! – I am becoming sententious. And all I'd meant to say was thank you, and to ask you to lunch. Please do write and let me know that you'll come.

With my fond regards,
Lydia

He read the letter once; then a second time, savouring it. That she had written to him at all felt like a reprieve. That her words had been wrung out of gratitude and tenderness was the wonderful bonus. By mentioning Teddy's death she seemed to have cleared the air between them. All that mattered now was life, and the determination to live it. And he also detected between the lines an underflicker of something else – affection, quite possibly. *It would make me happy to see you again.* Was he reading too much into it, or did he hear a kind of urgency, as though she might have some vital message to communicate? *I feel that we have much to discuss . . .*

245

He waited a few days before replying. He thought it sensible to let his feelings cool, in case he had been overzealous in interpreting her letter. He didn't want to blunder in and frighten her off. When he did write back it was in a friendly but composed mood, congratulating her on her progress, and modestly disclaiming the credit she had tried to bestow upon him – he had merely pointed the way, the initiative had been all her own.

Yes, he would certainly make time to meet her when he came down to London. (Here he had to concoct a pretext for his trip: he claimed to have been 'invited' by a publisher to discuss his memoir, a fortnight hence.) And lunch would be *his* treat, to celebrate her new life at the FO. He ended his letter by asking her to convey his regards to Mrs Tarrant, almost daring Lydia to remember the disobliging way he had spoken of her mother when they last met. But in their new spirit of reconciliation he thought he could get away with it – and Mrs Tarrant's influence was by now plainly in eclipse. To the victor the spoils!

The day of their meeting in London had been appointed. He found himself restless as he waited, and occupied the days preceding in household tasks, cleaning the windows, throwing out old junk, replacing his old blackout curtains with patterned ones from the Bon Marché. While he was there he ordered new carpets, a rug for the living room, various paints: he thought he might refurbish the kitchen and bathroom. His thoughts kept returning to his trip. He envisaged a happy reunion, but tried not to ponder it overmuch. He was passing the window of a gentlemen's tailors on Bold Street when he happened to spot a smart sports jacket, and thought he might try it on. As he was admiring it in the cheval mirror he remembered something he'd read, about bewaring all enterprises that required new clothes. He gave the shop assistant a rueful smile as he handed it back.

As the day drew near he became convinced that Lydia would find an excuse to cancel. She might justly claim pressure of work as the reason – she had alluded to the long hours in her letter – and he imagined the gracious manner of his reply: *It can't be helped*, and *We can always rearrange it.* Up until the eve of his visit he braced himself for some note of apology, a telegram perhaps, and the inevitable deflation of his spirits. Why wouldn't she cancel? She was busy – she surely had better things to do than entertain some retired copper she barely knew.

But no last-minute excuse intervened, and he caught the train from Lime Street just as planned. Arriving at Euston he briefly considered the Underground, but it was a bright autumnal day and the idea of a walk enlivened him. He had reserved a table at a grand old chop house in the City, and as he headed eastwards he felt a strange lightness beneath his steps. The London he had found gaunt and hostile on his previous visit seemed now to call him on, and he felt enfolded in the romance of streets unknown to him and his own anonymity among the indifferent crowds. Trams and buses whose advertised destinations (HIGHGATE – KINGSWAY – TOWER HILL) he half knew conjured a glamorous shadowland of pubs and dining rooms and intrigues and appetites.

Yes, a lightness in his hurry that felt like (could it be?) his student days, striding over the lovely acres of Sefton Park arm-in-arm with her, with Esmé. He'd almost forgotten how happy he had felt, in those bright hopeful days just before the war ... though he had never forgotten her. Sometimes her face came back to him in a dream, unfaded by the long decades. He wondered now if those months they'd known one another had actually been the turning point of his life, and asked himself why he hadn't been bolder in his pursuit – why hadn't he put up a fight for her? Too long ago to remember now.

He found the tavern in its narrow courtyard off Cornhill, a lunchtime hideaway which had been serving its mostly male clientele since the days of powdered wigs and snuff. Within he saw Lydia, already seated at one of the wooden booths; on spotting him she gave a shy little wave.

'Hullo there,' he said. 'How nice to see you again.'

'Likewise,' she replied, smiling. 'But how on earth do you know this place?'

He followed her gaze about the room, with its ancient brass fittings and etched mirrors. Aproned waiters drifted in pale attendance. 'Oh, I came here once about twenty years ago – always remembered it. It hasn't changed a bit.'

She pulled a comical face. 'I don't imagine it's changed since *Boswell.*'

They ordered drinks. He focused upon her, noting the open regular features he had once mistaken for plainness, the straight nose, the expressive brow, and the eyes that gaily appealed for understanding. But there was something different about her. In telling the story of her application to the FO and her early anxious weeks in the post she radiated a self-assurance, born (he supposed) of her new responsibilities. Then again, she had spent so much of her life in service to her mother that the virtues of patience and co-operation must have become by now second nature to her – working with colleagues would not present half so many difficulties.

'I'm glad that you get on with Lawrence,' he said. 'I thought you would.'

'Oh he's been a brick, though we don't see a great deal of one another. He's much too high-up to be bothered with our department. He's awfully fond of you, of course ...'

Key returned an affable shrug. He wondered what Lawrence had actually said about him, whether he had joked of his friend as a 'contented bachelor' – was that the epithet? – or exampled him as the living disproof of the line *No man is an island*. He supposed some might consider him out-of-date ... though when he thought back to their time on the boat he didn't recall any such condescension on Lydia's part. They had behaved towards one another as perfect equals; if anything it was Teddy who had seemed the odd one out, the boy in their familial triangle.

Something else had changed. The girlish pinafore dresses and cardigans she had sported on board had given way to a tailored jacket and skirt, and a navy blouse pinned with a sapphire brooch. The look was rather *femme d'affaires*, but without any sense of striving or calculation.

'You look very ... grown-up,' he said, conscious of himself reaching for a neutral word.

She retracted her chin in amusement. 'Well, I'll be thirty-one in December.' She narrowed her gaze suddenly. 'Did you think me so immature?'

'No, no. You were always nicely dressed, only now you – seem to have more confidence.'

This distinction seemed to appease her, and she gave her

hair a little comic primp in response. Thirty-one, he thought, wasn't old, but as far as Lydia was concerned it wasn't young either. To him the number seemed an irrelevance. When you loved a woman she was always the age you preferred her to be. And once love died her age was neither here nor there – the question ceased to carry any weight. As for himself the world could think what it liked; in matters of the heart he was as various as he'd always been. A man could become a different sort of man in every circumstance that involved him.

She asked him about his meeting in London, and about the memoir. Who were his publishers?

'Oh, Harrap,' Key said, reaching for one of the names he knew. 'It's still at the preliminary stages.'

'But how exciting,' she trilled, 'even to have their interest. I wonder, would you let me read it?'

'It's a long way from being finished, I'm afraid.'

'Yes, but once it is? I'd be a good editor for you.' There was almost a pleading tone in her voice.

'I'll bear you in mind,' he said, and felt a tweak of regret that the book was a lost cause.

He had not noticed himself eating until the waiter came to clear their table – apparently he had had the plaice and boiled potatoes. Lydia had taken out her cigarettes and was offering him one. In the office they all smoked 'furiously', she said. As she blew out smoke a faraway smile touched her mouth.

'D'you remember Teddy and his Lucky Strikes?'

'Of course. And his co-respondent shoes, and the golf sweater. It's a pity he never got to Hollywood – I imagine they would have loved him.'

'It's coming up for his first anniversary ...' Her expression, at first thoughtful, turned puzzled. 'Isn't it odd how people you've known for only a short time can make such a strong impression? I mean, more of an impression than people you've been around for years?'

He found her staring at him. 'You mean – Teddy?'

'Yes, Teddy, to a degree ... but I was thinking more of –' She broke off, maddeningly. 'I just wonder if it's generally observed ... '

'You mean someone whose force of personality impresses you?'

'Well, it's not necessarily *a force* at all. In fact it might be someone whose influence is quite subtle. It's not always the centre of attraction who ends up being the most significant.'

Key had gone from wondering who she could be talking about to judging it a near-certainty that she meant *him*. If she had been looking directly at him at this moment he would have known for sure, but her gaze had dropped and he couldn't quite read her. Might this airy theorising even be her roundabout way of declaring herself to him? She had spoken with such meaning in her tone it was possible. No, it wasn't possible – he must have misapprehended her. Lydia was fond of him, he knew, but any notion of her *falling* for him was wildly out of the question. Unless ...

He gave a nervous laugh. 'Would this "someone" be on your mind for another reason?'

'What other reason?' she said, looking up. Her directness disconcerted him, but he pressed on.

'I merely wondered – perhaps you're thinking of the sort of man you might like to marry.'

Lydia's eyes widened in surprise. 'What makes you say that?'

He felt his throat constrict with tension. Had he got this altogether wrong?

'Well, only that – you said just before that you'll be thirty-one soon. I wonder if you've reached an age when you're thinking of getting married . . . '

The astonishment of seconds before had thinned into wryness. 'I should have remembered how intuitive you are,' she said, then paused. 'I suppose my thoughts have been tending that way, of late. I fear I've missed out on my twenties, what with –' Their eyes met, and the unspoken reference was understood – 'so I'm going to have to play catch-up in my thirties. I can't afford to waste more time.'

Again he nodded, as if he grasped her meaning entirely – and yet he wasn't sure that he had. Was it to marriage in general she was referring, or to a man she had specifically in mind? If the latter, it was tantalising to think how close he might be. But she was too diffident to flirt, and he was too afraid of humiliating himself to break cover. It was an impasse, but one that still held the possibility of resolving itself. He needed to tread very carefully, and wait his moment; if what he had gleaned from this afternoon was reliable he might be more promisingly placed than he realised.

The lunch was over, he wasn't sure how. In a kind of half dream he found that they had wandered out of the courtyard onto Cornhill, where the chug of taxis dinned in their ears. The sun had gone in since his arrival.

'How are you getting to Holborn?' she asked, and he looked at her. Holborn? His air of confusion prompted her. 'To your publishers. Aren't they on High Holborn?'

'Ah. I hadn't thought . . . '

'You could catch a number eight from Bank,' she suggested, and they began to walk down the hill. She had reverted to the subject of his manuscript, hoping that she might change his mind about 'having a peek'. He fenced with her a little, wondering how far he could spin out the story of his phantom publisher. Her enthusiasm for his writing seemed quite genuine.

They had reached the junction where the traffic began to thicken. An Underground station entrance was drawing people down into its vortex. 'That's where I'm going – unless you'd like me to see you to Holborn?'

He shook his head, not willing to risk his subterfuge being blown. 'I'll be fine. Let's say goodbye here.' He offered his hand but she batted it away and hugged him. A gleam had come to her eyes.

'Do let's meet again,' she said. 'Next time it will be my treat.' Once again he felt the pressure of something not being said, something just ghosting on the limits of candour. The number eight arrived as she was about to turn. He stepped on, and when the bus pulled away he returned her wave from the platform. Then more people massed at the crossing, and she disappeared from view.

From the upstairs window he watched the life of the streets flow by. He wished he had agreed to let her accompany him: it would have required no great effort to raise a diversion about the publishers. The more he turned over her cryptic talk of marriage the more convinced he became of the direction in which her feelings tended. Why else had she lied for him at the inquest, pretending to the court she no longer had the incriminating notes on the Wallace story? It had been her intention all along to save him, and yet he had been so slow to understand why.

All the way back home on the train he replayed the hours of their lunch. He tried to recall not just her words but her tone of voice, not just her appearance but the shifting ambiguities of her expression. And as often as he dismissed the idea as mere self-indulgence he found on reconsidering that his conclusions were sound: *it might be someone whose influence is quite subtle.* Who else could she have meant?

24

After the excitements of his London venture he resigned himself to the uneventful days of retirement. Until now he had felt, if not suited to the solitary life, then perfectly capable of enduring it. But his meeting with Lydia seemed to have changed the element in which he moved – the colours of the street had taken on an altered hue – and he became distracted.

In the meantime his routines went on. He'd been drinking one evening in the White Star, his old stamping ground, when he happened to see a familiar profile flash by. He called out to him, and the man stopped as if someone had put a gun to his back. Ged McMahon faced him. 'I thought it was you.' Ged's expression underwent a rapid sequence of changes, from surprise to a qualified pleasure; then to awkwardness, and guilt. 'All right, son? Long time, eh?' He'd already worked out Key was there on his own. They yarned away for a few minutes, catching up with the latest from Cheapside, with what he'd been missing. The subject of his meeting with Shankland came up, and he felt Ged's scrutiny of him sharpen. It seemed there had been talk of indiscretion . . .

'They say you're writing a memoir,' said Ged. 'About the Wallace case.'

'Well, I've been trying to. There's a long way to go.'

Ged gave an uneasy laugh. 'A book about Wallace. That could throw the cat among the pigeons . . . Am I in it?'

Key looked at him. 'Of course. I've mentioned all of the old crew. It's about the case – the inside story, you might say.'

Ged nodded, but said nothing. They turned down safer avenues of reminiscence, to those cases that were cherished for somebody's moment of inspiration, or of stupidity, and they joked about the unlikely persistence of certain criminal careers. They talked about their colleagues – Alec Moran, Jimmy Dent and the rest – and for a while Key was back in his former life, reliving the old camaraderie.

When a silence eventually intervened he realised there was something on Ged's mind. 'Listen, I'm sorry about what happened,' the latter said. 'I know they didn't do right by you, and I was sick about it.'

'We all have to retire at some point,' Key replied evenly. 'Mine was just a bit premature.'

'You deserved better than that. And now the Super's got the wind up about what you're gonna say . . . '

'I'd say he's not the only one,' he suggested, lightly.

Ged looked sheepish. 'Yeah, sorry I've not been in touch. You know what it's like.' He gestured with a mock-weary sideways nod that encompassed the job, the grind, the constraints on his time. And perhaps he also meant the silent judgement that he and the others had passed on their former colleague.

Key could have made his resentment felt at this point – could have berated his old pal for not sticking by him. It seemed that Ged had fallen into line and shunned his company like the rest.

But all that he said was, 'Yeah. I know what it's like.'

Seeking an antidote to his restlessness he took a holiday, for no reason he could fathom, in the southwest of France. He was attracted to the names of those places in the Pyrenees – Ciboure, Bayonne, St Jean de Luz, Biarritz. In the last of these he installed himself at a modest seafront hotel, and drifted among crowds marinating in the unlikely warmth of late September. He hid his eyes behind sunglasses. In his bedroom the slow rotation of the ceiling fan seemed to mimic the indolence of the place. The casinos and the gambling rooms reminded him of his cruise the previous year; the seductive click of the chips tempted him again to the blackjack tables, and he wasted a few francs in memory of Teddy. Music jangled on the streets, revellers drank and danced, empty-eyed couples strolled up and down the shore. In his solitary wandering he felt himself a stranger in a strange land, but after a while he began to enjoy his isolation, unknown and unremarked.

One morning on the breakfast terrace his resolve cracked and he wrote a postcard to Lydia, breezily conversational in tone. He reminded her of the poet's lines on travellers who changed only their skies, not their minds – he had quoted it to her on the boat not long after they met. 'I am unarguably abroad, but my thoughts linger back at home.' That was as much feeling as he dared admit to her. Impulsively he added a PS, that he would stop in London on his way back north. So he had coerced himself into seeing her. He walked down to the beach and gazed for a long time at the Atlantic, its monotonous blue-green breakers seething back and forth. He asked the ocean if it wanted him today. No reply came. On his last night he played roulette and won two hundred francs. He took it as an omen that his luck was in.

He had reserved a room at the Grosvenor so he could drop his bags immediately on arriving at Victoria. It was colder in London than the last time he'd visited. He telephoned Lydia at her office, and when she came on the line she laughed on hearing his voice. 'I'd just been thinking of you!' she cried. 'Your card arrived this morning – from Spain?' 'Near enough,' he replied, and at once he was plunged back into muddle. He dreaded her guessing what he felt before they'd had a chance to talk, and yet it would lift a weight off him if she did, some-how, *understand*. It seemed impossible that she could be blind to the reason he had broken up his journey to meet with her again. As she gaily took charge of tomorrow's arrangements he felt the future speeding towards him, requiring an energy and decisiveness he didn't possess.

They were about to ring off when Lydia said, in a much quieter voice, 'I've been hoping to talk with you, as a matter of fact, about –' She paused, meaningfully. The hesitation seemed to have stopped his heart.

'About what?'

'Um, I can't really say –' And now he knew for sure. The background hum of her office precluded intimate confession.

'Then why don't we meet this evening – if it's that impor-tant.' He waited, hardly daring to breathe.

'Well, I've got to be in Chelsea about eight ... would you be able to meet for a drink beforehand?'

He could, and he would.

It was not long to wait. He tried telling himself it would be merely a prelude to their lunch the next day, but he couldn't ignore the sense of a great trial ahead. He hadn't eaten since he'd set out that morning. By the time he reached Dover he was ravenous. Since their telephone call, however, the hunger pains had vanished, and in his stomach sat an implacable dread. *Bound in to saucy doubts and fears* ... The line from *Macbeth* had fastened onto his brain and couldn't be dislodged.

As he set out from the hotel it repeated itself. On the street he shook his head, as if he might tip the words out of his ear. And why 'saucy' in any case? The word was too light, too frivolous, to be paired with doubts and fears. Distracted by this riddling language he struck out west as the evening darkened and the weary trees shivered. It was the gloaming hour. Street lamps were coming on, and he could see his shadow lengthen in front of him.

The pub she had appointed was on a quiet Chelsea street, so close to the river he could smell it. He had arrived early and hung back, watching people push through the doors. It reminded him of being a copper on surveillance duty, back in the long-ago; the hours he used to spend, waiting, checking his watch. And yet now there was no need to skulk across the street. He could have waited more comfortably inside. *Bound in to saucy doubts and fears* – it was the imminence of the test that stayed him. Could he hold his nerve? He was impatient to see her. At the same time he was tempted to walk away and not look back. A lifelong habit of refusing, of shunning the crowd, had made him unsociable. The chance to be otherwise was here, right now, and it made him almost faint.

'Hullo?' Key jumped at the voice. Lydia stood there, pert and puzzled. 'Are you not going in?' She nodded towards the pub, and he forced a smile.

Inside, he went to the bar while she got them a table by the window. The room wasn't busy, though small knots of drinkers were grouped here and there. He noticed her glance at her watch as he was carrying their drinks over. Perhaps this was the excuse he needed.

'You're in a hurry. We should have left this till tomorrow,' he said.

She squinted at him. 'Not at all. It's just a dinner around the corner. We've got an hour to spare.' Then something softened in her expression. 'I couldn't really talk about it on the telephone.'

His raised eyebrows asked the question.

'Well . . .' She took a breath and set herself. 'You remember when we were at lunch and you asked me if I'd been thinking about – marriage? I couldn't be quite honest, because I wasn't sure myself. I know it's ridiculous, really, when one considers how brief a time one has known a person . . .'

'You know you can tell me anything,' he said, with the braced stealth of a man putting his foot on a frozen pond.

She nodded. Across the table her eyes glittered at him. 'I dare say even you might not guess what's coming next.'

His heartbeat had climbed up to his throat. He was about to place his hand over hers, but instead he only murmured, 'I think I *have* guessed.'

Her eyes widened in astonishment, and she looked at him perplexedly. 'But how? Have you spoken to him?' Him. *Him?* Then Lydia said, 'You've spoken to Lawrence?'

The name snatched the breath from his body. Inside, it felt like the shock of plunging headlong into icy water. Lawrence. His old friend. A widower. A man of his own age. Her lover. Not only – her intended. Saucy doubts and fears were nothing like as terrible as this. He was abruptly aware of not having spoken for long moments. He looked for his voice, hidden somewhere deep in his guts.

'Lawrence – Lawrence Haydon?' The surname was immaterial. He knew already it was Lawrence. 'No . . . I haven't spoken to him. About anything.'

Lydia, alarmed now, had started gabbling out an apology, though the true meaning of his shock was lost on her. Of course she ought to have told him before now – quite honestly what had happened had surprised both of them – they hadn't even told Lawrence's children yet – and of course there was the problem of the office, she was pretty certain there'd been gossip already – but he was being so nice to her about it, he was a proper gentleman, although she didn't have to tell *him* that as one of his oldest friends –

He faced her over the table, seeming to listen to her.

It had occurred to him at times that he might be fooling himself, but only on the assumption that she would have met a man her own age, some amiable young shaver like Teddy. But if she could fall for *Lawrence*, who had already had his turn at marriage, who was the least likely suitor imaginable, why not – could she not –

'You know he's very close to his children, don't you?' Key said abruptly, interrupting Lydia mid-sentence and causing her to rear back, startled. His brusqueness of tone had caught her off-guard. 'I reckon Jane, his older daughter, must be about

261

thirty. A penny for *her* thoughts once she finds she'll have a stepmother the same age as her.'

He had never felt his two selves so distinctly at odds. He understood he ought to congratulate her on her news, and yet here was his other self bursting through the public front ready to goad and wound. Lydia, having had a moment to absorb his provocation, found her voice. 'I suppose it might be awkward,' she said, quietly. 'But Lawrence is very tactful, and the children are adults. I'm sure their love for each other will see them through.'

His impulse was to sneer – *I might have known you'd settle for blind optimism* – but he curbed his tongue. The rage was gone as suddenly as it had flared. His disruptive self had vanished back into its hole.

After a moment he said, in a collected voice, 'I dare say you're right,' and she brightened again, his brief loss of civility smoothed away like a wrinkle from a dress.

He wasn't sure how he managed to get through the remainder of their hour. When Lydia looked at her watch again and said that she ought to be going he rose to his feet, and like a blind man feeling his way he picked up his coat and followed her to the door. On the street, they prepared their short dance of parting, and he was composed enough at last to offer her an avuncular kiss of congratulation.

'I feel so relieved to have told you,' she said, smiling up at him. 'We can talk about other things tomorrow now that this isn't a secret.'

Other things? he wondered. What other things could possibly concern him now? But he heard himself murmur the emollient words she expected of him – and that yes, he did look forward to talking it over with Lawrence.

He walked back in the direction of his hotel, through the endless anonymous life of London. He had come here in search of revelation, and had found it. For one who prided himself on his instinct – his vital weapon, in the Army and in the force – the failure of it now felt punitive, disabling.

He had lost himself in a run-down maze of streets that cowered as the night darkened to indigo-black. On the other side of the road he saw a squaddie taking a piss against the wall of a dishevelled pub. A moment later his two squaddie mates came out, and after a mumbled confab they walked off. Hardly knowing why, Key decided to follow them, just close enough to overhear their talk, as profane and banal as his own comrades' from thirty years ago. One of them was staggering from the drink. They were passing by a bottle-shop, its lights out, where a vagrant lay abandoned half-asleep in the doorway. Key held back as the trio stood over the ragged heap, poking and taunting him; here was their sport for the evening. Laughter broke out as one of the soldiers, swaying back, began pissing on the unfortunate wretch. Then kicks and spittle rained down on him. He groaned, imploring them to stop.

When at last the men had finished and gone, Key sidled up to the crumpled victim, almost insensible from his ordeal. Trickles of urine pooled black under the street lamp. He stood over the man for some minutes, listening to him whimper, and felt a sharp spasm of disgust. He felt in his pocket and tossed half a crown onto the heap; and walked on.

Arriving back at the hotel he asked the receptionist to provide him with an early wake-up call: he had a train to catch from Euston.

Next morning he left a telephone message at Lydia's office,

263

apologising. A family emergency had obliged him to change his plans and return immediately to Liverpool. He was sorry to back out of lunch with her, but it couldn't be helped. For a moment he imagined Lydia receiving his message, and feeling a small prickle of disappointment – she was no doubt hoping to have a good long chat about Lawrence, to get a picture of his early years. That was not to be endured.

None of it was to be endured.

25

It turned out that Lawrence could not be avoided for ever. Several invitations to stay the weekend had been declined, and Key at last believed himself safe. The next overture proved impossible to escape. Lawrence had come up to Liverpool for the week and had kept his evening engagements entirely free, so he only had to pick a night and the *fait* was *accompli*. They spoke on the telephone. Once the ice was broken and the old confidences were restored Lawrence made a tentative inquiry into his old friend's state of mind. 'Lydia told me how much she enjoyed corresponding with you. I gather you've gone quiet lately.' Key played innocent: 'It wasn't my intention. I've just been embroiled in this wretched memoir.' He wondered how long he could use this as a deflective shield. For ever?

They set a date for dinner on Thursday. In the meantime Key decided to have a clear-out of the basement at Falkner Street, packed with all the junk and memorabilia of his professional years – old uniforms, insignia, medals, photographs, police reports, notebooks, correspondence, a winner's cup from a departmental darts competition. His service revolver. The chamber was empty.

Most of it he ought to have chucked out years ago, but he also discovered less sentimental items that had accumulated down there. Some of it had been confiscated during arrests, like brass knuckledusters, flick-knives, sets of skeleton keys, a jemmy and a bottle of rock oil, a fold-up burglar's ladder. Most interesting of the lot was a Malacca cane he found propped behind a set of golf clubs in a cupboard. Ostensibly a Victorian walking stick, its silver handle could be unscrewed to reveal inside a thin stiletto blade of about sixteen inches. He remembered taking it from some villain years ago during a routine shakedown in Toxteth. It felt nice in the grip, and he had habitually sported it at the races and the golf course: a curious thing, to go about in possession of something apparently genteel that was in fact a deadly weapon.

He spent an afternoon boxing it all up; the stuff was no use to him now, and he might make a few quid on it at auction.

The appointed evening came round, and they met for old times' sake at Wo's, the Chinese on Duke Street they used to frequent as students. It pleased them to see that hardly anything there had changed. The shouting from the kitchen dominated the cramped dining room, the windows blurred with condensation, and the service offered few concessions to politeness. But they still made the best prawn dumplings anywhere.

'This takes me back,' said Lawrence, sipping a beer when Key arrived. 'I must bring Lydia up here, she said she wants to visit . . . And there's always an old friend we can seek out.' He said it with a twinkle.

Key shook his head. 'I'm sure you'll have better things to do.'

Something in Lawrence's expression shifted. 'Nonsense.

Quite apart from our history, Lydia is very particular about keeping up with you. She finds you interesting.'

'Interesting?'

'Extremely. As I said, she enjoyed corresponding with you. And I believe she felt some bond of ... after what happened on the cruise. She told me the story of that unfortunate chap, um ... what was his name?'

Key paused, staring across the table at his friend. He didn't like the way the talk was turning, but he kept his voice level: 'Teddy. What did she tell you?'

'Oh, just that you'd made friends on board with him – with Teddy – in films, wasn't he? – and you'd had quite a time together until – well, an absolute tragedy, of course. It upsets Lydia to talk about it ...'

'You heard about the inquest?' As he said this he studied Lawrence's face to check for any hesitancy or awkwardness, and found none. Lawrence only nodded, and murmured, 'I gather it was recorded as an accident.'

I gather ... Key wondered exactly how much his friend knew. If, as he admitted, it upset Lydia to recall Teddy's fate, the likelihood was that she had shared – in the intimate hours of pillow talk – her suspicions around the case. He could not forget her uncertainty that day of the inquest, nor her troubled admission to him as they left the court – *you make me feel that I've been complicit in something*. That was the danger with honest people: they were inclined to take matters of doubt very seriously.

He listened somewhat distractedly to Lawrence confessing his happiness and surprise at the belated second chance Lydia had offered him. At some point in this account Key realised that his attendance at their wedding had already been assumed. Insupportable, as far as he was concerned. It astonished him that Lawrence could dwell so blithely on a subject about which his own hopes had been so recently and painfully disappointed. It was cruel – unknowing, but cruel.

Their talk had drifted to the war – the First War. Lawrence had been in the St John Ambulance in Belgium, and later on the Somme. Like other veterans they were reticent about that time, even amongst themselves, but this evening Key felt a strange prompting towards candour. He told Lawrence that amid the clear-out at Falkner Street he had found a sheaf of drawings by his friend, Hugh Endall.

'A great friend, really. He used to run a stables back home, and he drew these marvellous pictures of horses. He bequeathed them to me.'

Lawrence allowed a solemn pause. 'He didn't make it back?'

Key shook his head, and after a moment continued: 'We were in the heavy fighting at Glencorse Wood. I saw Hugh's lot up the line take a terrible pounding. When I found him he was in a shell-hole, kneeling there. He'd taken one in the gut, his face was badly cut up. He began to fade, all the blood he'd lost, and he muttered something, "Finish it." I think that's what he said ... He was dying, but I couldn't bear to leave him there. I stood behind him and took out my revolver. Fired – and the bloody thing jammed.'

'Oh, God,' said Lawrence in a whisper. 'What did you do?'

Key stared past his shoulder. He didn't speak for some moments. 'There was nobody else around to help. No other weapon to hand but the gun ... so I used that. On his skull. I don't know how many times I hit him before he was dead.

When I got back I remember someone looking at me queerly and saying you've got blood all over you.'

Lawrence had fallen silent.

Key picked up a cigarette and lit it. 'I've never told anyone that before.'

They had finished dinner. Key suggested that they go on for a nightcap, he had just the place in mind. As they set out Lawrence glanced to his side and asked him, 'Are you injured, old fellow? I've not seen you with that walking-stick before.'

'No, not injured. Something else I found in the clear-out.'

'Very distinguished,' he remarked with a smile.

As they walked Lawrence did most of the talking. He had become more voluble, Key noticed, since the change in his life. Perhaps it was to do with contentment; perhaps Lydia had renewed his social energy. For minutes at a time he let his companion yarn away ... something about the Civil Service? He was barely listening. A mournful foghorn indicated they were approaching the docks. Ahead of them a corner pub glimmered through the murk.

'Here we are.'

Lawrence looked up, inquiring. 'The Baltic Fleet. Good Lord!'

'An even older vintage than Wo's,' said Key, pushing through the door.

'This place felt nostalgic before I was *gone*,' said Lawrence. 'But I don't remember you and me drinking here.'

'No? Maybe not. I always think of it as the last pub the old emigrants would have called at before they got on the boat.'

They had just been served drinks when the bell rang for last orders. They settled at a table by the window, watching the occasional car or van straggle along the Dock Road. Lawrence was telling him another story – about what he had no idea. He was content merely to sit there, nodding at intervals, appearing to listen. But then something changed in Lawrence's tone, and he realised he had missed a question.

'Sorry. Miles away.'

'I was just asking how the memoir's going. Lydia said you were talking with a publisher about it.'

'It's a non-starter. In the unlikely event of my finishing it the might of the Liverpool police force would make sure it never gets published.'

Lawrence made a face. 'I see. Is this because of the Wallace thing?'

Key put down his drink. 'What do you mean?'

'Well, I read the newspaper report on the inquest, and of course ...' He hesitated, flustered, before continuing, 'Lydia mentioned it to me.'

'Oh, she "mentioned" it, did she? Anything in particular?'

The note of sarcasm made Lawrence flinch. 'Please, my dear man, that isn't what I – let's just forget it.'

'No. I'd like to hear. What did she say?'

He had looked embarrassed; now he looked alarmed. 'Nothing. Nothing she wouldn't say to your face. She defended you in court, for God's sake!'

Key stared at him in silence. He could tell by the way Lawrence blustered that he was hiding something. Under pressure his friend's old-fashioned calmness and cool had deserted him. No matter how deep you buried a secret – at the bottom of a pool, for instance – you could never guarantee against it bobbing up to the surface. He had not been able to forget the notebook Lydia had kept of their talks about Wallace, innocent-seeming at the time but now radioactive with implication. She had claimed in court, under oath, to have lost it, but Key had never been convinced. It was out there still, waiting to incriminate him.

Lawrence had also gone quiet. His friend's sudden change of mood had knocked the wind out of his sails. The pub in the meantime had emptied; they were the last in the room.

'I suppose we'd better call it a night,' Lawrence muttered.

They put on their coats and went out. The night had closed in, and the street corners seemed to lie in wait; a single sulky lamp pointed the way. Lawrence said he would look for a cab, but Key told him there was no chance of finding one round there. 'Your hotel isn't far. I'll walk back with you.' Lawrence began to protest but Key effectively overruled him by setting forth along the road. For a few minutes they walked in step, without a word between them.

They had turned into a cobbled alleyway, one of many in the maze between the docks and the city centre. They were now steeped in shadows; their faces had become indistinct to one another. He sensed Lawrence's unease, the feeling of something that should have been said, and now was too late. There wasn't another soul about, and Key saw his moment. He stopped abruptly.

'Something I've been meaning to show you, Lawrence. I think it might amuse you.'

Lawrence seemed to register the oddness of his tone. 'At this hour? I think I'd prefer to push on home . . .'

Key ignored him, and waved his stick in front of them, like a stage magician. 'You remarked on it earlier,' he began, unscrewing the cane's silver handle, 'and I was tempted to show you then. But I decided to save it' – he unsheathed the blade from its scabbard – 'for the sake of drama.'

The steel glinted in the dark. Acting the duellist Key made a few playful swipes at the air. Lawrence, startled, unconsciously took a half step back. Of all the things he might have imagined being shown, *this* was not among them.

'What on earth – Why are you carrying that?'

'It's a swordstick,' he said, admiring the blade. 'Useful thing, should you find yourself alone, in a hostile neighbourhood. Here, look – not a speck of rust on it.'

He had held it forward for inspection, but Lawrence held up his hands disowningly. 'Thanks, I'll take your word for it.'

'It's the element of surprise I like. You can imagine the scene. Some rogue sees a feller tapping along on a walking-stick and thinks he's fair game – his mark, his mug. He doesn't realise he's picked on an armed opponent. Next thing, instead of running off with a wallet he's bleeding from his gut.'

'I suppose you're speaking from experience.'

Key heard the note of contempt. 'Ah, so the mask drops at last. I've sensed for a while this has been on your mind –'

'I've had enough of this –' Lawrence's tone was curt, and he made to step past him. But Key in a flash blocked his path and shoved him against the wall. He heard Lawrence gasp in horrified surprise as he felt the blade cold against his neck.

'As I said, it's the element of surprise that works best. Now, you'll think it's none of my business, but I really must insist on knowing what Lydia told you. About the murder case. I had hoped to find out directly from her, but that didn't work out. So you'll have to tell me instead.'

Lawrence's voice, when it came, was strangled and halting, the consequence of a knife-point at his jugular. 'She said – all she said – you knew Wallace – you were friendly with him, and his wife. That's all I know.'

'But Teddy told her something, didn't he? Something to do with a man named Qualtrough? Come on, you'd remember *that.*'

Lawrence gasped again as the knife grazed his skin. 'I swear – swear to you I don't know. She never told me anything like that. For God's sake, she thinks you're her friend . . .'

He waited, staring at Lawrence's tensed face, listening to his shallow breaths. It was dawning on him that he had got Lydia wrong. Perhaps she didn't suspect him after all. Or, if she did, she had decided it was her secret, and no one else's. A pity that he'd had to draw a knife on his oldest friend to make sure, but there it was.

He felt restored to calm, and replaced the blade inside the stick, screwing down the handle. He looked up. For some reason Lawrence's appalled expression triggered a lightness in his lungs, and he began to laugh, properly laugh, his shoulders shaking. When at last he stopped Lawrence was watching him, the look in his eyes no longer fearful but enlightened. And he knew then that his friend would never be his friend again.

It was a brisk spring day in April. He stood before the upstairs window; below he could hear children playing on the cobbles of Falkner Street. He did not see much of anyone these days, but he would later visit his parents in Calderstones, as he did every Saturday. They would listen to the football results, his father would do the pools, his mother would make them tea.

They might go out in the garden now that the weather had picked up. They were getting on, his parents, deep into their eighties. But they loved their life, he realised, in a way he had never loved his own. She did her parish work, he pottered in the garden. They still attended Mass up the road at Bishop Eton Church. The previous week the old man had been on his way there to make confession when he asked, to Key's surprise, whether he would care to join him. But I've got nothing to confess, he said, and they laughed.

On his way home he decided to walk through Menlove Gardens, tranquil in mid-afternoon, and was struck anew by its prettiness. A line of mature trees kept watch over its wide sloping lawn. A world away from that black January night, and a tall man shivering in the cold, loveless and lost.

He had just finished writing to Lydia: it seemed he couldn't help himself. He was searching for a stamp when he spied, in the drawer, a pencil portrait of a face. One side of the paper was jagged from where it had been torn from a sketchbook. Qualtrough, caught in Teddy's quick, confident strokes. He took it out to examine. It was a better likeness than he first thought, happening to glance up that moment and catch himself in the window's reflection.

Acknowledgements

I owe this book to a conversation I had late one evening with Thomas Grant KC. He happened to make a glancing reference to the William Herbert Wallace murder case, which triggered in me a sudden memory from childhood. It was a case my parents once talked about, probably because we lived five minutes' walk from Menlove Gardens, L18. Having lain dormant for nearly fifty years, the story came out like a revenant from the darkness of forgetting, and I knew I had to retell it. My thanks to Tom for this and for reading an early draft of the novel.

Thanks also to Richard Beswick, Jon Wood, Peter Rook, Jon Appleton; to Nithya Rae and Zoe Hood at Little, Brown.

Of invaluable help in writing this was Roger Wilkes's book *Wallace: The Final Verdict* (1984). Also very useful were The Julia Wallace Murder Foundation website; *Checkmate* (2021) by Mark Russell; and *Humphrey Jennings* (2004) by Kevin Jackson.

My thanks and my dearest love always to Rachel Cooke, the best reader I know.